"What a curious people these are," Constance said almost involuntarily. "They seem to be, how shall I put it, hostile."

"Oh, the villagers," replied Dr. Murchison, indifferently. "That, after all, is only natural. You must remember that the people in these remote villages are still in the Middle Ages. They believe even now in witchcraft and are full of curious superstitions. They don't like us, or Dr. Edwardes, for that matter. They are afraid of Chateau Landry and of our patients there, and nothing would induce any one of them to go near it after dark. They are convinced that mad people are possessed by devils."

"But that hardly explains their hostility to us," replied Constance. "You can't describe them as friendly, can you?"

Dr. Murchison smiled.

"No," he answered. "So you see we shall have to stand together. We are not likely to make many friends on the outside . . ."

Read the original book from which Alfred Hitchcock produced his famous film classic with Zebra's MOVIE MYSTERY GREATS!

MYSTERIES
By Mary Roberts Rinehart

THE CIRCULAR STAIRCASE (1723, $3.50)

Rachel Innes became convinced that her summer house was haunted, and the explosion of a revolver along with a body at the bottom of the circular staircase ensured she would have many sleepless nights. She had acquired a taste for sleuthing and her niece and nephew were prime suspects in the murder.

THE HAUNTED LADY (1685, $3.50)

When wealthy Eliza Fairbanks claimed to have found bats in her bedroom and arsenic on her strawberries, Miss Pinkerton was promptly assigned the case. But apparently someone else was watching too. For the old lady's worries were over, but so was her life.

THE SWIMMING POOL (1686, $3.50)

With a deadline to meet on her detective story, Lois had no patience with her sister's strange behavior. Except the mystery Lois was writing was not nearly as deadly as the mystery about to unfold. For ravishing, willful Judith was about to disappear from her locked bedroom, and a woman's body would be found in the crystal blue depths of the Swimming Pool.

LOST ECSTASY (1791, $3.50)

When Tom was arrested for a not-so-ordinary murder, Kay's life turned upside down. She was willing to put her own life in danger to help Tom prove himself, and to save him from those out to silence him or those after revenge.

MISS PINKERTON (1847, $3.50)

Old Miss Juliet had endured quite a shock when her nephew committed suicide and her nurse, Hilda Adams, was determined to keep an eye on her. But the old lady wasn't as frail as she looked, and Hilda wasn't sure if she had murder or suicide on her hands.

Available wherever paperbacks are sold, or order direct from the Publisher. Send cover price plus 50¢ per copy for mailing and handling to Zebra Books, Dept. 2002, 475 Park Avenue South, New York, N.Y. 10016. Residents of New York, New Jersey and Pennsylvania must include sales tax. DO NOT SEND CASH.

MYSTERY MOVIE GREATS
SPELLBOUND

FRANCIS BEEDING

ZEBRA BOOKS
KENSINGTON PUBLISHING CORP.

ZEBRA BOOKS

are published

Kensington Publishing Corp.
475 Park Avenue South
New York, NY 10016

First Zebra Books printing: February 1987

Printed in the United States of America

Prologue

HOTEL IMPERIAL,
ANNECY,
June 22nd, 1926.

DEAREST HELEN,

How delightful to get your letter, which we found waiting for us at Thonon. I am sorry about Bingo, poor old boy. I'm afraid you'll miss him dreadfully. But he was getting old, wasn't he, and after the vet.'s opinion I don't see what else you could have done.

John is an angel, but I shouldn't care to take a honeymoon with *anybody*; so don't be rash, and if ever you feel in the consenting mood, which so often happens, pull yourself together and think it over. Fortunately, John and I agree about all the most important things. What I mean is that we both like to sleep with the window open.

We are being shamelessly vulgar. I hate trains and we can't afford a car. So we are doing the Alps in a charabanc. It was John's idea, and those P.L.M. autocars are wonderful, so comfortable, and it is the other people who get all the dust. We ran from Paris to Dijon. Such a sweet place, famous for eating, and

John and I made pigs of ourselves at the Hotel des Cloches. We were only trying to not be beaten by the natives, but it was no use. John's handicap (in courses) must be about minus two.

Last night we slept, or rather "lay" I believe the expression ought to be, at Thonon-les-Bains, near Evian, on the Lake of Geneva. It is a funny, quiet little place with an old eighteenth century square and a strange, tumble-down church which no one has troubled to finish.

We stopped three hours at Evian, which is very fashionable. We met the Bryces there. She is looking much better and was most charmingly dressed (half a page of details is here omitted). John lost fifty francs at boule, which he says is a rotten game, but we did not try baccarat.

Then we went for a short trip on the Lake, and saw the Dents du Midi and the Rochers de Naye. I've never seen so many mountains; and I'm afraid John is going to be difficult. He was hinting the other day at what they call a "petite ascension." You wear horrid clothes, and the most dreadful boots, and hang things on your back till you look like a travelling ironmonger. I prefer the charabanc myself.

But this is not what I was going to write about. For we have had an ADVENTURE. It happened on the way from Thonon to Annecy, via the Col des Gêts. We started late in the morning, as it is not a very long run, and we went up the most lovely valley with woods on each side. Sometimes the road went through tunnels. It was most exciting. I suppose it must have been about mid-day when it happened. We were turning a corner and I saw a big notice stuck out on the cliff with "Gorg du Diable" written on it. The Devil, by the way, is pretty frequent in these parts. He has gorges and rocks and chimneys in every direction. This one was particularly fiendish. On the left there was a precipice which went down for many hundreds of feet to the river which flowed at the bottom. The precipice was covered with enormous trees, and John was saying (you know how witty he is) that the devil had an obvious liking for *shady* surroundings, when we took another corner rather sharply, and the next moment I felt a sudden jerk and John's hand gripping my knee.

The autocar had stopped, and everybody in front began to talk at once. John got out with some of the others to see what was happening, and I followed him. I rather wish I hadn't, for it was really rather horrible.

There was a car on the side of the road drawn close into the precipice, and one of the back wheels was off. I think they must have had a puncture or something. There were two men by the car—one with a white face, holding a spanner in his hand, dressed in one of those light raincoats and a soft hat, and another lying apparently insensible on the ground. The man with the spanner was breathing hard as I came up, just behind John, and was talking rapidly to our driver. It's lucky I understand French, because I had to tell John what he was saying.

"He was mad, quite mad," the man kept on repeating, and I realised he was talking about the other man on the ground, who was, I now saw, bleeding from a dreadful cut on the forehead.

"He suddenly became violent and attacked our

driver," continued the man with the spanner. "We were taken completely by surprise, and it all happened before I could lift a finger. He killed the driver, and then I had to defend myself."

He held up the spanner, and I saw that it was dull red at the end, and there was that other man lying on the ground. It made me feel quite sick.

The man spoke with a funny accent, and I soon realised that he was English, though his French was very good.

After he had examined the man on the ground and put him in an easier position, he began to explain to us in detail what had happened. Of course, he didn't make a great long speech, as I shall give it here. It was all broken up in little bits of dialogue, which was as good as a play. That, however, is beyond me.

But first you must imagine what a fearful place it was. A great cliff towering up on our right, bare, except for oak scrub, going up for many feet to the sky. And then a narrow road (much too narrow John said), and then the cliff going down hundreds of feet to a river below. Only below the road it was all covered with trees and very lovely. And opposite was another high mountain on the other side of the valley, and last of all you must see this man with the English accent and the spanner and the silent figure at his feet.

"It's like this," he was saying; "I am a doctor, a specialist in mental cases, and I have just been engaged by Dr. Edwardes, whose private asylum is just up there," and he pointed to a little track which ran very steeply up the hill to our right till it was lost in the bushes.

"Dr. Edwardes," he continued, "has taken me for

8

his assistant, and I am on my way to join him now. Just as I was leaving England, however, he asked me to bring over a patient, a new patient you understand, also an Englishman, who was coming out from London. That is the man who is lying there. Normally he is quiet and not at all dangerous—mad only on one subject, and we did not expect to have any difficulty, especially as Dr. Edwardes had sent Jules over to help me.

"Jules is the head keeper of the asylum, an ex-sergeant of the French marine. He came to London and we travelled together by train all the way to Thonon with our patient. Everything went well until this morning, when we reached Thonon, where we were to pick up the car which was to take us to the asylum. Then our troubles began, for the chauffeur was not to be found. Jules picked up the car at the usual garage, but nothing had been seen of the man in charge of it since the night before. So we started out alone—the three of us, Jules, myself and the patient. Jules drove the car, while I sat with my patient at the back. All went well till we got here, but just at this corner the back tyre burst and, if Jules had been less handy with the steering, we should have been over the edge. But he pulled up just in time, and then we all got out and I started to help him change the wheel. Our patient also left the car and began to look about him.

"We had been at work I suppose for five minutes when it happened. My patient, who had been looking over the edge, to where you can just see a thin trickle of the river after it has leapt in a waterfall from that rock which is nearly hidden, sprang up, and his face

9

changed. I shall never forget how his face changed. *'The gorge of the devil! The gorge of the devil!'* he screamed. *'Master! Master! The sacrifice!'* And in an instant, before I could stop him, he rushed at Jules who was unscrewing the spare wheel, and with a single bound leapt at his shoulders and hurled him over the edge."

The man paused in his story, and there was a gasp from the passengers of the autocar. I know I clutched John's arm hard. Then, almost mechanically, we all moved forward and looked over the edge. At first I could see nothing. It was all beautifully green undergrowth and trees and short grass interspersed with patches of bare rock, but it was frightfully steep, almost perpendicular. Then suddenly a fat Frenchman with a thick beard pointed with his finger.

"Mon Dieu, look!" he said. And then I saw an arm and a head, all twisted unnaturally, sticking out of a bush. I must have turned white, for John caught me and pulled me back, telling me rather harshly to get into the car.

I am not quite certain what happened next, but I heard the young English doctor explaining that in self-defence he had been obliged to knock the lunatic out with a spanner or he would have attacked him too. It had all happened only a few minutes before we arrived.

After that John spoke to the man with a spanner, explaining that he was a doctor, too; and they had a short consultation together while the driver got us back into the car. Presently John came up and told me that he would have to go to the asylum with the young Englishman and his patient, who was quite insensible, but, as far as he could see, not badly hurt.

"I don't like leaving you," he said, "but I feel I must help this poor fellow. He is very much shaken by this horrible affair. He is very good, and has offered to send me on to Annecy in the car when I have helped him with his patient."

Of course, I said that I did not mind, and so it was arranged. I went on in the charabanc, leaving John and the young doctor to take the unconscious lunatic up to the asylum.

We reached Annecy about five that evening, and John joined me at seven. Everything had gone quite all right, he said, and the asylum was a very well-ordered place, though it was miles away from anywhere. It was a big old chateau belonging originally to one of the Counts of Savoy, but, of course, *converted*.

They got the lunatic, who was still insensible, into bed all right in the old wing, in a room which John says had once been a dungeon, though they had knocked a great hole in one of the walls to make a proper window. The young English doctor was, of course, terribly shaken, and it seems that his principal, Dr. Edwardes, was away, so he had to take charge of everything the moment he arrived.

John said the place was terribly desolate, but there was a large staff of servants. They were all very much upset by the death of Jules, though John said they did not seem to be particularly surprised, as some of the lunatics there are very violent, and accidents have happened before. It seems rather awful looking after a lot of dangerous lunatics in an old castle in the middle of the mountains, and the young English doctor was so nice—much too nice for such a horrible occupation. I can't think why he should have chosen it, but men are very peculiar.

Well, *that's* the adventure, and I am glad it's over. Annecy looks lovely. We are to stay here a whole day before going on through Aix-les-Bains to Grenoble. I will write to you again from there, and give you our news.

All the love I can spare (but John is very greedy).
Your affectionate
SUSAN.

Chapter I

I

Constance Sedgwick, M.D., aged twenty-six, was staring at herself critically in the long mirror. As a young doctor of medicine, with a degree for which she had worked hard and long, she prided herself on being objective. She was looking at herself, so she said, as she had been taught to look at a bacteriological culture under the lens, very steadily and without prejudice.

"How you strike a contemporary—that's what I want to know," she said, addressing the figure in the glass. "If I saw you in the street, should I turn to look at you again. You appear to be intelligent, and there is clearly no nonsense about you—or not more than is necessary. If I were a woman I think I should dislike you—yes, you are sufficiently attractive for that. If I were a man. . . ."

But here she paused. She had, she assured herself, no very great interest in what she would think of herself if she were a man.

"The really important question," she went on, talking still into the mirror, "is what Dr. Edwardes will think of you? You don't look in the least like a person who is devoting her life to medical science, and you would be a fraud if you did. You failed twice before you even got your degree. You took up medicine because you wanted to be independent, and because it was the only profession in which a woman can hope to do really well for herself. And you look it. The shape of your head is all wrong—no high, or even a middle brow, but just as low as they are made; a good chin but that only means that you are obstinate, and one sees at once that your manner at the bedside will probably discourage the cheerful patients, and kill the pessimists. Perhaps it's just as well that they are going to be lunatics."

And here, again, she paused, for now it was time to decide finally what she intended to do. She turned from the looking-glass, and going to her writing-table by the window, read again the two letters which she had received from Dr. Edwardes.

"You have now your medical degree," he wrote. "Never mind about experience; I can promise you plenty of that at Château Landry. I suggest that you should come to me for six months on probation and then we shall see."

She owed that, of course, to her father, dead these twenty years. If Dr. Edwardes had not been her father's friend, he would certainly have hesitated to engage a young person who had only just got through the London school by the skin of her teeth. For this

14

was a unique opportunity, which any one of the dozen brilliant young students of her year would have given their heads to secure. Château Landry, House of Rest for the mentally deficient, was famous in the history of mental disease. Specialists in the treatment of insanity in all its forms came from the ends of Europe to visit it and to sit at the feet of its director. Château Landry was no ordinary asylum. Dr. Edwardes chose his patients with care. They were special cases, and no ordinary lunatic need apply. To obtain admission into Château Landry you must first of all be medically interesting, and secondly, as this was a first-class establishment, you must be rich. Fortunately for Dr. Edwardes, lunacy is not confined to the poorer classes, and he had treated in his time more than one poor gentleman who, if he had not been sitting so comfortably in Château Landry, might have been sitting rather less at his ease, though possibly quite as much at home, in the House of Lords.

So much for the first of the letters which she had received from Dr. Edwardes. No girl in her senses would hesitate to jump at such a chance. The second letter, however, was less inviting. Dr. Edwardes had engaged her; but Dr. Edwardes, by the time she arrived, would not be there. The old man, in his zeal for science, had seriously overtaxed his strength, and he had been obliged—no one better qualified to give advice in such a matter—to order himself a rest.

"If I don't take a holiday and that immediately," he wrote, "I shall soon have to consider myself as a suitable patient for my own establishment. I am, therefore, leaving my work for three months. Do not, however, hesitate on that account to come to Château Landry. I have engaged a specialist from England, a Dr. Murchison, in whom I have every confidence. He will be in charge by the time you arrive, and I am leaving him precise instructions as to your duties."

This letter put rather a different complexion on the whole affair, and her friends had not been backward in discouragement. She would be going now to a strange house, a very strange house, if all she had heard of it was true, in the charge of a person unknown, and, though her chin was firm, she felt not perhaps anything quite so definite as hesitation, but certainly a tendency to waver. She had qualms. Yes, that was the word. Qualms. She had them now as, for the last time, she weighed the position all over again.

On the one side were these qualms. On the other was a salary of £150 a year all found, and the beginning of a promising career. There were also the protests of her friends who said that she must on no account set forth upon an adventure, so rash and so unmaidenly; observations which made her all the more eager to go.

The struggle was short and decisive. This was a chance which really could not be neglected by anyone who felt in the least capable of looking after herself. She had her living to get. She was twenty-six. She was qualified. She was Constance Sedgwick, M.D., and this was her first job. She would sit at the feet of the master (as soon as he returned). Meanwhile, she would show this Dr. Murchison that she merited all the kind things which Dr. Edwardes had doubtless said in her favour.

And now, having made up her mind, she gave free play to her imagination. Her dissections might be lacking in neatness and precision, there were gaps in her knowledge of the pharmacopoeia, and she knew nothing at all of mental science. But she intended to do well in her profession, and the chances were all in her favour. She was to assist Dr. Edwardes in his investigations, only a secretary perhaps, but what an opportunity! And what a setting for that awful riddle by which her young intelligence was already intrigued—the riddle of human minds, ruined or deformed, in which, nevertheless, a personality, or soul, call it what you please, must somewhere remain intact, and by some means accessible. She had formed already a picture of Château Landry; it was, she knew, a castle, in fact as well as in name, which had weathered the Middle Ages, and survived even the destructive zeal of Richelieu. She saw it as described by Dr. Edwardes, high up among the rocks and pines of Savoy, secluded at the end of a secret valley, with one small village about two miles away, a small collection of châlets, with half-a-dozen stone houses and a single inn.

There behind the impenetrable walls, in rooms formerly strewn with rushes and hung with tapestry, she would find, incongruously, every modern comfort and device—modern science in possession of an ancient stronghold.

Modern science, perhaps, dauntless, inquisitive, throwing its feeble ray into the heart of darkness. But where was its victory? Central heating and electric light, a little reasonable care of sick bodies, a little

17

insight into the mechanism of a brain diseased—were these the sum of its achievement in face of the enigma with which it was confronted in that House of Rest?

II

It was a bad crossing, whatever the offensive young man next behind her when she crossed the gangway might maintain. His remark, "Nothing like a good breath of sea air; freshens your face up so," delivered in the tone of one who was a good sailor, or a hearty Christian, or a crashing bore, irritated her almost to the point of comment. Why not, at least, be accurate? Sea air was not good for the complexion, and the rolling of the channel steamer was worse, even though you did not happen to be really ill.

Luckily, however, the ordeal was brief, and soon she was struggling forward to the firm land of France, tightly wedged in the crowd, trying not to be parted from her handbag, despatch case, passport and landing ticket—murmuring below her breath, as though it were of mystical significance, the number 179 stamped in greasy brass on the cap of the Calais porter who had possessed himself of her suit-case while he had gestured with some one else's towards the douanes. Thrust eventually past a shabby French official, redolent of garlic, sweat and sour wine, who glanced at her passport upside down, she found herself, bewildered by the noise and squalor of her surroundings, trying hard to overcome her conviction that the English were a superior people. The neat

officials of Dover, its clean customs house, the digni-
fied figure of the English stationmaster in his dark
blue uniform, these were behind her, symbols of the
law, order and familiar standards of the land for
which she was already homesick. In their place was a
seething rabble, unwashed and insolent, yet oh so
eager for the hundred sous with which its services
must be rewarded.

"Must pull myself together," thought Constance,
some minutes later, when she had successfully passed
through the customs house without having had to
open her bag, "or I shall develop a francophobe
complex."

She found her registered luggage, which was
opened and very perfunctorily searched. But there
again she happened to be unfortunate, for the official
fumbling among her silk underclothes shot a glance at
her capable of only one interpretation. "Filthy
beasts," was her comment, aimed, to be fair, less at
the man in front of her than at the sex in general.

Constance had viewed with mingled dislike and pity
such young men as had attempted any sentimental
advances towards her, but anything in the nature of
the purely animal instinct disgusted her. Men were
like that, children in the open expression of their
impulses, curiously unable to hide their primitive
emotions.

The train for a wonder arrived punctually at the
Gare du Nord, and at a quarter to seven Constance
found herself at the little hotel on the Quai Voltaire
where she had stayed on a previous occasion when she
had found herself in Paris. Her windows overlooked

the Seine, and, as she brushed her hair and got herself ready to dine in one of the little restaurants of the *quartier* before going to the play, she watched the barges drifting slowly down the Seine between the zinc cases of the second-hand bookstalls and the classic outline of the Louvre on the farther bank. The evening sky to the west was a golden haze, and the city lay like Danaë beneath the shower. The floating dust was of gold, and the golden light on the river was filtered through the thin veils of the poplars beside the water. Through the open window came the noisy riot of Paris, so different from the dull roar of London or the staccato rattle of New York. Each noise was individual, and swiftly identified. The sharp querulous hoot of taxis, the rumbling of a great autobus over the cobbles, with its rear platform packed with humanity like the over-grown garrison of a mediaeval castle as depicted in the margins of illuminated MSS, the slow click-clock of hoofs with the crack and rattle of a cart carrying empty bottles and siphons, and every now and again the beat of waves against the stone parapets as some river steamer bustled on its way to Auteuil.

She dined in a little restaurant in the Rue Jacob where, calling for an evening paper, she saw that a new play of H-R. Lenormand was being performed at the Odéon, near at hand. She was not particularly "up" in the French theatre, but she had heard of Lenormand from one of her medical friends in London, who had taken up psycho-analysis. "Pretty useful point of view," he had told her. "He dramatises the subconscious, you know. It's like a lot of complexes walking about; very chatty they are, too, and most informing."

She bought a *fauteuil* and was soon watching a performance of *La Dent Rouge*. Now and then she wondered at the chance that had brought her to that particular place on that particular evening. For it seemed curiously to fit in with her present adventure. It might even be taken for a gipsy's warning. Was she not on her way to wrestle with just those powers of evil which all through the play were militant and in the end victorious? There, too, on the stage, was just that mountain village which lay at the gates of Château Landry. That girl on the stage might be the shadow of herself.

She watched the progress of the play with a curious, intimate excitement. That girl had come back to her native village. She had, in the ordinary sense, been educated. She had outgrown the primitive superstitions which still linger in the remoter Alpine valleys. And that young peasant had married her, drawn towards beauty and freedom, defying the ignorance and cruelty of his kind. Would they not together be able to defeat the suggestions of the credulous folk who through the long winter went softly in fear of the demons of the mountain? But no; inexorably as the winter closed down on them, bringing with it the terrible, intimate seclusion of a primitive community cut off from every form of intelligent life, the demons of the mountain recovered their dominion even over the souls of those who had seemed to elude it. And now the young peasant, for all his proud defiance, was dead, and the girl a sorceress who had slain him with

21

an evil thought.

Constance, that night, slept badly. Most of the time, indeed, she was in a state between waking and dreaming. Pictures and phrases came and went in her tired brain, and she allowed them to pass, occasionally trying to give them form and coherence. Was she dreaming now, or was she really lying under the rafters in an Alpine valley? The old man had died, and, because it was winter, and the ground frozen to the hardness of steel, they were unable to bury him in the earth. Besides, they would not bury him in any case, though she had begged them to do so. It was his right to lie up there, out on the roof, just above her head, rigid and brittle, staring up at the sky. Did they defraud the old man of his right he would wander in a cold wrath for ever among the mountains, or come down among the hamlets, pressing his haunted face against the pane. So he must lie up there till the earth was soft enough to bed him. And now she was explaining all this to Dr. Edwardes, who smiled and pointed to the roof of Château Landry, where, neatly, in long rows, they lay side by side, smiling stiffly up at the stars. "Every modern convenience," he was saying. But she had thought it was only a dormitory. And there was Dr. Murchison. She looked quickly at his left foot, but it was really human, and he seemed to be quite a pleasant young man, and she asked him whether it might not be insanitary. "No," he said at once, "not till the spring sets in, and then, of course, we shall be obliged to put them in the ground." And suddenly it was spring, and there was a huge fellow who came down from the forest with a gigantic pick slung over his shoulder. He attacked the ground with heavy blows . . . knocking . . . knocking.

It was the chambermaid who entered, with coffee and rolls.

III

She travelled all that day, with the exception of an hour spent in the restaurant car, with two American tourists and a French officer on leave. The chatter of the tourists got on her nerves, and she answered abruptly the few questions which they put to her, mostly about the country through which they were passing. The French officer paid no attention to anyone, but sat reading a book whose title stared at her almost pointedly: *Sous le Soleil de Satan*.

She arrived at about four in the afternoon at Thonon, having been fortunate enough to catch the connection at Bellegarde.

And now she was on the threshold, and she gazed about her with interest.

Beyond the steep built town shimmered the Lake of Geneva, a trap for all the rays of the sun; embracing it were the gracious lines of the Jura, while, far away, across the water, the light, striking the windows in houses at Ouchy and Lausanne, signalled meaninglessly across the air.

She went into the station courtyard, dusty and surrounded by shabby houses. There appeared to be no one to meet her, but as she stood, uncertain what to do, a dusty Citroen, with the hood up to protect the driver from the glare of the summer day, came to stand beside her with a grinding of brakes.

"*Pour le Château Landry?*" said the man at the wheel, who in his linen coat with blue cuffs and flat cap presented a very tolerable imitation of a smart chauffer.

Constance assented, and the man, taking her luggage, which he stowed at the back of the car, opened the door and invited her to enter. Constance, however, elected to sit beside him, considering the windscreen would protect her from the dust.

They drove off, and the chauffeur apologised for not having brought the big Voisin, which, he said, was under repair.

The car turned to the right and began to run up a river (the Dranse, so the chauffeur informed her) through a narrow valley into the hills. The lake was behind her, and the pleasant plain with its villages and vines and orchards. In front was the climbing road, overawed by limestone crags. The road ran on beside the stream, alternately to the right and to the left, through rough-hewn tunnels, and they passed great rocks whose feet were set in foam. Soon the road began to climb more steeply, and, leaving the river, they reached the narrowest part of the valley, which was here only some two hundred yards broad.

"*Encore dix minutes,*" said the chauffeur, and he pointed vaguely ahead.

Here the mountain side rose abruptly on her right, covered with undergrowth and scrub, with bare patches of grass and rock and straggling pines, while on the left the river was lost amid a tangle of rocks and

24

trees. They swept round a bend, and came upon a notice board painted in red and clamped to the naked rock: "Gorge du Diable", and an arrow pointed to the left down the mountain side which now dropped sheer from the road. Constance glanced over the edge of the car. The gorges, whatever they were, were below her, hidden in the woods, but above the distress of the little Citroen she could hear the sound of water, remote and terrible, crying through the leaves of the wood beneath her, whose giant trees seemed from that height to be no more than shrubs and whose leaves held no bird or any living thing.

The place was terrible in its desolation, yet kindly in the sunlight, for it was green with the late grass of a mountain summer, and the trees bore their full panoply of foliage.

Then, suddenly, a new sound broke on her ears. Thin and shrill it rose in the afternoon air, a queer note of desperate hope and a sadness which would never be appeased. The car swept round a bend of the road and abruptly stopped.

Before her moved a strange company. First came an old man in a faded livery of scarlet and black, bearing a rusty halberd fringed with frayed crimson cord, and an old rapier at his side. There followed after him a mountain lad with red cheeks and the eyes of an ox, his great boots roughly cleaned and the frayed ends of his corduroy trousers showing beneath a black cassock, too short by a foot, over which he wore a white surplice. He bore in his hands a black pole surmounted by a silver crucifix, the polished figure of the dying Christ flashing in the afternoon sun. At his side walked two small boys, out of step, one carrying a censer which he swung noisily from side to side, and which glowed red, and the other a pewter basin holding a wet draggled brush at the end of a brass handle. Next came six peasants in their Sunday black, their heads bare and glistening with the heat. They walked in step, very slowly, bearing upon their shoulders a pine coffin, very new, with a brass plate on the lid and two ornate handles. Then came three children, carrying wreaths of immortelles, the waxen flowers twined fantastically about with black wire. There followed three or four women, dressed in black, one of whom was weeping, and finally the priest, in a crumpled alb, dusty and bedraggled at the edges, trimmed with soiled lace, a great black cope edged with silver askew across his shoulders. He held a book whose greasy pages were covered with unfamiliar black notes and hieroglyphics, and as he passed the car his voice rose, thin and out of tune, crying out the melody *In paradisum perducant te angeli*. But his voice cracked on the final word. The crowd, before and after him, tried to follow the chant, fumbling with the books they held, clasped in fat fingers with broken nails.

The chauffeur, as the coffin passed him, took off his hat and crossed himself. Constance bowed her head, but quickly raised it again, gazing with wide curious eyes on the pageant.

It was then that she perceived, following apart, a tall young man, with a black frock-coat and a bared head. His silk hat glistened in his hand, and he looked what he evidently was, the smart young medical practitioner, as strange an apparition among the dusty villagers as could well be imagined.

As he passed the car he turned his head, and his eyes met for an instant those of Constance.

He smiled and made a little motion of his hands, and she noticed that above his right eye was a big strip of plaster. Then he passed on with the procession, among the dust and the singing.

"That is the new doctor," said the chauffuer in a low voice. "He is following my murdered colleague to his grave."

Chapter II

I

For a moment she hesitated. Already the chauffeur had left the car, and had joined the procession with the villagers. She did not wish to intrude upon a ceremony in which she had no real call to participate; but, equally, on the other hand, she felt she must avoid remaining too conspicuously aloof.

Finally, she descended from the car and unobtrusively followed the crowd; and, very soon, she began to lose her sense of being an interloper, and to be affected along with the rest.

The procession plodded forward in the dust, away from the village, and up the hillside, where the grass was a vivid green, until presently they turned a corner and found themselves entering a little cemetery. It was surrounded by a white wall of stuccoed stone and contained a series of graves, most of them hung or overlaid with the wire skeletons of decaying wreaths, and shabby immortelles.

Here she waited for some moments, gazing at the great shoulder of the mountain behind, the blue sky without a cloud, and far away a hawk or an eagle, she did not know which, swaying on spread pinions, balanced in the easy air.

It was not like an English funeral, she reflected. People were not silent with grief. Rather they were disposed to comment, without reserve, and, when the hymn was done, the chatter became quite general as the bearers lowered the coffin on to a framework of low trestles by the open grave. The young man with the cross stood now at the head, and the old priest, clearing his throat and spitting to the side of the path, began the prayers which consign the body to its native earth.

She could not follow the mumbled Latin, nor understand the practised, mechanical gestures of the priest as he sprinkled with water the wooden shell, and presently motioned with his hand to the bearers to lower it into the grave.

The young doctor stood bareheaded, a little apart, while the villagers filed one by one before the open grave, casting into it handfuls of earth which rattled dryly on the coffin lid below.

She noticed after a time that the villagers eyed him curiously, and not, she fancied, without hostility. One woman, indeed, wearing the customary black of the Savoy peasant, pulled her child, a small boy of eight or nine, sideways as they passed him by.

The young doctor appeared to take no notice of this, but gazed with absorption at the priest and at the acolytes, who, now that the ceremony was over, were preparing to depart with a callous disregard of the solemnity due to the occasion. The acolyte bearing the cross slung it across his shoulder, as though it were a vine pole or a pitch fork, and pushed quickly towards the gate of the cemetery, cuffing automatically one of the smaller boys who got in his way. The cross which he was carrying cast an edged shadow on the white wall of the cemetery, and his sudden movement disturbed the balance of the pole, so that the shadow flickered and then ran swiftly up the body of the young doctor from his feet to his head, to become still and clearcut again as the acolyte paused to settle the pole more firmly on his shoulders. The young doctor started nervously, almost as though it had been the heavy metal cross itself and not the shadow which had struck him.

II

At that instant he caught sight of Constance. For just an instant he paused, and she was aware of his eyes looking deeply for a moment into her own. Then he held out his hand.

"I am sorry," he said simply. "This is hardly a good beginning."

"You are Dr. Murchison, of course," she answered.

"And you are Dr. Sedgwick," he replied.

He fell into step by her side, and they began to descend the hill together.

"I am glad you have come," he went on. "I may hope now to share my responsibility."

It was kindly said. She felt grateful to the man who welcomed her, almost on equal terms, as a colleague, and looking at him in the light of his observations, she was disposed to be less critical than usual. Not that she had anything to criticise. The man was good looking, and he carried himself sufficiently well to obliterate the effect of the clothes he wore. She could not say that, even on that mountain side, his frockcoat made him ridiculous or definitely out of place. He moved easily, and with a curious precision. The eyes, which she had seen very directly for a moment, were observant, but they were the eyes of a man who, in his time, had visions. His features were very regular, in fact, almost inhumanly faultless; and his hair was dark, with a tendency to curl which apparently he helped it to resist.

He surprised her in the course of her covert inspection just as she was noting again the strip of plaster over his right eye.

"You have had an accident?" she said, as though to justify her interest in his appearance.

"Why, of course," he answered, in some surprise. "Is it possible you don't know what has happened?"

"I have only just arrived."

"But the chauffeur," he began.

"He was not very talkative."

"But you passed the place where it happened."

His eyes which had been looking at her with curiosity suddenly contracted.

"Don't you remember," he added, "down there in the Valley—the Gorge du Diable?"

"Yes. I remember the Gorge."

"I was bringing a patient out from England. He took me by surprise, and killed one of the keepers— Jules, poor fellow, who has just been laid to rest this afternoon. I had to handle him at last myself."

The young doctor appeared to be much moved by his memory of the scene. She saw that he was trembling, and that his hands were tightly shut.

"How perfectly dreadful," she said, feeling at once that her words were curiously stilted.

"It was all over in a minute," he assured her.

Then with an effort, as though he were trying hard to recover control of his nerves, and to be normal again, he added almost jauntily:

"I laid him out with a spanner."

Constance gave a little cry of horror, and Dr. Murchison ran on hastily.

"It was the only thing to do," he said. "Luckily the man was not severely hurt—just a slight concussion. But I shall have to be specially careful of him in future."

He looked at her a moment, as though to see how she was taking it.

"I told you it was a bad beginning," he said.

They were still walking down the hill, and Constance noted that the villagers along the road drew well aside, affecting for the most part not to notice them at all as they passed.

"You will understand my distress," continued the doctor, almost as though he were trying to account for his previous emotion.

"Why, of course," she replied, feeling now that she had herself been rather callous.

"You see," he went on eagerly, "this is my first real chance, and I was naturally very anxious that everything should go well from the start. And then this happens."

She felt herself suddenly warm to the young man. He was, it seemed, in the same position as herself. This was also *his* start in life.

"Anything I can do," she murmured.

For a while they were silent. They had left the last of the villagers behind them on the road, and Constance felt strangely relieved to be rid of them. No one had saluted them, and their aloofness, obviously not mere indifference, for she was conscious all the while of their furtive interest, had begun to get on her nerves.

She would, however, have made no comment on their behaviour if it had not been for her encounter— for it seemed almost like an encounter, though no word was spoken—with the woman who during the ceremony by the graveside had drawn her child away from contact with the doctor. This woman had preceded them down the hillside and had already reached the door of her house, a wretched structure of wood. As they passed it she raised her head and looked at Constance with something like an appeal in her eyes. Constance met them steadily, but the woman's eyes did not fall as she had expected. They continued to stare at her. Then, all at once, the poor creature shook her head violently two or three times, as though reproving a naughty child from a distance. Constance passed on, but as she walked down the road, she felt that the appealing eyes still followed her, so that it needed a distinct effort of self-control to prevent her turning round.

"What curious people these are," she said almost involuntarily. "They seem to be, how shall I put it, hostile."

33

"Oh, the villagers," replied Dr. Murchison, indifferently. "That, after all, is only natural. You must remember that the people in these remote villages are still in the Middle Ages. They believe even now in witchcraft and are full of curious superstitions. They don't like us, or Dr. Edwardes for that matter. They are afraid of Château Landry and of our patients there, and nothing would induce any one of them to go near it after dark. They are convinced that mad people are possessed by devils. Indeed, Dr. Edwardes told me that when he first began his work here the village priest called on him to offer his services as an exorcist."

"But that hardly explains their hostility to us," replied Constance. "You can't describe them as friendly, can you?"

Dr. Murchison smiled.

"No," he answered. "They are, as you say, hostile, but I find it only natural. They cannot understand the great work Dr. Edwardes is doing in Château Landry. To them it is full of terrors, and we, who live there, are suspected of I don't know what—commerce with the Evil One at the very least. Then, of course, this last affair has made a very bad impression. The man who was killed was a native of the village—very popular in spite of his being a servant of Dr. Edwardes. I am told that he used to laugh at the misgivings of his friends, who said no good would come of his service at the castle. I suppose they regard his death as a kind of judgment."

He turned to her with an engaging smile.

"You see we shall have to stand together," he conclude. "We are not likely to make many friends outside."

III

By this time they had reached the car in which
Constance had travelled from Thonon. They entered
it, and, turning to the right just short of the village,
soon found themselves climbing a steep road which
ran in a series of zigzags up the mountain side, first
through upland meadows of short unbelievably green
grass starred with flowers, and then, as they mounted
higher, through the first outposts of the fir trees,
which in serried ranks marched up to meet the naked
rock at the summit of all. And as they slipped from
the afternoon sunlight into the shadow of the forest,
Constance felt suddenly an emotion to which she
could give no name or cause. It seemed as though she
entered into another world, a world of clean air and
sweetest fragrance, shut in by mountain tops of stone
which she knew (and the knowledge was in itself a
pang of swift delight) would soon turn orange and rose
till they faded to sombre gold and a violent shadow.

She turned impulsively to the doctor at her side,
who, as though he had followed and shared the feeling
which possessed her, pointed silently ahead to where
the road, which had been running through a narrow
gash in the hillside, turned abruptly and disclosed a
tiny mountain valley, an offshoot of the one by which
they had come.

Constance caught her breath, for, indeed, it was
beautiful. Before her ran the road, climbing once
more in two loops towards a large mound on which

stood an antique castle. Battered and harsh, but set in the shadow of the fir trees, it lost in those surroundings all fierce suggestions, and stood as a pathetic reminder of the age of chivalry. Here on the smooth grass, on which the road lay coiled like the white neck of a swan, "ladies dead and lovely knights" had walked and quarrelled and loved. Here had lived the barons of Château Landry since the end of the tenth century—Geoffrey of the Arrow, who had leapt second on the walls of Jerusalem, and who had died in the moment of victory; Fulk the Black, who had fought at Zara, and lay buried within the shadow of Santa Sofia; Cosimo, Condottiere of Gian Galeazzo Visconti, and a hundred others. They had learned the handling of weapons, the rude art of war on that upland meadow. Here had passed Jacques de Landry, the friend of Molière, here the pale Aminte, mistress of Louis XIV. Here, finally, another Geoffrey, last of his race, had seen the smoke curling from the roof as he was dragged by his own peasants to the guillotine at Chambéry.

All this and more Dr. Murchison told her as they sat there in the car which had stopped at his orders, and looked at the place which was to be her home for a time indefinite.

The castle had been carefully restored by a rich banker in the late 'nineties, who had died suddenly, and, after many vicissitudes, it had been bought by Dr. Edwardes and converted to its present purpose. But he had been careful to change in no respect its essential form and character. The central donjon still stood isolated in the midst of it, reached only by a drawbridge. The drawbridge led to a balcony, which surrounded an inner stone court of the early sixteenth century, with a famous winding stair up which a man might ride a horse.

She wondered at first why anyone had thought of building a castle in that far corner of the mountains. But she ceased to wonder when she saw the sheer walls of rock which led up on each side to the naked hilltops, only just too low to escape perpetual snow. The castle must have been impregnable, the only way in being the narrow cleft through which the road ran like an arrow aimed at the heart of it. Doubtless that way had once been barred in the old days by some form of fortified gate or barbican. To-day a white-painted gate and a strong fence of steel wire, twenty feet high and too closely meshed for climbing, blocked the entrance to the castle and the grounds surrounding it. There was a little lodge by the white gate, from which issued an elderly man in the dark green uniform or livery worn by all the male servants of Dr. Edwardes' establishment. The steel fence went right and left till it was lost among the pine trees and cemented into the naked rock.

The gate was always kept closed and could only be opened by a special electrical contrivance controlled from the lodge and from the desk in the study of Dr. Edwardes in the castle.

All this Dr. Murchison explained as the car stood stationary before the gate. Then, just as he was about to give the word to move forward again, Constance put out a hand and stopped him.

"No," she said, "this is all so beautiful that I would like to walk on alone, if you don't mind. I won't be more than half-an-hour."

Dr. Murchison at once assented, and he drove on, leaving Constance standing by the white gate. She turned her back on the castle and walked a few steps away from it down the road, drawn by the view of the little valley with its village and the distant mountain peaks beyond, whose names she did not yet know. She stood there for some minutes, and was about to turn round and pass through the gate, when she became aware of footsteps and heavy breathing. She paused, and, at that moment, round the corner of the road came a peasant woman, her face red from the effort of climbing the slope.

It was the woman who had stared at Constance a short time before from the door of her house in the village. On catching sight of Constance by the gate she stopped, and came to a halt a yard away, breathing heavily, with two broad hands pressed to her labouring heart.

"Qu'est-ce que vous voulez?" said Constance, but the woman had no breath to speak. She stood in the road, shaking her head, as she had done in the village, and pointing, as she did so, to the castle.

Constance turned and looked in the direction indicated, but saw nothing except the building itself, mellow with age and with the light of the dying day.

Then suddenly the woman began to speak, a thick harsh patois, and Constance, who found ordinary French difficult enough to follow, could not understand one word in ten. The creature was immensely in earnest and she seemed afraid. That much Constance perceived.

"What is it you want?" said Constance, feeling very helpless. "Is anyone ill or in need of help?"

The woman shook her head and broke out again into vehement observations.

"*Je ne comprends pas,*" said Constance. "*Je vais chercher le gardien ou le médecin.*"

This seemed greatly to trouble the woman. She became even more voluble and difficult to follow.

"No, no," she said with an increasing vehemence. "I will speak to you alone."

Then followed a further exhortation of which Constance caught only a sentence here and there.

"It is for your good, mademoiselle. Do not go in, I implore you. . . . They told me that only last night the stone was red again."

"I do not understand," repeated Constance, as completely baffled by the few words she could catch as by the stream of syllables which conveyed nothing to her whatever.

"The stone, the white stone, the old white stone," repeated the woman. "It was red—*rouge du sang* I tell you, all streaked and spattered."

Constance gave a little gesture of despair. She assumed that someone must be ill or in need of something, and she struggled to convey to the woman that, if she really needed anything, she had better come up with her to the castle.

On this the woman stared at her, suddenly silent, and now, as it seemed, suspicious. Then abruptly, without another word, she turned on her heel and shuffled off down the road.

Constance watched her a moment or two, then she herself turned and, passing through the white gate, made her way up towards the castle.

The light had been rapidly fading during her interview with the woman at the gate. The rocks above the castle had gone grey; the grass was no longer green; and the castle itself was a black shadow that squatted in the path.

Chapter III

I

It was nine o'clock next morning when Constance awoke.

Dr. Murchison had told her to be in no hurry to join him, but to take all the rest she needed after her journey.

She spent her time, as she dressed, by the open window, in the cool mountain air, collecting her thoughts for the professional interview which she was shortly to have with her chief. She must try to be ready and clear and efficient, making a good impression from the start.

She prided herself, above all, on being clear. It was her habit to put her thoughts, as she termed it, into boxes—one box for each thought or subject. This metaphor had been to her from childhood the greatest comfort and assistance. She imagined her mind as a large room containing rows and rows of boxes all neatly ordered, and each of them marked with an appropriate label; and, as she moved forward in time, the boxes which contained her past grew smaller. There was a box for her brother, but that box was seldom opened now, for he had been killed on the Somme. Already it was smaller than the others. There were many boxes for her work and boxes for her various friends. The contents of some of the latter, if opened, might perhaps have startled those to whom they were allotted. For her thoughts during the day she kept a large general box into which they were hastily thrown to be sorted out and stored at the first available moment.

This morning, somehow, the system seemed to have broken down. She was curiously unable to collect or to govern her ideas. She felt like a nervous orator, who has prepared his speech, but who, at the last moment, sees his points and phrases escaping all control and weaving wilful patterns of their own.

"But this," she assured herself, "is ridiculous. Dr. Murchison has given you no reason to be afraid of him."

"On the contrary," she said, securing the last button of her dress, and falling into the old habit of addressing her reflection, "I think that already you please Dr. Murchison—not in the French sense, of course. That would be too tiresome. But he seemed perfectly satisfied with his colleague."

She took another look at her thought boxes, but only to think how odd it would be if somebody, unknown to her, had happened to change all the labels.

She contrived, however, to laugh at that, and went downstairs, walking with a light step into the dining-room of the private set of rooms reserved for Dr. Edwardes, his assistant and his secretary.

These rooms were set apart in the south wing of the castle. They comprised three living-rooms. One was large and spacious, lined with books and looking straight out over the meadow fifty feet below. The other two were considerably smaller, one being used as a dining-room, the other as a laboratory and dispensary. Above them were three bedrooms, one of which had been given to Constance. It was a pleasant room, commanding from its windows the whole green meadow in which the castle stood, bounded by its rampart of rock and roofed with the blue sky.

As she entered the dining-room a man standing by the window came to meet her.

"I am Mr. Ambrose Deeling," he said. "You, I take it, are our new colleague, Miss Sedgwick?" and he bowed formally over her hand, so that Constance had a glimpse of his bald head, over which a few strands of hair were drawn in neat parallel lines.

"And now," thought Constance, "I know exactly what is meant when they say that every hair was in place."

She had never seen anyone so utterly correct. This was not a man, but a figure in geometry. He wore a black coat with striped trousers, faultlessly creased. His face would have delighted a cubist painter in search of a subject. Two prominent cheekbones and a noticeable chin made an issoceles triangle, while an unnaturally straight mouth ran parallel with his level brows.

"I am the laboratory assistant of Dr. Edwardes," he stated. "I have been with him for eleven years. There are eight patients with us at present."

"Item one, item two and item three," said Constance to herself. "His boxes seem to be quite in order."

Aloud she said something polite, and asked whether he had yet had breakfast.

"I breakfast at seven-thirty," he informed her. "I perceive, however, the motive of your inquiry," and he crossed to the white stone hearth and pressed a bell.

It was as though he had said: "You don't, of course, really want to know whether I have had my breakfast, but merely to intimate that you would like some breakfast yourself."

Constance decided that she was going to dislike this man. He was one of those people who expected you always to go at once to the point. She ought to have walked straight up to him and said: "I am Constance Sedgwick. I am hungry. I want some breakfast."

He sat with her as she ate. He did so in the manner of one who had set apart just these twenty minutes in order to make her acquaintance, and as though he had decided to give her just such items of information, mainly about himself, which were in his view necessary to her at that particular stage. Running over afterwards what he told her, she arranged it thus:

"He was forty-nine. He had not got a medical degree, but he was a licensed chemist. His position was one of great responsibility because there was no other licensed chemist nearer than Thonon. The patients called him Dr. Deeling. There were only eight patients. One of them was the nephew of a marquis. He mentioned him first for that reason. There had been a serious accident, but doubtless she had heard of it already. The patient responsible for the accident was very well connected, but Dr. Murchison had knocked him down with a spanner. Also a keeper had been killed. Dr. Edwardes was a very remarkable doctor. Nearly all his patients were ladies and gentlemen. It was a privilege to belong to so distinguished a house. He had great influence at Château Landry—in fact she really owed her appointment to him. He had insisted that Dr. Edwardes was overworked, and he had suggested an increase of staff. If Dr. Edwardes had sooner taken his advice Dr. Edwardes would not now be taking a rest. He hoped the new doctor would be satisfactory, and he especially hoped the new doctor would treat the patients with respect. They were mad, of course, but they all belonged to very good families, etc., etc."

He came to a sudden stop, as though he had finished saying just what he had intended to say, and it was then that Dr. Murchison come into the room.

Constance, as she rose to greet him, was aware of a friendly penetrating interest in herself, and a side-glance of amusement, in which her complicity was invited, at Mr. Deeling.

"Good morning, Miss Sedgwick," said the doctor. "I hope you slept well."

"Too well apparently," she answered. "Mr. Deeling has just been telling me that he breakfasts at seven-thirty."

"Mr. Deeling is most exact," said Dr. Murchison.

"If I might make a suggestion, doctor," began that gentleman.

"Certainly, Mr. Deeling."

"As I have already informed Dr. Sedgwick," Mr.

45

Deeling went on, "I haven't got a medical degree, but the patients here are in the habit of addressing me as Dr. Deeling, and I think it strengthens my authority. Unless, of course, you have any objection."

"None whatever," said Dr. Murchison.

Mr. Deeling looked at his watch.

"Thank you, Doctor. I will now, if I may, attend to your prescriptions. I may say that some of them are new to me, but you may rely on their being accurately made up."

Dr. Murchison looked after the retreating figure with a queer expression. Then he turned to Constance.

"Well, Miss Sedgwick," he said. "What do you make of him?"

"He is certainly a bore," she answered, and then wondered at her carelessness. It was her habit to speak her mind very frankly, but it was indiscreet, as she at once perceived, to comment thus upon a colleague to a chief to whom she was as yet almost a stranger.

But he looked at her with a smile, and she felt that he was not so much of a stranger after all.

"Surely not a bore," he protested. "I should rather regard him as an interesting case. He raises, too, a question which I am often tempted to consider."

"Namely?"

"If that man is sane, are we really justified in trying to cure the others?"

Half an hour later Constance sat with Dr. Murchison in the spacious room of Dr. Edwardes. One half of it was known as the office, and contained a large desk and typewriter. The other was fitted up as a comfortable living-room. This part of it was lined with books, and there were several sofas and easy chairs placed about a huge hearth. There were also one or two good oak chests, and several trophies of mediaeval weapons on the wall.

There was a smaller desk and chair near the large desk of Dr. Edwardes, and it was here that Constance was installed.

"I understand from the terms of your engagement," said Dr. Murchison, "that you are ready to do what secretarial work is necessary in addition to assisting me with the patients as your medical degree qualifies you to do."

He spoke quickly and to the point, which was agreeable to Constance, and confirmed the good impression she had formed of him on the previous day.

"Yes," she said, "I am here to make myself useful in any capacity."

"I suggest," he went on, "that we set aside an hour, say from 9.30 to 10.30 a.m. each day, for dealing with correspondence and other matters. Dr. Edwardes apparently deals with everything, even including the running of the house, but I have handed over that side of the business to Mr. Deeling. I want to devote my time almost exclusively to the patients. You will find all the particulars about them in that cabinet over there, which contains a complete file for each case. There are three women, who should, I suggest, be your own particular charge. One of them is very silent, and spends most of her time in her own room— an ordinary case of religious mania. She is under the impression that she is a reincarnation of St. Theresa,

47

and is much given to contemplation. Another is more interesting. She thinks she is growing backwards and becoming younger each day instead of older. At the moment she has reached the age of ten."

"What do you mean?" said Constance.

"That she is going backwards," he repeated. "She is ten this year, she will be nine next year and eight the year after."

"Oh, I see," said Constance. "And what happens when she reaches 0?"

"That is the question, and it worries her."

"She thinks she will die."

"I have asked her what she thinks is going to happen, and she says that she will change. I don't know what she means by that. It is a curious case. You will find all the particulars in file B.3."

There was a short silence, broken by a sudden crackling like dry wood burning. Constance looked up. Dr. Murchison was gnawing the end of his pencil, and the sharp tiny crack, as it split in half lengthwise, sounded unnaturally loud in the quiet room. He was not looking at Constance, but above her head, seemingly at a far corner of the ceiling, while his strong white teeth rent the wood. Constance moved in her chair. Dr. Murchison laid down the remains of the pencil and looked across at her.

"The men patients are rather more interesting," he said, "and there is one case, at least, which is dangerous. The men I propose for the moment to keep altogether under my own personal control. I hope you will not misunderstand."

He seemed nervous, and looked at her as though anxious to see exactly how she would take it.

"But, of course, Dr. Murchison," she answered, "I quite understand. It's perfectly natural that you should wish me to begin with the simpler cases, and leave the others to you. And please don't bother about my feelings in a matter which is purely professional. I am here to learn and to be as useful as possible."

He regarded her gravely for a moment.

"Of course," he went on, "there is nothing to prevent you studying any of the cases. Two or three of the men are simple enough. There's an extremely tiresome fellow who calls himself 'Colonel' Rickaby."

"Isn't he really a colonel?" demanded Constance.

"He is an old Anglo-Indian, who seems to have had a poor time of it among a rather hard-living set of military men in the Punjab. He now tries to believe that he was the finest fellow of them all, and talks as though he had been in the habit of shooting big game in the intervals of saving the Indian Empire. Then there is a painter-poet or poet-painter who will, I think, interest you. He suffers badly from persecution mania. The High Churchman is not so interesting. Melancholia is very common among parsons. I suppose it is due to their frequent money troubles and their large families. The other cases are more difficult, and I think you would do well, as I have suggested, to leave them entirely to me. I would, indeed, ask you for the moment to devote most of your time to the women patients who have hitherto, I gather, been somewhat neglected. Dr. Edwardes, strictly between ourselves, did not pretend to take the same amount of interest in all his cases, and his notes on these women are not nearly so full as I should like."

"What exactly do you wish me to do?" she inquired.

"I assume we are more or less bound to continue the system of our chief. As you know, he notes with the most painstaking accuracy his observations on each case. These observations, recorded over a number of months or years, have enabled him, so he maintains, to form the most accurate and convincing picture of their various mentalities. Their peculiarities are carefully tabulated, and they are then divided and sub-divided according to a system of his own, which is a derivative of the symbolist method of Freud. He then tries to cure his patient of the delusions which, as shown by his notes, occur most frequently. It is necessarily a long process, and one which gives slow, but durable results. I believe he has effected some remarkable cures. During his absence, I shall naturally confine myself to continuing his records, and I shall be very grateful for your assistance, more especially in the matter of the women and the old colonel."

For the next half-hour they discussed details. Dr. Murchison, who followed a somewhat different school from Dr. Edwardes, had ventured to introduce, if not a radical at least a somewhat marked change in the routine of the Château. It appeared that Dr. Edwardes had always treated his patients, though kindly, with a certain severity. Dr. Murchison was proceeding on different lines. The inmates of Château Landry were henceforth to have considerably more freedom; to be humoured as far as possible, and only dealt with firmly when the necessity arose. The routine and discipline of the Château was to be generally relaxed.

"I have, for example, ventured to suppress morning and evening prayers," said Dr. Murchison. "They annoyed the colonel, and I don't think they did much good to anybody else. We are going in future to make all these people as happy in their several ways as possible."

"But you will not, I suppose, go so far as to encourage their illusions," objected Constance.

"No further than we do in dealing with people who are sane," said Dr. Murchison smiling.

"I don't quite understand."

"If in ordinary life you meet a man who is under the impression that he thinks for himself, or a woman who believes her conduct to be rational, you do not necessarily feel bound to destroy that illusion. On the contrary, I should have said that human society is mostly based on a mutual respect for one another's misconceptions. I only ask that we should extend to our patients the common politeness which we practise towards the world in general."

"Of course," said Constance smiling, "if you only wish me to be polite. . . ."

"Politeness," intercepted Dr. Murchison, "consists in respecting the illusions of your neighbour on the understanding, of course, that he will similarly respect your own."

She hardly knew whether he was serious. He spoke lightly, but there was an undercurrent of wilful mockery which did not seem to be altogether assumed.

"One other point," said Constance, after a pause. "Mr. Deeling was talking to me about the patient who tried to escape. I understand that he is rather seriously hurt. Do you wish me to attend to his nursing?"

Dr. Murchison did not answer at once, and Constance felt for a moment as though she had been guilty of an indiscretion. He must, she reflected, be feeling pretty sore over that unlucky business.

Finally he rose, and walked across the room. His back was turned on her. He stopped short but said nothing, and Constance waited in silence.

Then abruptly he wheeled about and faced her.

"I should prefer not to discuss that case," he said at last. "In fact, it is best that you should have as little to do with it as possible. You will understand my feelings in the matter. I all but failed in my duty, but by a miracle I succeeded, at the cost," and here his voice faltered for a moment, "at the cost of a human life."

He ceased, and Constance looked down at the notebook on her knee, in which she had been taking a record of their conversation.

Suddenly, to her surprise, a hand touched her lightly on the shoulder. She looked up. Dr. Murchison was standing over her.

"I would not," he said, "have you needlessly disturbed by what that poor soul suffers, but believe me he is bound to the powers of darkness, bound and chained," and he paused a moment and threw back his head, "and yet he glories in it. What is strangest of all, in his lucid moments he studies his own case. If he were not a hopeless madman he might be the most remarkable of living alienists."

He turned and walked straight from the room. At the door, however, he paused.

"He is in his room recovering from the effects of the journey," he added. "I must beg you to hold no communication with him until I see fit for you to do so."

"You may rely on me," replied Constance, and the door closed.

II

Half-an-hour later Constance was on the southern terrace. This had been originally a space between the outer barbican and the inner wall, but it had been filled in to the height of the former and planted as a formal garden, with clipped hedges some two feet high, a sundial and half-a-dozen statues in the Versailles manner.

A bright-eyed man seated on a stone bench rose as she began to walk down a broad path between clumps of bright flowers. He had a pointed beard and moustache. He wore a white shirt, open at the neck, and flannel trousers, rather the worse for wear.

"The first of the lunatics," thought Constance, as she bowed to him.

He came towards her eagerly.

"So you are the beautiful lady," he said, "who has come amongst us. They have told me about you, but I would not believe it."

He gazed at her long and earnestly.

"Yes," he continued as she stood bewildered, "you are the beautiful lady. She let down her shining hair; but he could not climb, and they were always watching her. We must be careful. You should never have let them know that you were coming."

She wondered what to say to him, but he did not

give her time.

"Sit down," he said, "and I will tell you of the most beautiful thing that has ever happened."

She seated herself mechanically as he bade her.

"When I was a boy," he went on, standing in front of her and speaking with a curious, dreamy intonation and little gestures of his hands, "I used to walk over Westminster Bridge. Every day I walked across it through the sunlight or the fog of London, and every day I passed a cab-rank, and every day I read the notice which was nailed above it. 'All heads,' it said, 'must face east.' There it was, just a printed notice fastened to the lamp. And nobody seemed to know what it meant. But I think you would have known. All heads must face east—towards the desert, the palm-trees and the lurching camels, east to golden Samar-kand and dusty Bokhara, east to the Pamirs and the roof of the world, east to the blue tiles of China and the drifting blossom of Japan, east to the brown girls who dance in the sunlight. I read it and obeyed. I faced east, but I never went. I never went . . . and now it is too late. You know the reason why, for you have seen them. They are watching me now, as I speak to you," and he sank on to the bench by her side and covered his face with his hands.

"Nonsense," said Constance gently, more touched than she liked to confess. "Nobody can see us here."

A shiver went through him. He took his hand from his face.

"They are waiting for me," he said in a whisper. "They are always waiting for me—just beyond the white gate and all outside. They are waiting. One day they will get me. One day I shall be caught."

He leapt to his feet and his face was working.

"They will come," he shouted. "They will come tumbling down, thousands and thousands of them, over the rocks," and he pointed to the yellow crags above the fir trees which barred the horizon on either side.

"Over the rocks," he shouted again. "Over the rocks."

He turned away from her abruptly and disappeared down the path.

Chapter IV

I

"Upon my word, the dashed brute—excuse my language, Miss Sedgwick—measured sixteen feet four inches from his whiskers to the tip of his tail, and weighed close on fifteen hundredweight, and killed—killed, mind you—stone dead with a twelve bore shot gun at five paces. How's that for a tiger," and "Colonel" Rickaby drained the remnants of his whisky and soda, his "chota peg" as he called it, with as much satisfaction as if he had just performed the deed.

"How's that, padré, for a tiger," he repeated, blowing out his walrus moustache, and turning his prominent eyes on the lean man in the Roman collar sitting opposite.

He met with no response. The padré appeared not even to have heard him, but sat silent, staring at the untasted food on his plate, one hand playing with a little gold cross he wore on his watch chain.

"Most interesting," said Constance, trying to be kind.

"Interesting," thundered the Colonel. "It was the most extraordinary thing that has occurred to me in all my thirty years' Shikar experience. Did I ever tell you the yarn about old Tommy Erskine? Tommy, we always called him, because his name was Thomas. When Tommy and I were stationed at Bangalore, or was it Jullundur? Upon my word I can't remember. Yes, yes, I do, I remember perfectly well. It was Jodpore, in eighty-nine, or was it eighty-seven? No, no, it was ninety-three, the year of the smallpox epidemic, or was it cholera? No, I remember now; it was blackwater fever, blackwater fever, and I remember that Mrs. Brown, wife of John Brown, of the I.C.S.—no, it was someone else—can't remember who—anyhow she had twins and died of it."

"Excuse me, Colonel," put in a thin voice from the end of the table, "blackwater fever is a disease indigenous to Africa."

The speaker, even thinner than her voice, removed her pince-nez from a high nose and wiped them with severity. She was dressed in a severe garment of black taffeta, with innumerable jet buttons running from the chin to the waist. Incongruously her fingers were blazing with false gems. She crinkled uncomfortably as she sat back.

The Colonel turned his eyes in her direction.

"Stuff and nonsense, Miss Truro."

"My name is Truelow," she corrected him coldly.

"Truelow, Truro, Truelow," said the Colonel, "what's in a name? It's facts that count. Facts. You

57

think I don't know what blackwater fever is? Had it four times, madam, four dashed confounded times, and the last time I was all but drowned in it. Black water, devilish bad it was and full of whacking great trout. Caught one of them myself—on a little green-heart, only four feet long, or was it four feet six? Weighed a hundred and ten pounds when gaffed. . . ."

Constance looked appealingly at Dr. Murchison. This was one of the Colonel's bad days, during which he was rude to everyone, and especially to the Rev. Mark Hickett and to Miss Laughter Truelow, the thin lady, who seldom failed to contradict him.

Taking advantage of a momentary pause for breath in the interminable flow of the adventures of Tommy Erskine, who had by now become George Baghot, of the old forty-second, or was it the fifty-first, she inquired hastily of Mr. Curtis, the robust looking man seated opposite, whether he would care to come for a walk that afternoon.

Mr. Curtis, who had been eating in steady silence throughout luncheon, shot a furtive glance at her across the table.

"Would you mind repeating that last observation?" he said.

Constance, with an effort, did so.

"Go for a walk?" he repeated. "Go for a walk. That is a most unusual proposition. I must refer it to my directors."

"Stimson," he said over his shoulder to an imaginary person, "Stimson, make a note of that, it is very important, very important indeed."

"Oh, God," thought Constance, "how long shall I be able to stand it?"

She had never realised what this vocation which she had chosen might mean. She had at first been bewildered, then full of pity, but now, as she must own to herself, most crushingly bored. Scientific enthusiasm was all very well, but devotion to duty, when it meant meeting day after day the same poor minds, closed within a circle of their own into which it appeared quite impossible to penetrate, hardly sufficed to sustain her.

Her patients had exhibited degrees of madness varying from something almost sane to something approaching dementia, but she had not been able to add anything to their personal files of any real significance. Miss Laughter Truelow was the nearest to sanity. Severe garments and a terrible zeal for propriety were characteristics of her lucid intervals, and Constance had been puzzled to know why she was there at all, until one day she had come upon her posing before a mirror in her room, her everyday clothes discarded, wearing some kind of oriental transparency and repeating with curious gestures snatches from the Song of Solomon.

She was roused from her reverie by the voice of Dr. Murchison. He was addressing Mr. Curtis.

"By all means go for a walk with Miss Sedgwick," he was saying. "It's a lovely afternoon, and the exercise will do you good."

A sudden silence had fallen on the table. It was like the shutting of a door upon an uproar for they all talked at once and talked unceasingly, maddeningly, all except the Rev. Hickett, who would seldom talk at all. The face of Mr. Curtis assumed a look of strained attention.

"If you really have no objection," he stammered. "But we must be careful, Doctor. Business is business, you know. And my absence may be misconstrued. The Board is apt to be suspicious. I have suffered . . . suffered. . . ."

He broke off, and a look of misery came into his eyes.

"That will be quite all right," said Dr. Murchison soothingly. "I will see the directors myself."

Mr. Curtis nodded his head vigorously, brightened into a smile, and spoke again over his shoulder.

"Stimson," he said, "make a note of that and remember to put it in the minutes."

All the others at the table, except Constance, were leaning forward and gazing with awe at the doctor. Their attitude was one of extreme deference, a strange expectancy in which it was difficult to say whether confidence or suspicion predominated. Even the Rev. Hickett, abandoning the pose of detached sorrow which he had maintained ever since Constance had arrived, stared with the rest, his fingers plucking nervously at the high Roman collar about his thin neck. Miss Laughter Truelow passed a dry tongue across her withered lips. Colonel Rickaby assumed the expression of a junior officer awaiting important instructions from his General.

Mr. Curtis sighed heavily and sat back.

"Thank you, Miss Sedgwick, for the suggestion. I shall be delighted to walk with you, delighted . . .

delighted."

The attention of the others relaxed. They ceased gazing at the doctor, and the uproar broke out again. Constance felt a thrill of envy. What extraordinary power Dr. Murchison was beginning to exercise. How all these poor souls looked up to him, with what pathetic eagerness they waited on everything he said. Of herself they took little or no notice.

A servant handed her a dish, little rounds of steak cut thick on toast. Constance shook her head. She rarely ate meat at middle day, and she did not like it underdone.

"I am sorry," said Dr. Murchison, noticing her refusal. "Let me order something else for you. What about an omelette? But I can assure you that the steak is excellent, very tender and *saignant*," and he helped himself as he spoke to a large portion.

Constance flushed, obscurely resenting this comment on her refusal of a dish. And *saignant* . . . bleeding. How disgustingly the French described meat that was underdone.

"No, thank you," she said. "I'm not really hungry, you know."

"Stuff and nonsense," broke in the Colonel, "stuff and nonsense, my dear young lady, good roast beef of old England, never hurt anybody. I agree with the doctor, emphatically if I may say so, quite emphatically," and he thrust his fork into his own portion with a gusto that was somehow revolting.

She turned hastily to Miss Truelow, and inquired after her little dog. Birdy boy, it appeared, had refused his breakfast again, and Miss Truelow was

61

much distressed.

"When I was campaigning against the Mahsuds, or was it the Wazi Wazi," said the Colonel. . . .

II

At half-past two Constance stood on the terrace awaiting Mr. Curtis. She had recovered from her mood of the luncheon table, and was now trying bravely to achieve the true medical spirit which, devoid alike of pity or of anger, views its cases as so many milestones along the road to discovery. In a word, she had pulled herself together. She would not, she said, in future, allow the patients, however tiresome they might be, to get on her nerves. As a doctor she had no right to nerves. She was waiting now for Mr. Curtis with an equable mind, determined to draw him out as much as possible during the walk, and give as accurate an account as she could of the result.

This was her third experience with Mr. Curtis, and the mere fact that Dr. Murchison had allowed her to take him for a walk proved, as she assured herself, that he was satisfied with the way she was working.

Mr. Curtis came bustling out of the groined Gothic doorway five minutes late. He was dressed in rather startling tweeds, and in his cloth cap were stuck several dry flies.

"Sorry to be late. Sorry to be late," he said bustling across the gravel of the terrace. "There were some last instructions for Stimson. Stimson, you know. He needed some last instructions."

Constance felt a momentary return of her exasperation at the manner in which he ceaselessly repeated every remark, and his constant references to the imaginary Stimson. But she fought it down and met him with a smile.

"You are not very late, Mr. Curtis," she said, "and there is plenty of time."

"But I never like to keep a lady waiting. Never keep a lady waiting," he said hastily. "But Stimson is so stupid. I shall have to give him a wigging. That's what he wants, a good wigging."

They fell into step side by side and began to descend the terrace by a stone stairway leading to the meadow beneath.

"In which direction shall we go?" said Constance, as they paused at the bottom.

"Anywhere you like," said Mr. Curtis, with a vague gesture of the stick in his right hand. "Over there perhaps," and he pointed to the further end of the valley, where the rocks rose sheer through the forest of fir, not far short of half-a-mile away.

"I like the smell of the firs," he went on. "It is a pleasant smell. Or perhaps you don't agree."

He looked at her anxiously, and Constance hastened to say that she also found it a pleasant smell.

Instinctively, as they went along, she ran over in her mind the salient points of his history as far as she knew them.

He had been the senior partner in a not very prosperous firm which had gone bankrupt not long after the war through bad speculation. The catastrophe had unhinged his mind, more especially as his junior partner had been prosecuted for fraud and had only escaped conviction for lack of evidence. Mr. Curtis during the trial had apparently been quite unable to understand the transactions in which his partner had involved him, and his mental collapse was the consequence of prolonged worrying over small details and horror at being suspected of dishonesty. He had been sent to Château Landry by some rich relatives, anxious to put him out of the way and to forget the scandal of his bankruptcy. He now believed himself to be a Napoleon of finance, brilliant, ruthless, controlling the markets of the world.

Dr. Murchison had informed Constance, however, that this delusion was the least important of his symptoms. There was, it seemed, a psychosis, the origin of which must be sought further back than the period of his bankruptcy.

"I wish there was a trout stream here," he said suddenly. They were walking now across the level grass, where, not far away, Colonel Rickaby was engaged on a solitary round on the nine-hole golf links which was laid out in the castle grounds.

"I didn't know you were a fisherman, Mr. Curtis," said Constance, and her remark led him to talk easily and sanely of his pastime. He was a keen angler, and had once been a member of Driffield and accustomed to take three or four miles of a Norwegian river every summer. For a few moments Stimson was mercifully forgotten. Mr. Curtis strode briskly along, sniffing the fragrant air and pausing every now and again to illustrate with his stick a difficult cast, as he described his pursuit of a whacking great fellow, not an ounce

64

under four pounds, which he had hooked late on a May evening, and which had apparently cost him some trouble to bring to the net.

"I believe there is some fishing here," said Constance. "The man who drove me up from Thonon said that there were trout in the Dranse. We might perhaps be able to get you permission to fish there. Perhaps you would like me to inquire?"

They were now walking upon a little path scarcely broad enough for two, which wound up among the fir trees.

"The Dranse," said Mr. Curtis, "where is that?"

"It's the river down there," said Constance, and she pointed across the level stretch of meadow towards the main valley which was shut off by the shoulder of the mountain round which ran the only road to the castle.

Mr. Curtis stopped abruptly, and the anxious look which she was beginning to recognise as a symptom of some profound mental disturbance came into his eyes.

"Not over there, Miss Sedgwick," he said, "I could never go over there. You see, I know what happened down in that dreadful place. I know all about it, Miss Sedgwick, even the details . . . even the details," and he stood shivering as if with sudden cold.

Constance looked at him, at a loss how to reply. Was he alluding to the accident which had resulted in the death of poor Jules? She decided to ignore his change of manner.

"Come along, Mr. Curtis," she said, for he still stood as though rooted to the spot, "I find it a little chilly under these firs."

They were now cut off from the sunshine, and the

dark forest was cold and obscure after the open meadow.

"I would not fish over there," repeated Mr. Curtis. "not even if *he* gave me permission."

"Do you mean Dr. Murchison?"

"Who else should I mean?" said Mr. Curtis.

For a moment longer he stood lost in some vision of his own. Then suddenly he shivered.

"You are right," he said abruptly, "it is cold. . . . cold as death, cold as that poor, mangled fellow."

He lingered on the last two words with a strange unction. She knew that he was afraid, abjectly afraid, and yet he seemed to be prolonging some secret source of pleasure. She watched him curiously. Meeting her steady gaze he passed a hand rapidly over his forehead.

"You quite understand," he said, as though in apology, "my nerves are not for the moment very strong. I am here for a rest, you know. I have been overdoing it, of late . . . vast operations in the city, enormous responsibility, immense sums involved."

Constance sighed. The interval of comparative lucidity seemed to have passed. Mr. Curtis was back once more in his old delusion. He moved on rapidly, speaking to her now over his shoulder as she followed him along the narrow path.

"It is better to get away," he continued. "It is better to get right away. The Dranse, I think you said, I must remember the name . . . that is important. I will ask Stimson to make a note of it. You see the idea . . . make a note of it . . . But first we must get away. It will be safer up there. But even up there . . . you see

66

that great hawk, wheeling in the sunlight. He is looking for something to kill. Poor beasties! They do squeal, you know. Suddenly he pounces on them and then he tears them with his sharp beak and they bleed."

He paused a moment in his rapid ascent, and they stood on the path, breathing rather fast from the climb. He laid a hand on her arm and, avoiding her eyes, he said with the same strange unction which she had already noted:

"The Dranse, was it not? The River Dranse. I am going to forget it. . . . And for a while forget, the weariness, the fever and the fret. . . . The nightingale, you know. . . . It is very steep down there by the river, precipitous, quite precipitous. And the poor fellow went crashing down, right beyond the rocks till his head hit a large white stone and it cracked, just like that," and Mr. Curtis put his foot on a pine cone which crackled under his heel as he spoke.

"Horrible, horrible, most horrible," he went on. "That stone would have to be scrubbed . . . hardly the work for a maid," and suddenly he broke into a high cackling laugh.

"How do you know about the accident?" said Constance, for she felt sure that so terrible an event as the death of Jules would have been kept from all the patients.

Mr. Curtis looked very cunning at that—cunning and a little frightened.

"I mustn't tell you," he said. "It's a secret between me and . . . and someone else. We really oughtn't to talk about it at all. So you mustn't give me away. We must be very careful, you know. Both in the same boat, now."

What did he mean? He had evidently had a vivid account from someone of the murder of Jules. Or perhaps he had overheard the servants talking. Constance decided to speak to Dr. Murchison about it. The incident had evidently impressed Mr. Curtis, and it had obviously had a most deplorable effect upon his state of mind.

They were passing now through the firs and the path ran along the edge of the naked rock. It went, as it seemed, right round the whole circle of the mountain wall which rimmed the meadow, sometimes dipping low into the fir trees, sometimes rising above them to the bare stone. In the confined space of the valley this was the only walk of reasonable length that could be taken.

Suddenly Mr. Curtis paused again.

"One thing," he said, "before we leave the subject. It was evidently his own fault. . . . Nobody else to blame . . . blood on his own head. I tell you this as a friend, for it will be a lesson to us all."

"I'm afraid I don't know what you mean," faltered Constance.

"He disobeyed," said Mr. Curtis.

III

Germaine was a little late in starting. The servants had their evening meal at seven, an hour before the doctor dined himself, but she had been kept late with a press of work, mostly due, she decided, to the fantastic notions of cleanliness entertained by the young English "Miss," who also called herself a doctor, and to whom she had taken a dislike. She had not, therefore, been able to start for the rendezvous till close on eight o'clock.

She had started in a hurry, and in her anxiety to get away she had forgotten one of her duties. The new doctor had particularly asked her on no account to leave unlocked the little chapel where those poor mad folk, in Dr. Edwardes' time, had assembled every day for morning and evening prayers. She had dusted the chapel only that afternoon, and she had neglected to lock it up again. No one, however, she reflected, was likely to notice it, and she would see to it as soon as she got back.

It was almost dark as she crossed the meadow, but over the hills was a lemon-coloured light against which their rocky summits stood in frowning relief. But even this light was rapidly fading.

She set out at a brisk pace, making for the belt of fir trees. Every now and then she paused and glanced nervously over her shoulder as though to make sure that she was unobserved. She was not, however, breaking any rule of the house, for, provided the servants did not go beyond the lodge gates, which were closed every evening at sundown, and which could only be opened from the switch on Dr. Edwardes' desk, or from the lodge where there was someone on duty only during the day, they were free to go where they liked within the limits of the meadow.

That she should be nervous was less remarkable

than her being there at all. No other girl in the village would have dared as much. Ever since she could remember the villagers had shunned the castle and its grounds, and had avoided its inmates, a taboo which had only been broken by herself and a few other men and women, attracted by the high wages paid by the doctor. But even these bold spirits, who were ready to brave the obscure terrors of the place by day, never ventured out of doors by night. And of late there had been stories in the village, stories which had renewed its faith in an ancient evil. It was known that in that valley the Devil had once had special powers. She had often heard her grandfather tell of a dreadful visitation in his early youth when the whole countryside had been swept as by an evil wind and strange rites had been performed up and down the valley, but more especially within that very circle of rock which hedged the castle.

It was dark by the time she reached the trees, and she paused for one final glance round before plunging beneath them, so dark indeed that, had she not known the path so well, she must have lost her way.

The colour had died from the sky and the stars were showing, while behind the Dent Noire hung the new moon. Germaine bobbed hastily three times to the slender crescent, and wished with all her might. She wished that Pierre would be true to her and not run off to Thonon or Annecy and take up with some other girl, as he always threatened to do when they quarrelled. They had quarrelled the last time they had met, and her mind was full of doubts and fears as she stumbled on beneath the firs, her feet brushing softly through the needles.

She was late, too, and Pierre hated to be kept waiting. She knew that she was a fool to be thus abject, for everyone said that Pierre was good for nothing—a great strong fellow, who had come unharmed through the war, but was still content with looking after the tiny property of his old father. He had no ambition, the village had decided; besides, he was a sullen man and close-fisted. He never took her to town or bought her things, and when they met he would talk of nothing but the sickness of Sarah and Deborah, his fat Savoyard cows, except when he was angry; and then he would swear to go away and leave the land he so dearly, but inarticulately, loved, and become a chauffeur.

But she did not care what he did or what they said of him. She loved him, and as she moved forward now in the darkness her body ached for his arms and her mouth for his rough kisses, for the hands that held her so urgently and the harsh voice that broke under his passion.

She was now on the path that ran all round the circle of hills in a great horseshoe, barred at each end by the steel fence, with its close mesh.

She laughed a little to herself. That was her special secret, shared only with Pierre, who had been so clever and contrived it all. For these two had made a gap in the fence unknown to anyone. It had taken Pierre two days with wirecutters and a file. He had cut a little flap in the mesh, and when she lifted it up he could just crawl through to her. In the day time no one would ever notice it, so skilfully was it hidden, though it was less than ten yards from the end of the path.

She had by this time reached the clearing, and was only a hundred yards away from the fence. The clearing was a tiny space, not twenty yards across. You came upon it suddenly just as you seemed to be approaching the thickest part of the fir wood. There was nothing in the clearing but an old white stone in the middle. She could just distinguish it, grey against the darker turf surrounding it, as she moved quickly past, panting a little, for she had come at a sharp pace. She came that way to-night because it was shorter by some two hundred yards than the path, and because she was late and full of her meeting with Pierre. Normally nothing would have induced her to come near it after dark. She crossed the clearing quickly, and a moment later she was among the fir trees again. Fifty yards farther on she stopped and listened.

She heard nothing but her own heart, for Pierre had not yet arrived. Up to that moment she had been so full of Pierre and of her eagerness to reach the meeting place in time that there had been no room for any other feeling. He was the journey's end; he filled the darkness; he would be the next shadow that waited in the path; and, as she almost ran into the wood, it was as though she were running into his embrace.

But the wood was now no longer the covert in which he waited; the shadows about her were suddenly alien; the tree that stood darkly at her side was itself a presence. She was humanly alone and yet she was encompassed by shapes that scared her with their blank indifference. And between her and the castle with its fellowship lay the little clearing with the ancient stone. She knew now that some secret part of herself, even when she had been full of her lover, had been afraid as she had passed that empty space. The panic which had unconsciously quickened her breathing as she had moved again so softly into the covert now came to the surface. She *knew* now that she was afraid; that she would never again cross that space alone. Sooner would she stand there rooted forever, facing the night, with a nameless anguish in her heart, and a fear that spread like a pool upon the floor of her soul.

And soon it became intolerable. For just one further instant perhaps she would be able to keep control, to remain herself, Germaine who had come to meet her lover. And then she would be a driven thing, the body and soul of her fear, with a voice that screamed, and feet that ran and stumbled.

But just at that moment from somewhere in front came a stealthy sound, which changed the world—three bars of "Madelon" whistled softly below the breath.

"Pierre," she cried, and stumbled forward sobbing and with arms outstretched. A great wave of happiness spread in her, choking her so that she could not speak. She groped in front of her. Her hands touched a sleeve. A voice, a little above her in the darkness, said softly:

"At last, *chérie*. Where have you been all this time?"

73

Now she was in his arms, held so close that she almost cried out at the pain.

But to-night he could not hold her close enough, for there she was safe and he made the world human again with his kisses. She gave little cries and gasps of pleasure. Presently, however, when the first rapture was passed, she began to struggle.

"No, no," he said, and his voice was harsh and troubled. "You have kept me waiting long enough."

He had never kissed her like that before. She had never let him. She had instinctively kept him at arm's length not from conscience but from an unreasoning instinct of defence which she could neither explain nor understand. But to-night it was different. She had been late, and she had thought she was alone, and there he had been waiting for her the whole time, to be suddenly her refuge and a great relief. And it was all so dark and she could see nothing—only feel him and be aware of his great strength and the futility of her resistance.

So after a while she ceased to struggle, allowing his kisses once again to drown even the memory of her recent terror, and she scarcely noticed what path they were taking as he led her forward, away from the fence by which he had been waiting, back along the path by which she had come, back to the little patch of fragrant needles at the edge of the clearing, where they had lain hid together once before when they had heard footsteps and had been frightened.

Not even when they had reached the edge of the clearing, and she stood with him where she dared not have ventured alone, did she remember her panic of a short while ago. She was conscious of nothing but the man who held her and the harsh voice that broke upon her name, and she closed her eyes that she might be the more secluded in her pleasure.

There could never be anything in her world again but this seclusion. There was no more room for fear of misgiving.

Then suddenly she was aware of a change in him.

He had stiffened and the hand on her shoulder gripped her so fiercely that she gave a little cry of pain, but the grip was not relaxed, and she heard a harsh whispering, not close as before, but above her, breathed out into the night.

"Sacred God, what is that!"

She opened her eyes. He was looking away from her into the clearing. His arm trembled like a leaf, and she felt all the strength go out of him. And suddenly she, too, was afraid, and seemed unable to breathe. She thrust an arm about his neck and pulled herself up, so that she was half sitting and half lying against the tree, and then she looked out over his shoulder, following the direction of his eyes.

The clearing was not dark as when she had left it. There was a light in it, small and flickering, and of a bluish colour, somewhere above the white stone. It hissed and spat a moment, and then something rose up from the middle of the clearing, a tall black shadow that moved upwards in one great gesture, lifting sable arms. She saw the glimmer of a white object caught between them. The arms dropped suddenly above the stone. There was a beating of wings, and the white thing jerked, a soft thud, then the sound of steel striking stone, and a voice that said a single sentence in an unknown tongue.

The white thing was lifted wildly into the air again, and torn before her eyes so that it was scattered above the stone and fell in a whirl of snowy pinions. Then the light went out.

And Pierre was on his knees beside her muttering prayers to Our Lady and his patron saints with a fierce, mechanical intensity.

She flung her arms about him, needing him as a refuge from her terror.

"Save me, Pierre," she whispered. "Take me away."

But he was blind and deaf, and seemed unaware of her presence. Each was alone with a fear that held them in an implacable solitude of their own.

IV

The dawn rose late within that circle of hills. First the darkness went pale behind the mountain wall and the shadow of the wall itself was cut more clearly upon the sky. The light for a while was colourless, but the sun, hidden behind the wall, was soon able to reach the clouds or the more distant edges of the valley which from darkest purple lightened into warm russet, then into tender rose till at last the valley itself assumed colours of its own. The pastures were green, a white house stood upon the brown earth.

But still the circle at the head of the valley was in shadow and the little clearing in the midst of the firs was as yet unvisited. Then the sun looked over the shoulder of the mountain and the light poured over into the clearing as into a bowl. The turf was green and the firs were dark, and the stone in the midst of it was gleaming white.

But the white surface was that morning flecked with red, and on the green turf were white feathers and fragments which gleamed under the sun. And in the midst of the clearing a lean cat, bright orange against the vivid green, was nosing one of the fragments, about which a small army of warrior ants was busy.

Chapter V

I

Early next morning Constance was sitting on the western end of the castle terrace. Behind her was the wall of the chapel, pierced by a rose window of exquisite design, said to have been copied from the window in Santa Lucia at Syracuse. One of the de Landry in the service of King Roger of Sicily had seen it, and caused it to be reproduced in his own home. Just beneath the window were two white painted seats, on one of which Constance was sitting in the company of Miss Truelow.

In front of them stretched a rose garden, built in the Italian manner, the rose trees being planted in green painted tubs. Down the centre of the garden ran a little stream, trickling from the mouth of a wineskin held by a leaden satyr and confined to a stone bed bordered by red saliva and moss.

No one was in the garden, but just beyond the pergola which bounded it on the West Constance could see Miss Collett, the patient who believed herself to be growing backwards, and who had now reached the age of ten. She was an elderly lady, nearer sixty than fifty, dressed in a childish frock of linen, with a pink bow in her grey hair. She was playing battledore and shuttlecock all by herself, with the intense absorption of a child.

Constance would have liked to go and talk to her, but the other woman at her side in the black taffeta was claiming her attention. Miss Truelow, it seemed, was in need of a friend, and Constance, though she rather tended to fight shy of this particular patient, was pleased at her approach. It seemed to show that she was gradually gaining the confidence of these people, without which, she knew, no hope of a cure could be entertained.

Accordingly, she sat in the sun and did her best to listen.

"I need hardly assure you," Miss Truelow was saying, "that I have never given him the least encouragement. The attachment which he has formed for me is quite spontaneous."

It was to Dr. Murchison that she referred, and Constance, looking in perplexity at the prim figure beside her, was at a loss for an answer. For the moment, however, none was required. Miss Truelow was apparently quite content so long as she had someone in whom she could confide.

"At first," she went on, "I was reluctant to believe it, though, of course, it has happened before. I had trouble with that Hyacinth boy not long ago—most attentive he was, so that I never allowed him to find me alone. I fear that with the doctor it will be serious.

79

He was telling me this morning of a dream that he had last night. He came to a flight of steps that led up to the door of a tiny church. And suddenly he began to climb."

Her eyes were glittering, and all at once she had begun to breathe rapidly, her fingers tightly clenched.

Constance put a hand on her arm.

"Surely, Miss Truelow," she said, "you must be mistaken. Dr. Murchison never told you that."

"Yes, my dear, he did, and what is more, I know that the dream was true, for I was in the church myself."

She ended impressively in the tone of one who was giving the club to a mystery.

"You will realise," went on Miss Truelow, "that this puts me in a very awkward position. That is why I spoke to you. I wanted to ask your advice. What do you think I ought to do?"

As Constance considered her reply, the seat on which she sat vibrated, and she heard music, muffled as from a distance. It came from the organ in the chapel behind her, which was odd, for she knew that Dr. Murchison kept it locked. The player, whoever it was, had, however, no misgivings on the subject, for a great volume of sound swept out into the sunlight. Constance welcomed the diversion, as it gave her a chance to lead Miss Truelow away from her fixed idea.

"I wonder who that is playing the organ," she said.

But Miss Truelow was not to be deterred.

"Please tell me what you think I ought to do, Miss Sedgwick," she replied, laying a thin hand on the arm of her companion.

"Well," said Constance slowly, "I don't think I should worry too much about it for the moment."

As Constance spoke, the thin hand tightened on her arm.

"There is a further complication," said Miss Truelow.

"Indeed?"

"Yes," said Miss Truelow, "surely you must have noticed it."

Constance observed a change on her patient's face. It had darkened perceptibly.

"Haven't you observed how carefully she avoids him?" Miss Truelow suddenly inquired.

"You mean?"

"Why, Miss Archer, of course. She is frantic with jealousy, and one of these days something terrible will happen."

She paused a moment and added suddenly:

"This morning she was alone in the garden, and she picked a spray of white roses. We all know what that means."

"Surely," objected Constance, hoping to soothe her patient, "you must be mistaken about Miss Archer. She often gathers roses for the chapel."

Miss Truelow drew back, her eyes grew hard. She removed her pince-nez with hands that trembled.

"Very well," she said, "you leave me to take my own precautions. But I hope that you will give orders that Miss Archer is on no account to be allowed in the kitchen."

"The kitchen?" Constance repeated in bewilderment.

"I do not wish to be poisoned," said Miss Truelow,

and rising with immense dignity she added:

"It's a fine day, and I think I shall take a turn in the garden."

She strode rapidly away, and as she did so a childish lamentation came from beyond the pergola where Miss Collett, in pursuit of her shuttlecock, had tripped over a flower bed and fallen heavily on her face. She was now screaming like a child, more frightened than hurt.

Miss Truelow was already going to the help of Miss Collett, and Constance paused, uncertain whether to follow. She saw Miss Truelow, however, assist Miss Collett to her feet, pat her affectionately on the shoulder, and begin to brush her down. She felt, therefore, that her own intervention was unnecessary, and, leaving the bench, she made for the chapel door, wishing to find out who was inside.

She drew back the heavy curtain which covered the door. It was not very light in the interior, for the biggest window in the chapel was the rose window, the others being mere slits, the building having been originally included within the defences of the castle.

It was a small place, not more than fifty feet long, and built entirely of stone. At the east end stood the altar, a plain slab with the six candles upon it. There were a dozen rush-bottomed chairs in the nave, and beside one of these, close to the wooden rails shutting off the sanctuary from the rest of the church, stood a dark figure.

As Constance moved towards it, the right arm of the figure was lifted, and a voice cried out: "I forbid you to continue playing that infamous music!"

Constance recognised the voice of Miss Archer, the

religious devotee, who spent long hours in mystical devotions under the impression, at times, that she was a re-incarnation of St. Theresa.

"Why, Miss Archer, what is it?" said Constance, as she came forward into the chapel.

Miss Archer turned towards her a pale face, delicately lined and glowing with indignation.

"Please, Miss Sedgwick," she entreated. "Tell him to come down."

She was deeply moved, and her black draperies rustled about her as she pointed once more at the organ gallery.

The organ occupied most of the north transept. It was altogether out of proportion in size to the chapel. At the double keyboard sat Hyacinth Clearwater. He was leaning at that moment over the balcony of the loft, smiling impishly down at the two women.

Constance paused, uncertain how to deal with the situation. Except for some occasional bickering between Miss Truelow and Colonel Rickaby, she had never yet had to encounter anything in the nature of quarrels between the patients.

She saw at a glance that this was rather more serious, absurd as it might seem on the surface. Miss Archer was quivering from head to foot.

Constance decided to try her influence upon Mr. Clearwater.

"Come, Mr. Clearwater," she said, "don't you think it would be better to play some other tune, or won't you stop altogether. It's very pleasant in the garden this morning. Suppose we leave Miss Archer in peace. You can continue your practising later."

"Practising!" said Mr. Clearwater, assuming an

attitude of pained surprise. "Practising, beautiful lady. Is that how you refer to my music?"

He cast up his eyes as though in elfin mockery of the devout Miss Archer.

"O jasper tones!" he cried. "O sable harmonies! How are ye profaned!"

"Now, Mr. Clearwater," protested Constance, "you know very well that I was not intending to disparage your music. You shall continue it this afternoon, when Miss Archer is resting."

"I never rest," said Miss Archer abruptly, turning her white face towards Constance.

A shaft of sunlight, striking through one of the slit windows, fell in a radiance about her, so that she looked like a nun in the style of El Greco.

Constance tried another tack.

"Won't you come into the garden, Miss Archer?" she suggested. "It's so fine out-of-doors to-day, and I'm sure you would enjoy walking among the roses."

"The lilies and languors of virtue, the roses and raptures of vice," chanted Mr. Clearwater from the balcony.

"I will not leave this House to be profaned by that evil rhymster," said Miss Archer in a loud voice, and she fell on her knees and covered her face with her hands.

Mr. Clearwater rose with dignity.

"Rhymster," he echoed. "I allow no one to question my poetic gift. I would ask you to withdraw that expression, Miss Archer."

But she paid him no further attention. She was now muttering prayers between her fingers: *Si iniquitates observaris Domine: Domine quis sustinebit?*

84

Constance was disappointed. Mr. Clearwater had hitherto been her favorite among the patients, and she had found him quite easy to manage, fundamentally good-natured and tractable. She felt now as though he had been somehow removed from her control. This morning he seemed to be possessed by the very spirit of mischief. He faced her now like a difficult child, and Constance admonished him accordingly.

"Come down at once," she said, "and leave the chapel. If you can't behave decently, you had better go!"

He twisted round on the stool and looked at her stubbornly.

"I was here first," he said. "And I've got just as much right to be here as she has. I'm sure the Doctor would say so."

And turning round to the keyboard, he began to play again.

Constance stood below in the chapel, powerless to interrupt, though she felt that either she must continue to assert her authority or never stand again for sanity or discipline. She wondered how to meet the situation.

In that moment of hesitation she was lost, for already the pipes were in full blast, and she could not have made herself heard even if she had thought of anything to say.

She did not know the music he was playing—something, perhaps, by an unknown master or possibly a composition of his own. But she was caught by the power of it, a power in which there was clearly no relish of salvation. She found herself following helplessly a melody that leaped in strange intervals, but never at random, inevitable as the step of the statue of the commendatore on the stair. It sprang ungainly, it hobbled as on a crutch, it limped, it soared as on a broken wing. But always it advanced, and nothing could stay its progress. There was something in her that fled its approach, and yet was rooted to the earth as in a dream when the limbs refuse their office.

Then suddenly there was a cry, and Constance turned to see Miss Archer running swiftly forward to the altar steps. A chair fell with a clatter on the stone floor as she swept blindly through the chancel. Arrived at the foot of the altar, she stopped abruptly and gazed straight before her between the six candles. Then she cried out again and turned swiftly, her arms outstretched like some distraught bat, which had blundered into a lighted globe.

"The crucifix," she screamed, "he has taken it away," and, still screaming, she fell to the ground, rolling down the steps in some kind of fit.

The music ceased abruptly, and Constance ran forward to where Miss Archer lay, insensible, with foam upon her lips.

Then, as she bent over her patient, a voice came sternly from the end of the chapel.

"What has been happening here, Miss Sedgwick?" said Dr. Murchison.

II

The doctor passed quickly up the nave and reached the chancel.

"Miss Archer has had a fit," said Constance stupidly.

"So I perceive," replied Dr. Murchison coldly, and stooping over he felt the pulse of the unconscious woman. He put a silver whistle to his lips with his other hand as he did so, and blew three short blasts, which were answered a moment later by a warder.

"Tell Nurse Webster that I shall want her in Miss Archer's room immediately," he said to the man, "and then come here with a stretcher."

The warder went off, to return a few moments later with a companion.

During these proceedings Dr. Murchison said not a word. Constance stood by wretchedly, feeling miserably inefficient. Yet it seemed to her that, though she had apparently failed in her duty, it had scarcely been her fault. She did not see how, in the circumstances, she could possibly have avoided the crisis.

The warders entering caused her to look up, and it was then that she saw Hyacinth Clearwater. He was stealing softly on tip-toe down the winding metal stairs which led to the organ loft, holding on to the rail and testing each step as he went, the complete picture of a school-boy hoping to escape detection. He reminded her of the fox terrier at home when caught in the larder. But she had no time to observe the behaviour of Mr. Clearwater. As the men stooped to place Miss Archer on the stretcher she sighed and opened her eyes. She found herself looking straight into the face of Dr. Murchison, who was bending over her. For a moment she stared at him. Then with a long shuddering sigh she covered her eyes with her hands.

"The powers of darkness," she whispered. "Now

am I wholly forsaken, bound and delivered up."

The doctor smiled at her pityingly.

"Come, Miss Archer," he said gently, "you will soon be all right," and he put a hand on her forehead.

She shrank and shivered under his touch.

"Signed and branded," she moaned.

She half rose from the stretcher, and said in a clear strong voice: "I call upon St. Michael and his angels," and suddenly she began to pray hopelessly, incoherently, but continually to the effect that the Lord should protect her from evil which encompassed her on every side.

At last, in the midst of her praying, she paused, and sitting upright on the stretcher faced the doctor, as though she were defying her own imminent destruction.

"You have taken it away," she said.

"What does she mean?" inquired the doctor sharply of Constance, checking with a motion of his hand the movement of the stretcher-bearers who were about to remove her.

"She means the crucifix," said Constance in a low voice. "She was upset by the playing of Mr. Clearwater, and suddenly she ran to the altar and found that the crucifix was no longer there."

"You have taken it away," repeated the woman on the stretcher, and thrusting out her right arm she pointed full at the door. "You have broken it," she said, "and buried it, and you are damned eternally. God give me strength to pray for your soul."

She sank back on the stretcher and relapsed into secret prayer.

The doctor jerked his head, and the stretcher-bearers moved steadily with shortened step out of the chapel with their burden.

"And now, Mr. Clearwater," said the doctor, as the curtain fell behind them, "I will attend to you."

Mr. Clearwater, who had reached the bottom step of the spiral staircase, and was tiptoeing towards the door of the chapel, swung round and tried to look completely unconcerned.

"Come here," said Dr. Murchison sternly.

Mr. Clearwater came forward with an air of elaborate innocence, but with a careful eye on the doctor, like a puppy who is doubtful whether his master really intends to inflict the punishment he deserves.

"Now, Mr. Clearwater," said Dr. Murchison, "what have you to say for yourself?"

"Nothing," said Mr. Clearwater promptly, with a propitiatory smile. "I was just . . . er . . . playing . . . playing, you know."

"Wasn't that rather inconsiderate," said Dr. Murchison. "You must have known that your music was distressing to poor Miss Archer."

Mr. Clearwater looked quaintly at the doctor, almost as though there were an invisible wink in his eye.

"I wasn't playing for Miss Archer," he said, "I was playing . . . I was playing for the beautiful lady here," he concluded, indicating Constance with a sudden mendacity that took her breath away.

"Yes," continued Mr. Clearwater with a bright smile. "I was playing for Miss Sedgwick. You like my music, don't you, Miss Sedgwick?" he asked, turning to her like a child inviting a confederate to play up.

"I have not had much opportunity of hearing you," said Constance coldly.

"And may we ask, Mr. Clearwater, what it was that you were playing. I heard you as I came through the garden and it seemed vaguely familiar."

"Oh, nothing," said Mr. Clearwater, "nothing at all . . . just a little thing, nothing at all serious, you know."

"And what was its name?" persisted the doctor, quietly.

"Its name?" echoed Mr. Clearwater, changing uneasily from one foot to another.

"Look at me, Mr. Clearwater," said Dr. Murchison in the same quiet tone.

Mr. Clearwater looked at his toes and then unwillingly raised his eyes to the doctor.

"What was its name?" Dr. Murchison repeated.

Mr. Clearwater spoke now with a rush.

"They call it, 'Jumping Joan'," he said with a little laugh. "They played it in the old days when they burned witches in the streets. And it frightened them properly, just as it frightened that nasty old witch a moment ago. Oh, yes, it's a naughty little tune—very naughty indeed."

He was looking now at the doctor rather like a spoiled child who knows that he has misbehaved, but knows also that he will be indulged in his misdemeanours. And indeed, it seemed to Constance that Dr. Murchison with difficulty suppressed a smile.

"Very well, Mr. Clearwater," he said, "you may go."

Mr. Clearwater, like a schoolboy released by his master, turned on his heel and, leapfrogging over two or three kneelers and a *prie-Dieu*, landed lightly near the door of the chapel. Then he sped swiftly through the curtain, leaving Dr. Murchison and Constance alone.

"I am afraid, Miss Sedgwick," said Dr. Murchison after a pause, "that you have not had a very successful morning."

"I . . . I am sorry," said Constance. "They seemed suddenly to get quite out of hand. I cannot understand your control. It is marvellous."

He gave no sign that he appreciated her rather blunt enthusiasm, and she blushed uneasily.

"You will improve," he said. "It is merely a question of time. But I must have a serious talk with you very shortly on those two cases. They are quite simple to handle if you know how to take them."

"I should be only too glad," said Constance. "To-morrow morning, if that would suit you, during the office hour."

They were walking slowly down the chapel as she spoke.

"Not to-morrow," said Dr. Murchison, "I expect I shall be ill to-morrow."

His face looked strangely haggard, and his eyes were abnormally bright—or was it merely the effect of the light striking down through the coloured glass of the rose window as they moved westward towards the door?

III

Mr. Ambrose Deeling walked every evening once round the castle, or rather round that part of it inhabited by the patients, in order to see that they were all properly settled for the night. He was accompanied on these occasions by one of the two trained nurses, whose duty it was to look after those of the inmates of Château Landry whom it might be necessary to keep in bed either during the crises to which most of them were subject from time to time or when they were attacked by some ordinary malady.

Dr. Edwardes had originally been accustomed to visit the patients himself, or rather to look in at their rooms every night before they retired to rest, but of late years he had delegated this duty to Mr. Deeling, and Mr. Deeling set great store by its performance, partly out of respect for Dr. Edwardes, but more, as Constance suspected, owing to the fact that such a duty flattered his conceit, seeming for a moment to raise him from the status of a compounder and dispenser of drugs to that of resident physician.

On that particular evening, Dr. Murchison had retired to his own room immediately after dinner, so that Mr. Deeling was left to conduct a desultory conversation with Constance for the half-hour or so which preceded his rounds. He eyed her with more than a touch of irritation, as she sat opposite to him on the other side of the hearth, sipping his coffee and smoking the last of the three cigarettes a day which he allowed himself. She had from the first outraged his sense of the fitness of things, and he resented everything about her. She was a woman. She was young. She was a doctor. It was really absurd that she should be a "doctor," and, if she were a doctor, she should not be sitting there in an evening dress of green velvet with bare arms. She should be dressed in black, with perhaps a touch of white at the throat and wrists, and her hair should be pulled back from the forehead and fastened in a knot low down on the nape of her neck, instead of being waved and shingled.

He talked slightingly of the fine weather and of the new moon, of the remarkable purity of the air, of the lack of consideration shown by the servants. Only that morning, it seemed that one of the maids, Germaine, a village girl, had given notice for no particular reason, so far as he could see.

Constance replied in monosyllables, and presently, picking up a magazine lying on the table beside her, began to turn the pages. Mr. Deeling rose.

"Good-night, Dr. Sedgwick," he said delicately, stressing, as was his custom, the offending title.

"Good-night, Mr. Deeling," she absently replied, and as she bent forward the light fell across her hair and one round arm that lay across the back of her chair.

"Altogether too young," said Mr. Deeling to himself as he closed the door behind him.

He passed down the corridor to his own office, a little room on the ground floor of one of the four round towers which stood at each corner of the castle. It was fitted up as a laboratory, and contained, besides a number of locked glass cabinets which held the drugs used by Dr. Edwardes, two sinks, a number of glass retorts, pipettes and other apparatus, and a small pinewood desk with a single swivel chair in front.

Mr. Deeling crossed the room, sat down, opened a drawer of the desk and extracted his ledger. It was his daily custom to balance the amount of drugs which he had used in the dispensary, much as a merchant balances his accounts. He opened the ledger, at the same time taking a pile of little shiny leather note-books from a pigeon-hole in front of him. He had one notebook for each drug; that was his system. At the end of the day the amount used of each drug was noted in the big ledger; and at the end of the month he added up the totals and checked them against his stocks.

He opened the big ledger and frowned. He had forgotten the date. It was the thirty-first of July. He would have to make up his account of the drugs that night, and he was tired. It did not occur to him, however, that the operation could be postponed. Wearily he began to run his pencil down the items, adding drams and scruples.

He had not finished his task when there was a tap on the door, and Nurse Baxter, a pleasant English-woman of middle age, came into the room. It was time to make the nightly round of the castle.

He took his electric torch and followed the nurse out of the room, switching off the light and pulling the door, which closed with a spring lock, behind him.

He walked slowly down the corridor in front of the nurse, flashing his light officiously to either side as he went. The torch was not very obviously necessary, for there were lights in all the corridors, though they were shaded to little more than a soft glow. They passed from room to room, Mr. Deeling noiselessly raising the little flap which covered the spy-hole in the door of each of them, and looking quietly into each interior.

Nurse Baxter did the same for the women patients, whom Mr. Deeling had always resolutely refused to overlook, maintaining, as was her wont, a running commentary on their activities. These did not, however, amount to much—in fact they were all "quiet-like," she said. Miss Truelow, usually the most restless, was apparently engaged in the study of a large book propped up in front of her in bed, the title of which was invisible.

The men patients were equally tranquil. Mr. Clearwater was reading in bed; the Rev. Mark Hickett was as usual on his knees at his *prie-dieu* in the corner of the room; the Colonel, in his pajamas, was doing his nightly physical exercises with the aid of a rubber chest expander. The only one who attracted any attention was Mr. Curtis, who was crouching by his window looking out at the night. Mr. Deeling watched him for a moment, wondering whether to enter and ask whether he wanted anything. But Mr. Curtis shifted his position, so that his face became clearly visible. He was smiling happily, evidently enjoying some private thought, and Mr. Deeling decided to leave him undisturbed.

Mr. Deeling, having completed his round, returned at once to his accounts. He was tired, but he was also obstinate, and he was determined not to allow mere physical fatigue to seduce him from his routine. He continued, therefore, doggedly to total up his drugs, and presently he came to his stock of hyoscin, the powerful sedative used to reduce troublesome or violent patients.

He noted with satisfaction that according to his entries very little of the drug had been used during the past month, none at all in fact, except apparently for the Honble. Geoffrey Godstone, the maniac who had murdered the unhappy Jules. It was now over three weeks since Mr. Godstone had entered Château Landry, and throughout that time he had been kept continually in his room, suffering, so Mr. Deeling understood, from the effects of the blow which Dr. Murchison had been forced to deal him in self-defence. During the last week Mr. Deeling had twice been asked to make up a prescription containing hyoscin, presumably for the benefit of Mr. Godstone.

Half an hour later, the accounts were finished. Mr. Deeling rose wearily from his desk. All that now remained for him to do was to check the quantity of drugs left in the bottles against the amount shown in the big ledger as having been consumed, so as to make sure that they tallied. He crossed the room and began to unlock one by one the glass cases screwed to the wall.

Quickly he checked the various bottles. The work was mechanical enough, but, when he came to the bottle containing hyoscin, Mr. Deeling paused in surprise. He picked up the bottle and looked at it. There was appreciably less of the drug than there should be. He moved across to his desk and consulted his original entries in the notebook for hyoscin. There was no doubt about it. There should have been considerably more of the drug in the bottle than there was.

Mr. Deeling was puzzled. Such a thing had never happened before throughout the whole eleven years in which he had been at Château Landry. He moved to the centre of the dispensary, and held the bottle up to the light.

As he did so, a step sounded on the gravel of the terrace outside.

Mr. Deeling wheeled round sharply towards the long French window. It was open, for the night was sultry, and the light from the dispensary shone upon a bright triangular patch of gravel. Again there was a step on the gravel, and something black fluttered for a moment on the edge of the triangle of light, something like the edge of a sable cloak.

Mr. Deeling went at once to the window, and through it, to the terrace outside. He looked into the night, very soft and dark. On the edge of the lit triangle he paused, straining his eyes and ear. From far away down the valley came the tinkle of a cowbell, liquid and passionless. He took a dozen steps forward, bringing him to the edge of the terrace, and paused again. Still he could see nothing, hear nothing, but, even as he began to wonder what he should do, he became aware of a sudden illumination behind him. He turned round. Three rooms of the first floor of the castle were brightly lit, and at each of the barrel windows a dark figure stood in silhouette. Two of them were motionless.

"Mr. Clearwater and Miss Truelow," said Mr. Deeling to himself, "and the third is Mr. Curtis."

The figure at the third window stirred. It leaned far out, pulling itself forward by the bars till its face was pressed between them. From the unseen mouth came the appeal of a man forsaken:

"Master! Master!" it cried.

Mr. Deeling moved rapidly back towards the house till he stood once more in the triangle of light from the open window of the dispensary. Till then he had been invisible, but now suddenly the figures at the windows caught sight of him. All three turned simultaneously

97

and disappeared, leaving the three squares of light brilliant and empty.

A moment later the lights in the three windows went out and the upper floor of the castle was again in darkness.

Chapter VI

I

"It's dashed fine lie, upon my word it is. I have never seen such a fine lie in all my life," said Colonel Rickaby, as he gazed at his ball perched on the little worm cast in the middle of the fairway of the last hole.

Constance hastened to agree with him. They were approaching the end of a close match. The Colonel, an erratic player, had won the seventeenth hole and was consequently all square. Unfortunately, for him, however, he had cracked at the last hole, and he was now about to play five, his ball being still twenty yards from the green. Constance was on the edge in three and so could feel pretty certain of the hole.

The Colonel, whom four bad shots had depressed, became suddenly triumphant. Such a good lie was really remarkable. He gazed at the ball earnestly from several angles, and then approached his bag, held upright by patent arrangement of light sticks in the form of a tripod of which he was very vain, and began to select a club.

Constance was a little tired. The day had been more

strenuous than usual, and it was very hot. Dr. Murchison had, for the first time since her arrival, failed to put in an appearance either at breakfast or in the office immediately afterwards, and she had received a note about ten o'clock from one of the nurses informing her that he had contracted a slight chill and was keeping to his bed. He required no attention from anyone, he said, and hoped, if he felt better, to get up for dinner in the evening. Would Dr. Sedgwick be kind enough to carry on without him during the day?

The Rev. Mark Hickett, whose melancholia waxed and waned, had collapsed about eleven o'clock, and had been put to bed suffering from the physical effects of under-nourishment. Constance blamed herself severely for this, for he was one of her patients, and she felt that she ought to have observed him with greater care. He had apparently been conducting a self-imposed fast for the last nine days, during which he had eaten practically nothing, though he had contrived to conceal this fact from all of them. It was only upon his collapse that Constance had realised what was the matter with him.

She would have to report this occurrence to Dr. Murchison, and that would be another failure to her account, and it was not one to be lightly excused, for the reverend gentleman was notoriously liable to starve himself unless he were very firmly discouraged. He was awaiting some kind of revelation for which every now and then he would endeavour to prepare himself by fasting and prayer. She had often talked with him on this subject long but unavailingly. All she could get from him—and it recurred during their conversations with a maddening frequency—was that the time was at hand, and that now, more than ever before, it was necessary to be prepared.

Miss Archer was still in bed, for she had not yet recovered from the crisis in the chapel. With these two patients laid up, and with all the ordinary routine work on her hands, Constance had been kept more than usually busy. She had not felt it wise, however, to break a long-standing engagement to play golf with Colonel Rickaby. It was a rule at Château Landry that promises made to a patient should, if possible, be kept.

Now, as she waited for the Colonel to play his ball, she reflected that she would only just have time for a cup of tea before paying another visit to Miss Archer and the Rev. Mark Hickett and settling down to two hours of necessary office work.

The last hole was close to the castle, right under it, in fact, on the side away from the terrace and the rose garden, the castle wall rising sheer from the grass only ten feet or so away from the green. The wall here was blank except for two small windows.

The Colonel had selected a club and was addressing his ball. Constance noticed that he was using either a driver or a brassie.

"Don't you think you will overrun the green, Colonel?" she called. Indeed he was not more than thirty yards from the pin.

The Colonel looked up, a frown on his face. "How am I expected to make a good shot," he replied, "if silence is not observed when I am addressing the ball?"

"Yes," and Constance patiently, "but wouldn't it be better to use a mashie or a mashie-niblick?"

"Certainly not, Madam," replied the Colonel. "It's a dashed fine lie, and I am going to have a dashed good smack at it," and, puffing out his moustache, he began once more to address the ball.

Constance watched him in silence. He had been perfectly sane throughout the round, a bit garrulous, but that was all. Why, she asked herself, should he suddenly become so unreasonable?

The club head swung up and described a swift half-circle. She heard its impact with the ball. The colonel, usually an indifferent performer, had timed this shot perfectly. The ball flew straight, rising in a long low curve. It passed high across the green, straight for the castle wall. An instant later there came a tinkle of glass.

Colonel Rickaby had sent his ball through one of the windows.

Constance could hardly refrain from laughing. The colonel's expression was ludicrous. Pride at the excellence of his shot struggled with discomfiture.

"It's a dashed awful confounded bunker," he said at last. "I don't know how I'm going to get it out. But I'm not beaten yet, not by any means. You don't know how good I am with a niblick, Miss Sedgwick, upon my word you don't," and seizing the club in question he strode purposefully across the green towards the castle and the window in the wall, ignoring the fact that it was small, barred and quite out of reach.

Constance walked after him, wondering how she

could dissuade him from what was obviously impossible. They reached the wall of the castle together and looked up.

As they did so, a face appeared and two white hands were thrust through the broken pane, gripping the bars.

Colonel Rickaby dropped his niblick and stared aghast.

"Good Gad, I have hit somebody!" he exclaimed. "Your hole and match, I'm afraid, Miss Sedgwick. But the dashed fellow is not going to get away with my ball. By George he's not."

Whereupon the Colonel picked up his niblick again and strode off round the angle of the castle wall.

Constance was still looking up at the man at the window. She saw him more clearly now, a man with tousled hair, wearing pyjamas as far as she could see, and in a flash she realised who he was. This must be Mr. Geoffrey Godstone, the dangerous lunatic who was under the special care of Dr. Murchison. The window was, it seemed, almost beyond his reach, for he was holding tightly on to the bars, as though he had with difficulty pulled himself up level with the broken pane.

He was looking at her eagerly, a strained expression in his eyes.

"Tell me," he said huskily, and hurrying his words as though he feared to be cut short, "you are Miss Sedgwick, are you not? You were to join Dr. Edwardes so it must be you—unless you are a patient."

His voice sank to a whisper as he said the last

words, and his hands relaxed their grip on the bars. The sweat broke out on his face, which abruptly sank back out of sight.

Constance was bewildered. How was it that this patient knew so much about her? How could he possibly be aware of her engagement at Château Landry?

She had barely asked herself the question when Mr. Godstone reappeared, looking down at her, his face twitching with the effort he was making to hold himself up by the bars.

"Quick," he said. "You must get me out of this at once. Tell Dr. Edwardes that I must see him immediately."

"Dr. Edwardes is away," said Constance. "You came here just after he had left, and you have been ill."

Mr. Godstone was staring down at her in horror. "Dr. Edwardes away!" he echoed. "Then who has taken his place?"

"Dr. Murchison is in charge," she replied. "I am only his assistant, you know."

"Dr. Murchison," he said, "I don't understand."

"Why, of course," insisted Constance, "Dr. Murchison has been in charge for three weeks."

"But that is impossible," said the man at the window. "Merciful God, I must be going mad."

"No, no," said Constance soothingly. "You are already much better than you were. But you must be calm."

She could see in his eyes the effort it cost him to master his rising excitement. Outwardly he succeeded, for with quiet emphasis, speaking slowly and distinctly, he said:

"It is impossible for Dr. Murchison to be in charge, Miss Sedgwick, and I will tell you the reason why."

And as she stood looking up into his white face, and at the hands which gripped the bars of the window, he added:

"*I myself am Dr. Murchison.*"

II

Mr. Deeling was taking tea on the terrace outside the library. He was glad to be taking it alone, as this was the first occasion on which he had been able to consider, in what he called "suitable circumstances," the events of the preceding night. Suitable circumstances as defined by Mr. Deeling consisted in an absence of noise, a comfortable but not too comfortable chair, and, above all, the knowledge that work could conscientiously be forgotten for half an hour.

He looked tired in the strong sunlight. It had really been a very hot day, and he had slept badly the night before, not at all, in fact, until dawn, when he had fallen into a doze fitful with dreams.

What exactly had happened last night? Had he really seen or heard anything on the gravel? And why had the lunatics come like that to the windows? He could still see the three lighted panes which had so swiftly gone dark again. Then there was that matter of the hyoscin.

There were only three people in the world, besides

himself, who as far as he was aware had keys of the dispensary, and thus had access to the drugs—Dr. Edwardes, who was absent, Dr. Murchison and Dr. Sedgwick. He concluded that either Dr. Murchison or Dr. Sedgwick must have taken an extra supply— Sedgwick or Murchison, Murchison or Sedgwick, which would it be? Why, Sedgwick, of course. Possibly the girl had wanted it for herself. He remembered her saying that she had not been sleeping well. It seemed that nobody had of late been sleeping well at Château Landry. Yes, it must have been Miss Sedgwick, and she had a guilty conscience. That must have been Miss Sedgwick last night on the gravel. She had been watching him at his accounts, and then, on seeing that he had discovered the loss, she had run away into the darkness. But why had not Miss Sedgwick taken the drug openly, as she had a perfect right to do? Secretive, he thought, naturally secretive; she had hoped he would not notice it. The woman must be a perfect fool.

That was an odd dream that had come to him last night: something about a bird—a large black bird, with flapping wings. It had perched on the window sill of his room, and would not go away, though he had thrown one of his ebony-backed hair-brushes at it. Then of a sudden it changed into Miss Collett, in her white frock and bow, with her battledore and shuttle-cock. She had jumped down from the sill and had sat on the bed and asked him to tell her a story, for she would not go away till he did. He had felt so shocked. A lady, even as old and mad as Miss Collett, in his room in the morning when it was quite light—quite light, and he had been feeling sleepy then. Just when you ought to wake up. You should only feel sleepy in the dark.

Mr. Deeling's head nodded once, then fell forward on his chest. The hot tea, the warm afternoon, his broken night, had proved too much for him. He slept.

He woke with a start, a childish treble in his ears.

"Poor little birdie," the voice was saying. "Look Mr. Deeling. It hasn't got any head!"

Mr. Deeling opened his eyes and sat up with a jerk. In front of him stood Miss Collett in her girlish frock, bearing in her arms a dead cockerel, its feathers spattered with blood and a red stain where the head should have been.

"I found it in the woods," she said, as Mr. Deeling gazed at her. "We must have a funeral. Come and help me, Mr. Deeling."

Mr. Deeling rose to his feet. The sight of this grown woman in her girlish frock, crooning over that dreadful trophy, disturbed even his unimaginative soul.

"Drop that disgusting thing at once," he said sternly. "Go to your room and wash your face and hands."

For answer Miss Collett dropped the bird, and seizing the apron which she wore round her waist, burst into tears.

Mr. Deeling took a step forward uncertain what to do, but at that moment Constance appeared round the corner of the castle. She was in tweeds and carrying a bag of golf clubs. She walked straight up to him, and, taking no notice of Miss Collett or the thing at her feet, threw down her clubs on to an empty

107

chair.

"Come at once, Mr. Deeling," she said in a curiously tense voice: "I urgently need your advice."

III

Mr. Deeling paused a moment and then followed Constance rebelliously. This was no way to behave. Things should be done decently in a scientific institution. Presumably this was a crisis, but a crisis should be met without excitement. There was no need to be dramatic and intense, whatever might or might not have happened. But that was so like a woman.

One thing, however, was gratifying. Dr. Sedgwick needed his help. Well, that was not altogether surprising. He was only a chemist, but he was at least a man, and a man of experience.

They turned the corner of the castle, and Constance led the way, still at a rapid pace, into the library.

"Shut the door, please, Mr. Deeling," she said, and then, pointing to a chair, sat down herself at her desk. He could see now that she was thoroughly upset. Well, he would be calm, and thus give her a very necessary lesson in deportment.

Constance, now that she needed, perhaps, the help of this man, felt with something of a shock that he was hostile. She did not like Mr. Deeling, but she had never realised until that instant that he did not like her—which means, she told herself accusingly, that I am hopelessly self-centred and unobservant.

She leant across the desk, and smiled. She must

win him over now. He was her only hope, her only possible ally.

"Mr. Deeling," she said, "I very badly need your advice."

"It is my duty," he said, "to place it entirely at your disposal."

He bowed from the waist, so that Constance had an excellent view of the hair so carefully arranged on the top of his head. Yes, he was undoubtedly absurd, but it was equally clear that she had never given him a chance to be anything else. And now she needed him.

"You see, I have not been here very long," she continued desperately, "while you have been here in Château Landry for eleven years."

"Eleven years, six months and one day," said Mr. Deeling.

"Then I am sure," she urged, "that you can tell me what I want to know. Did Dr. Edwardes ever keep a patient isolated in his room for any length of time?"

Mr. Deeling responded with the exasperating air of a man doing exactly what was required of him and no more.

"If my memory does not fail me," he said, "a Mr. Boardmore was confined to his room for twenty-two days in 1913, and in the month of April, 1917, Miss Archer was isolated for seventeen days. Apart from the various attacks of ordinary illness to which sane and insane are alike susceptible, I can recall no other instance during my period of residence."

"Then normally Dr. Edwardes allowed his patients full liberty?"

"Certainly," said Mr. Deeling.

"And the confinement to his room of Mr. Godstone is unusual?"

"Unusual, but not unprecedented," he replied, "and I should say, speaking, of course, as a layman, that the circumstances of his arrival fully justified his isolation!"

He looked suspiciously at Constance. What was the purpose of these questions. The next one increased his bewilderment.

"Has Mr. Godstone been treated with hyoscin at all frequently since his arrival?"

Mr. Deeling raised his eyebrows. "I do not think that I can answer that question," he said, with the air of one who was being asked to betray a professional secret.

"But surely, you must know," she urged. "You make up all the prescriptions."

"I suggest, Dr. Sedgwick," he returned, "that you ask Dr. Murchison himself on his recovery."

"But that is just what I cannot do," she said in a low voice.

She leaned forward and to Mr. Deeling's immense confusion placed a hand on his arm.

"Mr. Deeling," she said, "this is a very serious matter. Believe me, you will best be serving Dr. Edwardes and Château Landry by telling me everything you know."

Mr. Deeling looked helplessly at the hand which still lay upon his arm. That simple gesture sounded within him an alarm against the wiles of woman. Women were like that. They took a medical degree and assumed equality with men. Then when it came to the point they put a hand upon your arm and expected you to be overcome. There was something here that needed investigation. Probably she was thinking of the hyoscin in his treatment of the Honble. Geoffrey Godstone.

"Are you trying to find an explanation, Dr. Sedgwick," he said, looking at her steadily, "for the disappearance of several drams of hyoscin from my dispensary some time within the last twenty-four hours?"

She looked at him, a new alarm in her eyes.

"Good heavens," she said, "this is worse than I thought. Do you mean to say that hyoscin has disappeared?"

Guilt could not assume a more stricken look. Mr. Deeling began to feel almost sorry for the culprit.

"Do you not think," he said slowly, "that you had better be quite frank with me?"

"Certainly, Mr. Deeling," she replied. "I will, of course, tell you exactly what I think. The fact is, I don't believe Mr. Godstone is being properly treated."

Mr. Deeling sat back in his chair. The woman was hopeless; she persisted in her deception.

"I cannot," he said stiffly, "presume to have any view on a difference of opinion between two doctors. Have you, in any case, discussed the matter with Dr. Murchison himself?"

"I haven't had any opportunity," said Constance. "I have only just seen Mr. Godstone. Colonel Rickaby broke his window with a golf ball. And Mr. Godstone, speaking to me through the broken pane, told me at once who I was."

"Indeed," said Mr. Deeling.

"He told me that I was Dr. Sedgwick, who had come here as the assistant of Dr. Edwardes. How on earth did he know that?"

"From the servants, from the warders, from Dr. Murchison himself," said Mr. Deeling. "I do not see that there is any difficulty."

"That is quite possible," admitted Constance. "But he told me something else. He told me that he was Dr. Murchison."

"What!" said Mr. Deeling, getting to his feet.

"That he was Dr. Murchison," repeated Constance.

Mr. Deeling looked at her in amazement.

"But surely," he protested, "you do not believe this ridiculous story."

"I . . . I don't know what to believe," said Constance.

"Then I can set your mind at rest," returned Mr. Deeling. "The Honble. Geoffrey Godstone arrived at Château Landry unconscious. He was brought here by Dr. Murchison himself, having attacked and killed the chauffeur who drove them from Thonon. He was put to bed immediately on his arrival."

"Oh yes, I know all that," said Constance. "But suppose it was the other way round?"

Mr. Deeling stared at her stupidly.

"I do not quite follow," he said.

"Don't you realise," said Constance, "that we have no evidence at all, either way. Two men arrived here at Château Landry in a motor-car. There were no witnesses of the . . . the accident to poor Jules. Suppose

112

it was Mr. Godstone who had knocked down the doctor and brought him here unconscious. Suppose Mr. Godstone is now impersonating Dr. Murchison?"

Mr. Deeling passed a hand over his forehead.

"Impossible," he protested, "Quite impossible."

For a moment they stood staring at one another. Mr. Deeling made to speak again, but at that instant there was a knock at the door.

"Come in," said Constance.

The door opened to admit one of the warders, a dark, wooden-faced man, English and entirely reliable.

"What is it, Jones?" Constance asked.

"It's the patient in No. 17, Doctor. He is making a great deal of noise," returned the man. "If you would come and look at him. It 'as occurred to me 'as how he might do himself an injury."

"No. 17?" said Constance, looking inquiringly at Mr. Deeling.

"That is Mr. Godstone's room," said Mr. Deeling.

Constance turned at once to the door. "Come with me, Jones," she said, "and you, too, Mr. Deeling."

Mr. Deeling followed in silence, and they passed into the corridor in the wake of Jones. No. 17 was at the end of it. Already they could hear the noise being made by the patient.

"He is as mad as a hatter," muttered Mr. Deeling as they went along.

A moment later they were in front of the door behind which Geoffrey Godstone was confined. A violent fusillade of blows sounded on the other side of the panel. Constance pulled back the shutter of the spy-hole.

"Stop making that noise at once, Mr. Godstone," she said sternly.

The noise ceased abruptly.

"Is that Dr. Sedgwick?" said a hoarse voice.

"Yes," she returned.

"Then for God's sake come . . . come at once," said the voice.

"Only if you promise to keep quiet," she returned.

"Of course, I'll keep quiet, anything—anything. I only want you to hear what I have to say," he answered.

Constance signed to the warder to open the door.

"If he shows any violence," she said in a low voice to the two men, "I shall ask you to restrain him. Do not move, however, until I give the word."

They nodded, and Jones threw open the door. The three passed in, Constance and Mr. Deeling together and Jones slightly behind.

Mr. Godstone was seated on the edge of his bed, looking eagerly towards them. It was a pleasant room, adequately furnished, though curtainless and without pictures. The walls were covered with thick grey felt, the corners rounded. Mr. Godstone did not present a very creditable appearance. He was dressed in pyjamas. There was a short untidy growth of beard on chin and lips. His hair was disordered, and there was a wild look in his eyes. He sprang up as his visitors moved towards him.

"Thank God, you've come," he said jerkily. "Thank God, it is not too late. Who are you?" and he pointed abruptly to Mr. Deeling, but did not give him

114

time to answer. "You are a warder, I suppose," he said to Jones, who stood impassively beside Constance.

"Quietly, please Mr. Godstone," she said. "What is it that you want us to do?"

"But I am not Mr. Godstone," he interrupted wildly. "I've told you that already. I am Dr. Murchison. I implore you to believe me. No, I will not ask you to believe me, for I can prove it. I can prove it in ten minutes. But you must give me the chance. I . . . I tremble for the consequences, if you don't."

He took a step forward, his hands outstretched and shaking.

Mr. Deeling, who was nearest him, recoiled.

"Look out," he said, "the man may be dangerous. Hold him, Jones."

The burly warder, forgetting Constance's instructions, moved forward and laid a hand on Mr. Godstone's shoulder, who spun round, his elbow, as he did so, striking Mr. Deeling a sharp blow on the chin.

"Better 'ave the weskit on him, Miss," whispered Jones hoarsely.

"No, no, I didn't mean to hit that man. It was an accident," cried Mr. Godstone, springing back towards the open window. "I am perfectly sane, I tell you, as sane as any of you."

Constance motioned Jones to fall back.

"Sit down, Mr. Godstone," she said quietly.

He looked at her a moment, then crossed to the bed reluctantly and did as he was bid.

"Now, for God's sake," he said, "listen to my story."

"What story?" said a voice behind them.

The three of them turned round.

Dr. Murchison, in a dark blue dressing-gown, was standing in the doorway.

IV

The first to speak was the man on the bed. He rose and pointed at the figure in the doorway.

"That is my patient," he said. "That is Mr. Godstone."

Constance, in the pause that followed, looked from one man to the other as they stood confronted. The man in the doorway had not yet moved. His face was calm, though it was a little haggard, as though he had passed a sleepless night.

The other, who had risen from the bed, was quivering from head to foot, his eyes shining with excitement, his outstretched hand shaking miserably, and the sweat standing cold upon his forehead. He turned suddenly to Constance.

"For God's sake," he said, "give me a chance to prove my identity. Confront me for five minutes with that man, or look only at our papers. I can prove at once what I say. I am Dr. Murchison."

The warder turned to the door.

"Best be careful of 'im, sir," he said. "Patient's inclined to be violent. Shouldn't cross 'im if I was you, Doctor. He's like one we 'ad here in '23. Thought he was running the establishment. Used to give me my orders, sir, every day, cool as you please."

"Thank you, Jones," said Dr. Murchison. "But I

116

will deal with this case in my own way."

He turned abruptly to Constance.

"Miss Sedgwick," he said curtly, "I don't think you can be of any further use to us here. Would you please go with Mr. Deeling to the library and wait for me there."

Constance made as if to speak, but suddenly turned to leave the room.

On seeing this, the man standing by the bed seemed to lose all control over himself. He took a step forward which brought him near to Constance. Instantly Jones slipped behind him and had him by the arms. The man, feeling himself caught, struggled a moment, and then went deadly quiet.

"Release him, Jones," said Dr. Murchison.

Jones doubtfully loosened his hold, and the patient stood, white and trembling, in the centre of the room. Dr. Murchison stood aside to allow room for Constance and Mr. Deeling to pass into the corridor.

She slipped quickly by the patient, but, as she did so, he suddenly seized her by the arm and in a tense whisper, almost into her ear, he said.

"You don't believe me, Miss Sedgwick. But look at his feet."

Jones, who had again moved forward to restrain him, if necessary, caught the words, and looking at Constance, tapped his forehead significantly. With a little shiver, which she could not control, Constance slipped to the door and so out into the passage.

V

She was waiting now in the library. To Mr. Deeling, who stood by the window looking out upon the meadow, she could find nothing to say. She was alone, very much alone, with her thoughts. How could she for one moment have attached any significance to the allegations of the madman in No. 17? Half a dozen incoherent sentences flung at her through a broken window pane, and she had at once allowed herself to be shaken. She could only infer that she had utterly mistaken her vocation. The whole place had got on her nerves to such an extent that she had lost all sense of reality. She had got into the frame of mind when anything, however impossible, might happen.

What was taking place in the room which she had left? She did not know, but of one thing she was sure. Dr. Murchison was dealing quickly and firmly with the situation. Probably he was administering to his patient another dose of hyoscin. It was not for her to protest against such a remedy. He would say at once that she herself was responsible for the crisis which had rendered it necessary.

The door opened abruptly, and Dr. Murchison entered, closing it behind him. He was still in his blue dressing-gown and wearing on his bare feet a pair of leopard skin slippers, rather crushed at the heels. He crossed the room without speaking, and sat down at his desk.

"Now, Miss Sedgwick," he said abruptly, "what does this mean?"

Then, as she did not immediately reply, he went on rapidly:

"Let me tell you, at once, Miss Sedgwick, and you, too, Mr. Deeling, that in the space of half an hour you have completely undone the work of several weeks. The condition of my patient was rapidly improving. I come down from my room to discover him in a state of high excitement, and to find you, Miss Sedgwick, apparently encouraging him in the most dangerous of his delusions—this, in spite of the fact that I had made it quite clear to both of you that he was under my own personal care, and that neither of you were in any circumstances to interfere with my treatment of the case. I must ask you both for an immediate explanation."

His tone was that of a man deeply moved by a legitimate, professional anger. To Constance it was like a whiplash. But though she felt that the censure was deserved, a spark of anger was kindled in her, and began steadily to burn. Though she was a hundred times to blame, he should not speak to her like that.

She was about to make a sharp retort, but found herself forestalled by Mr. Deeling.

"My own part in this affair," he was saying, "is easily explained. Dr. Sedgwick came to me (he glanced a moment at his watch) some thirty-seven minutes ago. She told me that Mr. Godstone had spoken to her and that he had declared to her that he was not Mr. Godstone at all, but that he was Dr. Murchison. She appeared to be much upset by this occurrence."

"Upset?" interrupted Dr. Murchison, impatiently tapping the desk with a pencil. "What exactly do you mean by that?"

119

Mr. Deeling glanced inquiringly at Constance.

"I will tell you exactly what happened," began Constance.

"Please allow Mr. Deeling to finish what he is saying," said Dr. Murchison.

He turned back to Mr. Deeling.

"You were saying that Miss Sedgwick was upset."

"Dr. Sedgwick had undoubtedly been very considerably impressed by the statement which the patient had made to her."

"You mean that she was inclined to believe it?" said Dr. Murchison.

"I should be very sorry," began Mr. Deeling. But Dr. Murchison cut him short.

"Did Miss Sedgwick believe the statement or not?" he asked.

"If you insist, Dr. Murchison, I can do neither more nor less than repeat her exact words. She said that she did not know what to believe."

"And you, Mr. Deeling," he said in a tone of dry indifference. "How exactly did *you* receive this declaration?"

"I regarded it as merely a painful symptom of the disease from which your patient is suffering," said Mr. Deeling.

"Very well," said Dr. Murchison. "As it doesn't appear to be necessary for me to convince you of my identity, I will not detain you further. But please be under no misapprehension as to what I think of your conduct. You have disregarded your instructions, which seems to show that you are very little the wiser for your eleven years' experience at Château Landry. I

hope that in furture you will realise the importance of carrying out quite literally the orders which you receive."

Mr. Deeling crossed the room. At the door he returned.

"I have never had any doubt as to your identity," he said, "and I am now more than ever convinced that you are Dr. Murchison. The Honble. Geoffrey Godstone, sane or insane, would never have addressed me in the tone which you have seen fit to adopt. Only my long association with Dr. Edwardes and the fact that I have some small reason to believe myself to be of value to him induces me to withhold my resignation. I have the honour to bid you good afternoon."

Dr. Murchison gave no heed to this, but waited till Mr. Deeling had closed the door. Then he turned to Constance.

"Is it true, Miss Sedgwick," he asked, "that you not only encouraged the delusion of my patient in No. 17, but that you were actually inclined to share it?"

"It was all a hideous confusion," began Constance, "I was taken by surprise."

"I'm afraid that will hardly do," said Dr. Murchison coldly. "If Mr. Deeling was speaking the truth, you actually went so far as to believe. . . ."

"No, no," said Constance, "I never believed it."

"You did not, in fact, know what to believe?"

Constance flushed, and then faced him suddenly.

"Yes," she admitted. "For a moment I was in doubt. But that moment is past. I beg that you will forget it."

"I don't think you quite realise what you are

asking," he said. "I feel that, in the circumstances, I
have no alternative but to ask Dr. Edwardes to return
immediately to Château Landry, so that he may deal
with the situation himself. You will agree that after
what has happened it is hardly possible for us to work
together."

"Let me explain," said Constance.

"I should be interested to hear your explanation,"
said Dr. Murchison, "though I do not see how it can
possibly affect us now."

"My communication with Mr. Godstone was an
accident," said Constance hurriedly. "Colonel Rickaby broke the window of No. 17 with a golf ball, and
Mr. Godstone spoke to me through the broken pane.
He knew at once that I was Dr. Sedgwick."

Dr. Murchison pressed a button on his desk.

"One moment," he said. "I propose to deal with
your difficulties as they arise. You apparently considered it strange that Mr. Godstone, who came here
before you arrived, and whom you had never seen
until to-day, should have addressed you as Dr.
Sedgwick. Let me first dispose of that."

"Is this necessary, Doctor?" said Constance, flushing, "I have admitted my mistake."

"I prefer to put the matter beyond all doubt," said
Dr. Murchison. "I shall refrain from making any
appeal to your confidence. I propose to give you the
facts. Mr. Godstone is suffering, among other things,
from two fixed delusions—the first that he is myself,
and the second that every woman he encounters in
this establishment is Dr. Sedgwick. You will remember that it was I who brought Mr. Godstone to

Château Landry. Unfortunately, I told him on our journey from London to this place that a woman doctor would shortly be joining our establishment. It was foolish of me to do so, and I have several times regretted it, for it has started in him another fixed idea.

"The delusion that he is Dr. Murchison is not in the least abnormal, and should have been familiar to you. It very frequently happens that a patient imagines himself to have changed places with his doctor. Jones alluded to a case that was here in 1923. I shall, therefore, make no further reference to that delusion for the present. The second delusion is merely incidental, but I will demonstrate to you in a moment that it is as strong and just as involuntary as the first."

As he spoke, Nurse Webster entered the room.

"You rang for me, Doctor?" she said.

"Shut the door, please, Nurse," he answered, "and sit down, won't you? I want you to give Dr. Sedgwick an exact account of what happened when you attended Mr. Godstone, the patient in No. 17. I remember rightly, you attended him only once, when I asked you to change the dressings on his head. Afterwards I did them myself, if you recollect."

"You want me to remember just what he said?" Nurse Webster inquired.

"Yes, Nurse, if you will be so good."

"The patient was very weak and didn't seem to be taking much notice of anything when I started. But then he comes suddenly to himself and stares at me a bit, wildlike. Then he seizes me by the arm and lifts himself up. And then he says to me: 'For God's sake,'

123

he says, 'tell me quick. You must be Dr. Sedgwick.' Then he shakes me by the arm. 'You *are* Dr. Sedgwick, aren't you,' he says. And that was all, for suddenly he came over queer and fainted right off again."

"And that, I think, was the only time you ever saw him," suggested Dr. Murchison.

"That was the only time, Doctor, seeing as you thought it would be best if you changed the dressings yourself so that the patient should not be encouraged in his ideas."

"Thank you, Nurse," said Dr. Murchison.

"Is that all?" said Nurse Webster, rising from her chair, "because if it is, Doctor, I think I ought to be getting back to Miss Archer."

Dr. Murchison nodded. "Yes, thank you, Nurse," he replied. "Get back to your patient by all means."

He turned to Constance as the door closed.

"Well," he said, "are you satisfied?"

"Why do you treat me like this?" said Constance in a low voice. "I have admitted my mistake."

Dr. Murchison rose swiftly from his chair and went towards her. He seized her almost roughly by the arm.

"Miss Sedgwick," he said, "on almost no ground at all you have allowed yourself to entertain a monstrous suspicion. You could never have believed such a tale unless you had wished to believe it. I must, therefore, assume that for some reason or other I have failed to win your confidence. That, however, is neither here nor there. Quite apart from anything personal as between you and me, I have the right, as head of this establishment, and as a fellow-doctor, to demand that you shall not allow your private dislikes to affect the performance of your duties. I put it no higher than that. You have been false to me as the person in charge of Château Landry, and you have been disloyal to your profession."

He released her arm and walked abruptly from her to the window.

"You wish me to resign," she said after a short pause.

He turned back from the window.

"How can we continue to work together after what has happened?" he asked.

She looked at him for a moment in silence.

"Very well," she said. Her voice was creditably even, and she looked him full in the face, wondering, however, how long she would be able to do so.

Then suddenly, to her amazement, she found him again beside her, and he had taken her gently by the arms.

"Miss Sedgwick," he said. "I must ask you to forgive me."

"Forgive you," she stammered, "I don't understand."

"I lost my temper just now," he continued, "I said more than I need have done—more than I intended. My responsibility here is very great, and the strain, perhaps, is beginning to tell. And then I suppose . . ."

He broke off, and Constance felt his grip tighten, as though involuntarily, on her arm.

"I suppose," he went on, "that I was more hurt by your attitude than I cared to confess. In fact, I have been something of a hypocrite. My feeling was not wholly professional, though, when I came downstairs just now and saw what had happened and felt that all my patient work on Godstone had been undone, you will realise that I found it a little difficult. . . ."

"Please," said Constance, "this is worse than before."

The pressure on her arms was urgent. She realised with a faint shock that she was almost in his arms. Almost imperceptibly she drew back, being aware, as she did so, of a faint tremor that shook him from head to foot. Abruptly he released her, and they stood facing one another.

Then mastering himself with an effort, he smiled winningly and said in a tone that was as light and friendly as she could possibly desire:

"I shall not accept your resignation, Dr. Sedgwick."

VI

The night was oppressive, and Constance had flung wide the window of her room where she was reading. The whole valley was very silent. The earth, breathing warm, lay like a huge animal asleep.

Dr. Murchison, following that interview in the library, had seemed anxious to show that he had in her now the completest confidence. He had talked to her frankly and in detail concerning his plans, and he had handed to her that evening the file containing the history of the two most difficult cases with which they would have to deal, those of Mr. Curtis and of the

Honble. Geoffrey Godstone. For the last half-hour she had been reading the first of them.

Her reading had been desultory, for every now and then she would lean back in her chair and allow her thoughts to wander. During her talk with Dr. Murchison she had for the first time been brought into intimate touch with the subliminal world in which the modern alienists were groping for a solution of their problems. He had discussed in the curious language of Freud and the later school of Zurich the secret forces which lie beneath the threshold of consciousness.

Standing now by the window, she brooded on that hidden life which lurked within herself, of which she would never be aware, which would never give any sign of its activity except in dreams, or some unbidden fancy when the conscious mind was asleep or relaxed its vigilance. Dr. Murchison had discussed at length the "Zensur" of Freud, describing it as the Warder who stood perpetually on guard at the gate which separated the unconscious self from the intelligent and regulated activities of the mind. Beyond the gate, blindly dynamic, moved and worked, insentient and with no knowledge of good and evil, the primitive will of the human creature to persist, to develop, to fulfil an unknown purpose, a darkness that stirred with primaeval memories.

He had talked much of the Warder and his office, for it was in his attitude to the Zensur that he differed from Dr. Edwardes. Dr. Edwardes had set his face against the method of Freud, which sought to lure the Warder from his post so that the secrets of the unconscious mind might come into the open and there be destroyed. Dr. Edwardes argued that this process of introspection and analysis merely encouraged the madman in his delusions, and that better results could be obtained by firmly and gently leading the patient away from his fancies and by giving him interests and occupations which would exercise that part of the mind which was unaffected. Dr. Murchison had admitted that for most practitioners this was undoubtedly the safer way; but there were others, he had said, who might claim to have special powers. And this point he had used a simile which had deeply impressed her. She could see him still, sitting in his chair, gazing in front of him, a confident, proud smile on his lips.

"You remember," he had said, "the legend of the sorcerer's apprentice. He stole the spells of his master and raised a horde of demons whom he was unable to control."

He had gone on to tell her of a case in which a doctor, who was endeavouring to effect a cure by the Freudian method, and who had thereby concentrated upon himself all the dormant evil of the sufferer, had been murdered by his patient in an access of dementia. He had added that those who raise the whirlwind must be prepared to ride it. Personally, he had no misgivings.

She came back to the table, and began to read again the file of Mr. Curtis. Much of the later notes of Dr. Edwardes and those added by Dr. Murchison himself were almost beyond her comprehension, but there were many suggestive details. She read of dreadful acts of cruelty, committed by him as a child on animals. There was a revolting story of a cat, and of a chicken plucked alive. Another curious detail was his abnormal readiness, amounting almost to craving, to be punished for his abominable acts.

She laid the file aside and took up that of the Honble. Geoffrey Godstone. For the next half-hour there was no sound or movement in the room, except for the occasional rustle of a page that was turned.

But at last there was a breath in the valley. Distantly it stirred the forest and came whispering over the meadow till it reached the open shutter of the window, which grated back upon its hinges and hit the stone sill with a clap.

Constance started. She rose and went to secure the shutter, and her hand trembled slightly upon the latch. The air that met her as she went to the window was hot upon her cheek. She turned back to the table and took up the file which she had been reading.

Then suddenly with a shiver she let it fall. She would not look at it again that night. Already she had looked it through completely from beginning to end, and she was appalled by what she had read.

Chapter VII

I

At half-past two on the following afternoon Mr. Deeling left the castle, a stout ash plant in his hand. He was proposing to take one of his constitutionals. These were of two kinds. On Mondays, Wednesdays and Fridays he allowed himself thirty-five minutes for exercise. On Tuesdays, Thursdays and Saturdays, however, some two hours and fifteen minutes were at his disposal. To-day was Thursday, and Mr. Deeling intended to walk as briskly as advancing years and a sedentary habit permitted until a quarter to five, when he would return, refreshed in body and mind, to his laboratory.

It was very hot that Thursday afternoon, really extraordinarily hot, even for the time of year and at that height. He could feel on his face the glow from the chapel walls as he passed them on his descent from the terrace to the meadow.

There was something happening in the meadow. A chattering group, headed by Colonel Rickaby, was making hay, tossing the great swathes which had been cut two days ago, but which were already almost dry enough to carry. The sight of the inmates of Château Landry thus engaged was displeasing to Mr. Deeling.

"Most inappropriate," he thought, as he continued on his way.

It was all part and parcel of this new system which the unspeakable, the quite unspeakable, Dr. Murchison was introducing. Dr. Edwardes would never have approved of it—people with weak heads working like that in the hot sun.

Dr. Edwardes would disapprove of a good many things when he came back. This Dr. Murchison would then be put very properly into his place. Let him wait. Let him only wait. Sooner or later Dr. Edwardes would return, and then this fellow would sing pretty small—very small indeed.

"Making hay while the sun shines—that's what he is doing," muttered Mr. Deeling savagely to himself, and he gave a short laugh at his own joke.

For a night and a half a day since his last encounter with Dr. Murchison, Mr. Deeling had brooded ceaselessly, continually discovering a new aspect of the indignity to which he had been subjected. The man was literally intolerable—not any too strong a word in the circumstances. He had dared to speak to Mr. Deeling, who had been eleven years at Château Landry, eleven years of devoted service, as though he had been no more than a servant. Thank God, he had kept his temper. Yes, he had left the room with dignity. He had remonstrated in a few well-chosen words, extremely well chosen considering that he had been taken by surprise, and then the door had closed upon him. Since then, except at meals, when he had maintained a lofty silence, he had not set eyes on Dr. Murchison.

Mr. Deeling paused in his walk and wiped his brow. It was certainly hot, most appallingly hot, in the open, but there, before him, stretched the dark shade of the belt of firs. It would be cool in there, and he would be able to consider his position more calmly.

He ran a finger round his soft collar which was sticking unpleasantly to the back of his neck, and moved forward into the shade.

Dr. Murchison had insulted him. He must do something about it. Should he write to Dr. Edwardes? *Dear Dr. Edwardes. . . . I regret to inform you of a most regrettable incident.* . . . No. That wouldn't do. He had used the word "regret" twice over. But the incident was certainly regrettable. Should he ask Dr. Edwardes to return, hinting perhaps at resignation? That was one way, but it was hardly fair to his old employer. Dr. Edwardes had gone away for a rest cure, on his recommendation too, and it would be most inconsiderate to recall him at the end of a bare month. Besides, how was he to justify such an appeal? There was nothing obviously wrong. The patients were all quite happy—happier than he had ever known them to be. The man Murchison was certainly efficient—*damned* efficient. There was little hope of ever catching him out. Everything was just as it should be. On the surface, at least—except perhaps for that little matter of the hyoscin.

Mr. Deeling paused to rest beside a tree, and moodily drummed upon the trunk with his fingers.

There came from the right as he did so a prolonged rustling, though there was no wind or any life in the forest, but Mr. Deeling did not notice it.

There could be no doubt about the hyoscin. Dr. Murchison had taken it. But he must have proof, and then, perhaps, one thing would lead to another. There must be something queer about a doctor who stole his own drugs. There was no sense in it.

He moved forward again. Was there anybody who would be likely to help him? Should he consult Miss Sedgwick? Mr. Deeling permitted a short laugh to escape him. Of all courses that would be the last. For the wretched girl was quite under the thumb of the new doctor. An hysterical creature. Only yesterday she had believed the man to be mad, and now she was eating out of his hand. There could be no possible reliance on a girl like that. In any case, she and the doctor were now as thick as thieves. Or perhaps she was not so stupid as she seemed. Suppose she had never really believed the doctor to be mad at all, but had just wanted *him* to believe it, so as to discredit him and expose him to the insult which he had received. Or suppose that the whole thing was a put-up job, a plot between the two of them to bring about his discomfiture. That, perhaps, was a little far-fetched. But when people behaved so unreasonably, one did not know what to believe.

One thing, at any rate, was clear. That girl, who had suggested only yesterday that the doctor was mad, was now his most devoted admirer. Why, only that very same evening he had seen them walking arm in arm—yes, arm in arm, mind you—in the rose garden.

Well, perhaps that was not quite true. Dr. Murchison had laid his hand on her arm for a moment, but, at least, she had not tried to shake it off. And, after a moment, the Doctor had withdrawn it. Then they had disappeared round the corner, where the statue stood of the nymph undressing. Pretty certainly they were arm in arm again as soon as they were out of sight. He only hoped it was no worse than that. There was something between those two, and he was prepared to believe the worst. He had seen the Doctor looking at the girl very strangely at times, and he knew what young people were. He had been young himself. There was that black-eyed girl in 1897 at Amalfi and their walk together by the water mills.

No, he must act alone—if it were at all possible to act.

He stopped again, for he had now reached the path which ran right round the circle of rocks, mostly in the fir wood. There was a fallen trunk by the side of it, and he sat down, taking off his panama hat and holding his handkerchief once more to his head. It was still terribly hot, even here, in the shadow of the firs. And it was unnaturally quiet in the wood. There were no birds, and no insects on the wing. It was not like an English wood, which at that season would be full of sounds and bird voices. It was as still and as lifeless as a stage setting. The firs spread all about him, climbing sharply to the naked rock, of which he caught a glimpse now and again between the tree-tops.

He shifted uneasily on his seat, and, as he did so, there was that rustling again quite close to him. This

134

time he heard it. Some animal, perhaps, and he did not like animals, especially animals you could not see. He looked round uneasily and heard the sound again, followed by a silence even deadlier than before. He could hear nothing now, nothing but the sound of his own laboured breathing, or was it the breathing of some other creature near at hand?

He sprang to his feet, and there was a faint stir in the undergrowth behind the trunk on which he had been sitting. He stood for a moment, still as a statue, and then, on a sudden impulse, prodded the undergrowth with his stick. He touched something hard, but not very hard, not rock at any rate. It moved under the point of his stick, and a hoarse sound in the nature of a grunt came from the thicket.

This was a nasty thing to happen. You poked at the solid earth and it moved. Like those men who landed on a whale.

Mr. Deeling turned and shambled down the path, almost at a run. Fifty yards away he halted and listened intently, but there was no further sound. He put his hand to his heart. His mouth was dry, and sweat, not altogether due to the heat, was running into his eyes. He wiped his forehead again, blew out his cheeks, and then, very deliberately, though with hands that trembled slightly, he felt for, found and filled a pipe. He struck one match and then another, and he would not look behind him. Then, when the pipe was alight, he moved forward again along the path.

His nerves were not as good as they should be. There could, of course, be no animals in the wood. No animals could climb the mountains surrounding the valley, or get through the wire fence which cut off the valley at the only point at which it was accessible. He was becoming fanciful. All that business about the doctor and the girl and the plot between them. It was undoubtedly far-fetched. He had lost his bearings. There was no sense in anything at all. That was a horrid thought, for in a world without sense one thing was just as likely to happen as another.

He walked on, more briskly now, down the path. He would walk to the end of it where it met the fence, then he would turn back, walk all the way round to where it joined on the other side of the valley, come down through the trees and reach the castle just in time for tea. He glanced at his watch, and saw that he would have to walk at a fair pace to carry out the programme.

He began to think again of Dr. Murchison, but he seemed unable now to keep his reflections clear and connected. The doctor, perhaps, would marry the girl. Why not? The Rev. Mark Hickett would be delighted to perform the ceremony. Was a marriage to be regarded as valid if performed by a madman? That was rather an interesting speculation. It would be odd for a couple to be living in sin without being aware of it. He had thought a great deal about sin in his youth. That black-eyed girl. How he had longed to live in sin. But he had not dared.

Why had the earth moved and what had been that curious sound? Man or beast, fish, flesh, fowl or good red herring? But that was nonsense. He must pull himself together.

He stumbled over a root and looked at the path. At his feet, branching off to the left, was a little track leading through the bushes and fir trees slightly down the hill. He followed it mechanically, though he did not remember ever having trodden it before. It led him to a little clearing—quite fresh, it would appear, for the stumps of the felled trees were not yet overgrown. It was perhaps twenty yards broad, and the afternoon sunlight beat upon it fiercely, so that the air above was dizzy with heat. In the middle was something white—or was it something red?—which Mr. Deeling found it difficult to put a name to all at once. He walked towards it, and saw that it was a flat white stone, about the size of a small table, a very ordinary stone with nothing to distinguish it from ten thousand others, except for those streaks of red that ran down the front and sides from an uneven blotch in the centre.

Mr. Deeling bent and touched the red patch hesitatingly with his finger. It was sticky. Paint apparently. Red paint. Very curious. But it could not be paint. What was it then? Once more he touched it with his finger. It was certainly very sticky, and a faint stale smell hung about it. Mechanically he put his finger to his lips. It tasted salt. "It's blood," said Mr. Deeling to himself in a whisper. "That's what it is—blood."

And as he spoke there was once more a rustling—this time in the thicket of bushes behind him.

He whipped round and faced the thicket.

"Come out," said something in his brain. "Don't play those silly tricks."

137

But no sound came from his lips, for he only thought that he had called.

Then he heard something, a voice that muttered in the shadow.

"Not yet," it seemed to be saying, "not yet. Neither the day nor the hour."

Mr. Deeling stared at the thicket, which moved under his eyes as though an unseen wind were blowing. Or was it the passage of some heavy body? The sweat trickled unchecked down his cheeks.

He walked quickly back to the path. He must not run, for that would be the end.

Soon he was again in the wood, but now he had a companion—something that stalked him invisibly, rustling beside him as he went upon his way. Where were the human voices and the pleasant light of day?

Mr. Deeling began to run.

II

The haymaking party had started early after lunch.

"A dashed sight too early in this confounded heat," grumbled Colonel Rickaby, who disliked having to hurry his cheroot and coffee.

Dr. Murchison had suggested it on the previous evening, and the patients had received the idea with enthusiasm.

The portion of the meadow lying towards the east, between the castle and the wire fence, had been mown several days before, unwillingly, by a party of villagers, whose desire as farmers to obtain an excellent crop of hay at a very low price had overcome their reluctance to enter the castle valley.

Everyone, except Miss Archer, was there, including Dr. Murchison and Constance. There were rakes and pitchforks with wooden prongs for the men, and it was proposed that the ladies should either help their male companions or sit on the hay wagon, which was in the charge of two surly young rustics and Warder Jones, and help to stack the hay.

Constance, who had fallen in very readily with the plan, was now a little doubtful. It was so very hot. The sun blazed down from a sky so blue and cloudless that it hurt the eyes. The hot air rising from the valley made it seem as though a shimmering veil were stretched between her and the yellow rocks above the belt of firs. The handle of the rake she was grasping was hot and dry to the touch, and she had doubts about the efficacy of the cream which she had put on her face and arms, which were bare to the elbow. She wore a tennis frock and a straw hat. Dr. Murchison was in flannels, his shirt open at the neck. He was at present talking to Mr. Rev. Mark Hickett, who, with Colonel Rickaby, was standing beside the pile of pitchforks and rakes.

"I recommend a rake," he was saying.

The Rev. Mark Hickett was looking at him intently, and for a moment he did not reply. There was more colour than usual in his pale cheeks.

"Just as you wish," he said, at last.

"Then I should certainly choose a rake," said Dr. Murchison gravely.

"Here you are, padre," said Colonel Rickaby, hand-ing him one of the implements in question. "Take a rake and let's see what you can do with it. The rake's progress, what?"

He burst into genial laughter at his own joke, and himself selected a pitchfork.

"The fatigue party will be in charge of Corporal Hancock," he declaimed, as he shouldered his pitchfork and moved off towards the wagon where Mr. Curtis was already tossing up hay to Miss Collett with desperate energy.

Dr. Murchison smiled at Constance, who set to work with a rake, urging Miss Truelow to follow her example.

Miss Truelow, she noted, was not very suitably dressed for the occasion. She was wearing, in fact, her usual clothes, the taffeta blouse with long sleeves, buttoned up to the neck.

Evidently Miss Truelow had a similar impression in regard to Constance herself.

"Your arms will be burnt to a cinder," she said, as she began to drag her rake aimlessly through the grass. "I advise you to cover them up."

"I rubbed in some cream after lunch," said Constance pleasantly.

"I never use cosmetics," said Miss Truelow. "I advise you to cover them up." She looked significantly away to Dr. Murchison as she spoke.

"Cover them up!" exclaimed Mr. Clearwater, who was playing with a rake near by. "That would be sacrilege. White arms under the sunlight in Arcadia."

He leaned upon his rake and looked with a boy's delight at Constance as she worked.

"You are, indeed," he cried, "the fair spirit of this valley. For you Daphnis and Menalcas contended with oaten pipes, drowning the cicala while their goats strayed seaward. Soon we shall dance, and perhaps the Maenads will reel with the drunken god from the forest and crown us with vine leaves."

"I trust they will do no such thing," said Miss Truelow severely.

Constance coloured in spite of herself, and the flush of her cheeks deepened as she saw that Dr. Murchison was also regarding her. He smiled gravely as he met her glance.

"When I was on leave in '89," said Colonel Rickaby from near the wagon, "or was it '93? No, it was '95. I was staying with the Bastupps at Bastupp Park—no, it was not the Bastupps. They have been dead for the last ten years. It was the Grimbsys, of Thornton Grange, of course, down in Devonshire, or was it Dorset? No, no Derbyshire. Anyhow, it began with a D; and we had an absolutely splendid hay party. For the children, you know. Three of them, there were, or possibly four. The eldest was Arabella, or was it Daisy? No, it was Ethel. She used to sit on the hay wagon and pretend it was a castle."

"I'm queen of the castle. I'm queen of the castle," chanted Miss Collett from the top of the hay wagon.

"Somebody must come and attack me," she continued, challenging the field.

The Colonel leaned confidentially towards Constance.

"I don't like attacking places," he said in a low, uneasy voice. "Too much blood, you know. You've no

141

idea how much a man can bleed."

He started as Dr. Murchison laid a hand on his shoulder.

"Come, Colonel," said the doctor kindly, "you mustn't be thinking now about your old campaigns. We're going to enjoy ourselves."

Mr. Clearwater leaning on his rake was looking at the doctor with an almost painful intentness. Then his eyes ran shiftily round the meadow, and he beckoned to Constance, who went towards him.

"Do you remember," he said, "the Cardinal in the Duchess of Malfi? He saw a thing, you know, armed with a rake, that seemed to strike at him."

"I could never read that play to an end," said Constance.

"Oh, but you should," said Mr. Clearwater, earnestly, and suddenly he began to declaim:

"I know death hath ten thousand several doors
For men to take their exits; and 'tis found
They go on such strange geometrical hinges,
You may open them both ways: any way,
    for heaven's sake,
So I were out of your whispering."

He looked at her wisely.

"We have improved on that," he said, "not even a whisper and yet we know that everything proper is said and done. You remember how it goes . . . *a mere glass house where the devils are continually blowing up women's souls on hollow irons and the fire never goes out?"*

"Come, Mr. Clearwater," protested Constance. "Some of those Elizabethans were just a little morbid, don't you think?"

Mr. Clearwater gave her a charming smile.

"It was the rake," he said. "But my dainty shepherdess will understand. She knows that I would never hurt a fly—not even spiders, that old Curtis loves to kill."

"Mr. Curtis likes to kill spiders?" said Constance. They had drawn a little apart from the rest, and were now raking together a long swathe of sweet-smelling hay, which would presently be tossed into the wagon by Colonel Rickaby, who was working busily just out of earshot.

"He stamps on them with his bare feet," said Mr. Clearwater, "and they pop like little bladders of seaweed."

He gave a little laugh and added hastily: "But what a silly thing to talk about on a summer's day!"

Constance agreed, and looking away down the meadow told herself that the hay-party was a great success. Miss Collett, shrieking with delight, was almost smothered with hay tossed up into the cart by the Colonel. Miss Truelow, following in the path of the doctor, was gleaning the stray wisps that escaped his fork. In the middle distance Warder Jones, who had worked upon a farm in his youth, was, with slow, tireless gestures, doing the bulk of the work. The sight of his sturdy figure turned this alien meadow into an English field. Then, as by a miracle, from somewhere far up in the blue, a lark was trilling, and the voice of

143

Mr. Clearwater rang out suddenly:

"And then I changed my pipings,—
Singing how down the vale of Menalus
   I pursued a maiden and clasped a reed:
Gods and men, we are all deluded thus!
   It breaks in our bosoms and then we bleed."

A little apart from the rest the Rev. Mark Hickett, pausing in his aimless labour, was looking up as though in search of the tiny creature whose singing had suddenly fallen from the sky. Was this a prelude to that opening of the heavens for which he waited? No: not thus would the revelation come. And yet, it was very near. But would it come from heaven? He must forget all his earlier expectations, put from his mind the dove descending, and the still small voice. Such thoughts might even delay the revelation. A great strong wind rent the mountains and brake in pieces the rocks . . . and after the wind an earthquake . . . and after the earthquake a fire. . . . He looked towards the doctor. There was the man who knew. On his face was authority. That man had only to call aloud and the revelation would be upon them all. Perhaps he would not even call aloud. He had only to send out his thoughts. Thoughts are things. That was the title of a book he had read—what his grandmother would have called a good book. The lips of the Rev. Mark Hickett curled in a sudden disdain, and that was rather alarming, for he had always respected his grandmother. Perhaps it was the scene—pastoral, of course, but somehow terribly pagan. . . . Sheep on the right hand and goats on the left; but this was not a country for sheep. There were goats everywhere in the valley. They browsed among the rocks, and stood in the path, primitive, shapeless creatures, older than sin.

An unexpected sound broke in upon his meditations. For Mr. Clearwater had taken from the pocket of his tweed coat a little flute, in two pieces, which he had screwed together. He was blowing it clear of the dust and grains of tobacco which it had collected, and it gave out a low, clear note.

"It's summer and harvest time," thought Constance, "and the world is very beautiful. If only it were not so terribly hot!"

At the sound of the flute the others looked up, and with one accord stopped working. Mr. Clearwater, having cleared the instrument to his satisfaction, blew three or four notes rapidly to try it, running his fingers up and down the stops. Then, putting it to his lips again, he blew in good earnest, and began to dance, raising his feet with odd ungainly steps. Having played a few measures, he paused for a moment and broke into a happy smile.

"My men like satyrs, grazing on the lawns,
Shall with their goat feet dance the antic hay,"

he said, and putting the pipe to his lips began to dance again.

"Reminds me of those summer evenings in the

145

hills," broke in the Colonel. "Those black fellows used to pipe to their flocks. Most confoundedly queer tunes they used to play, upon my soul, and with hardly a rag to their backs."

"Cover your arms," said a voice, and Constance found that Miss Truelow was again at her elbow.

Miss Collett now slid rapidly down from the hay wagon, and running towards Mr. Clearwater, began to dance to the music of the pipe.

Dr. Murchison again smiled at Constance.

"Well," he said, "what do you think of my party?"

"The tune," said Constance abruptly, "it's the thing he played in the chapel. Don't you remember? He called it 'Jumping Joan'."

Miss Truelow came suddenly between them.

"Certainly, Doctor," she said, "I will dance with you, if you insist."

> "Ring-a-ring o' roses,
> Pocketful of posies,
> This way, that way,
> All fall down."

broke in the childish treble of Miss Collett; and, in a moment, Constance found herself hand in hand with the doctor and the Colonel, dancing merrily around Mr. Clearwater. On the other side of the doctor was Miss Truelow, and, wonder of wonders, the Rev. Mark Hickett was also there completing the circle with the grey-haired child of ten.

Constance, self-conscious and unhappy, tried instinctively to free herself, but the doctor's clasp upon her hand was firm.

The ring broke as they dropped to the ground. The Colonel sprang up laughing loudly. He pulled Miss Truelow to her feet, who, dishevelled and breathless, seemed unaware that a fair proportion of the black buttons of her dress had burst asunder.

They started again, this time without Constance and the doctor, who fell out of the circle and stood apart watching the other four as they capered in a circle about Mr. Clearwater.

Constance now felt very much alone. She had often felt like that at a party, when, failing to catch the spirit of the thing, she had stood apart and watched. She was in some other world and did not know what they were doing. Only the doctor knew. For him all those separate, disjointed souls fell into place.

The doctor knew, but she was aware only that the surface was unreal. Those figures who capered and sang were beyond her—out of her range and sympathy. By what false memories or hopes were they thus beguiled into this semblance of a festival? The Colonel swung past, singing of posies, and Miss Truelow, a thin Maenad in black taffeta, leaned back from the circle, her eyes shut upon some secret ecstasy. The Rev. Mark Hickett gyrated as in performance of a rite, and Miss Collett swept by, dancing fatally towards the zero which would solve the mystery of her days.

Constance turned suddenly to Dr. Murchison and gripped him urgently by the hand.

"Stop them, Doctor," she heard herself entreating.

147

"Can't you see? It's all wrong?"

Dr. Murchison looked at her inquiringly.

"I don't like it," she said.

There was no time to see how he would take this appeal, for at that moment Warder Jones, who had come from his work in the meadow, and was waiting for an opportunity to address the Doctor, touched his cap and stepped forward.

"Beg pardon, Doctor," he said. "But may be you 'aven't noticed as how Mr. Curtis 'as given us the slip. 'E came out with the party, but I haven't seen him since we started. 'E's been a bit queer these last few days, and I don't like to lose sight of 'im."

But the doctor was not looking at Warder Jones. He was listening and looking away, over the meadow, towards the forest from which, as he looked and listened, there came a sudden cry, loud enough to be heard above the sound of Mr. Clearwater's piping and the merriment of the ring. The dancers paused abruptly. Silence fell as the whole group listened intently, and Constance was aware in that silence that the lark was no longer singing.

The Rev. Mark Hickett stepped forward from the circle straining his weak eyes in the direction of the cry. This then was the moment of revelation, the moment for which he had waited, and in which he must bear a part.

There was a further noise in the wood, as though some beast was forcing its way through thick undergrowth. The bushes at one point on the edge of the fir trees quivered and shook. Then abruptly out darted the figure of a man. He was panting, and one sleeve of his coat was torn. There was dirt on his hands and cheeks, and a great smear lay across one side of his mouth. He stumbled towards them, but, before he could reach them, he tripped and fell, uttering, as he did so, a choking cry.

It was Mr. Deeling.

For a moment no one stirred. The dancers stood in their circle, motionless, all except the Rev. Mark Hickett who had stepped out in advance of the rest.

He was a priest, and this was the obscure prologue to the harvest for which he had prayed. His voice rang out over the meadow and to the mountains beyond.

"Hymn No. 245. The Two Hundred-and-Forty-Fifth Hymn:

> 'Fair waved the golden corn
> O'er Canaan's pleasant land'."

III

That evening, after dinner, Constance and Dr. Murchison were walking in the rose garden. It was the first quiet moment since the sudden appearance of Mr. Deeling some three hours previously. Mr. Deeling had given a great deal of trouble. He had been carried speechless to bed by Warder Jones and his assistant, and after that it had been necessary to look for Mr. Curtis, who had ultimately appeared about an hour after the break-up of the hay party.

Dr. Murchison had taken charge of Mr. Curtis.

149

Constance had visited Mr. Deeling for a few minutes shortly before dinner. He had been strangely incoherent, and she had been able to get very little out of him. Only one thing was clear. Never again in any circumstances would he enter the wood. He had never been backward in any duty: he had worked tooth and nail, heart and soul, for the establishment, but no one could reasonably be expected to go back into the wood.

She had begun to talk about Mr. Deeling at dinner, but Dr. Murchison to her surprise had refused to do so. He had talked, however, abundantly of other things, and Constance, not for the first time, was astonished at the wide range of his thought and experience. He had talked of Pietro Aretino and the literature of the Renaissance—as marvellous, he had maintained, as its painting and sculpture—of eighteenth century glass and silver, and finally, though she did not remember how he came to do so, of Napoleon. Napoleon, she had found, was his hero, his greatest of men. Napoleon, he had said, had taken all life for his province, and his mind was everywhere at once. The doctor had quoted instances; how in the morning Napoleon would dictate letters and orders on such widely various subjects as the official caricatures to appear in the French press, the supply of artillery ammunition for the Spanish garrisons, a censure upon the high prices charged by Paris dressmakers, and a confidential memorandum on the attitude of Prussia to be sent through Talleyrand to Duroc. He was a master of mankind. He had in him the source of secret power, a curious expression which Dr. Murchison had used more than once, but which he had neglected to explain; and the talk had drifted on, by way of Napoleon's decree dated from Moscow, reforming the Comédie Française, to a discussion of the modern French theatre.

Constance had referred to the play of H. R. Lenormand which she had seen in Paris on her way to Château Landry. She found that Dr. Murchison was familiar with the work of this dramatist, but by no means enthusiastic.

"He writes of evil and its mysteries, but he is a trifler. He has seen the Ancient of Days and yet he remains helplessly a moralist. He is drawn into the darkness, it fascinates and intrigues him, but he goes into it with a lighted candle. You remember what Matthew Arnold said of the man who sinned against the Light. This man is sinning against the Dark."

After dinner they had taken their coffee on the terrace, and now they were walking in the rose garden, up and down in the scented darkness, which was presently chequered with silver by the moon which had climbed slowly above the barrier of the rocks.

Suddenly he turned to her and broke into a praise of beauty.

"There should be white peacocks about her with gilded beaks and she must be hung with pearls and emeralds and all pleasant stones. She should walk only in the light of the moon. Only the moonlight should touch her white arms and crimson mouth. For in the moonlight crimson is black, and we only feel it to be red."

He spoke in a kind of rhapsody, and her arm was

drawn within his so naturally that she did not realise that he held her imperceptibly near to him as they walked.

Suddenly he broke off.

"I must go and make the round of my patients," he said, "since Deeling is laid up."

"Let me do that for you," she began, but he shook his head.

"No," he said with a smile, "I can't allow you to lose a moment of all this. You should be sitting now at your window, looking at the roses that are trying to be red under the moon."

He withdrew his arm as he spoke, and Constance drew back a little. For a moment they stood silently together, then quietly he leaned forward and took her hands.

"I have seen beauty to-night," he said, looking her very directly in the eyes.

Then he bent his head, lightly kissed her fingers, and, turning quickly away, left her alone in the garden.

Chapter VIII

I

Mr. Deeling was lying in a rattan chair overlooking the rose garden. Three days had passed since the hay party, and he had spent most of the time in explaining very clearly to himself what had happened. He had overworked, and the heat had not unnaturally been too much for him. For two days he had lain in bed, while for the third and most of the fourth day he had been confined to the garden.

It was now nearly seven o'clock, and he would shortly go for a little stroll, nothing strenuous, because he was still feeling somewhat weak, probably from the effects of the powerful tonic which they had insisted on giving him.

He had not started earlier owing to the heat. It had grown no cooler during these last four days. He had come to dread the slow climbing of the sun to the summit of its brazen arc, for it seemed every day to make matters worse, and he had waited impatiently for its descent. It was hanging now like a golden apricot above the rocks which shut the valley at its western end. Even as he looked, its wheel of fire began slowly to roll down the farther slope to a swift extinction. In a few minutes it would be comparatively cool, cool enough at least for an evening walk.

Life was a very complicated business, so complicated that, unless one kept everything exactly in place, and behaved always according to plan, there would be chaos within and without. He must take care to keep his thoughts always perfectly in order. The mind was like a lens. One had to keep it steadily in focus; otherwise the object was indistinct, and the imagination, which was a dangerous and unaccountable faculty, might make of it any foolish or frightful thing it pleased.

Fortunately, it was for him comparatively easy to live according to plan. He was Mr. Ambrose Deeling, a man whose daily conduct had not varied for eleven years. All he had to do was to continue in the way he had chosen. His duty was plain. He was there at Château Landry to uphold its traditions, to keep the flag of Dr. Edwardes flying. The old routine was threatened. He did not trust Dr. Murchison, and he had even less faith in that chit of a girl.

He passed a soothing hand across his high wrinkled forehead and down over the severe, geometrical features, which relaxed for a moment and assumed a softer outline. Then he rose, very deliberately, and began walking with quiet, even steps down the garden path between the rose trees towards the steps which led to the meadow.

How heavy was the scented air. A vague line from some almost forgotten classic which had intrigued him when in the upper form of his grammar school came back to him. Something from Theocritus. Something about sleep, dripping from the leaves of apple trees. He could not remember how it went on. That's what it felt like in the garden now, only these were rose, not apple trees—rose trees, heavy with sanguine blossoms, waiting with curled petals and fragrant hearts for the evening dew.

As he walked, the sound of Mr. Clearwater's flute came to his ears. The notes rose and fell, with a plaintive iteration.

"It is beautiful," said Mr. Deeling to himself, just above his breath.

He found that he was walking awry, and that, having wandered from the path, he was knee-deep in the flowers that bordered it. For a moment he stood thus, listening to the music.

"Dear me," he said suddenly, "what am I doing here? And why am I listening to that confounded piping?"

He stepped briskly back on to the path, and, turning the corner, discovered Colonel Rickaby seated on a carved stone bench. He was in his shirt sleeves and his braces were lying across his knees. Mr. Clearwater was piping behind him. Mr. Deeling halted a moment and stood watching them.

The Colonel pulled the belt which he wore round the top of his trousers a hole tighter, felt in the pocket of his discarded coat and took out a piece of chamois leather with which he proceeded to rub the metal buckles of his braces, whistling the while through his teeth like an ostler.

"I wish you wouldn't do that," said Mr. Clearwater suddenly to the Colonel, stopping in the midst of a roulade. "It puts me off my playing."

"I don't like your playing," said Colonel Rickaby firmly, but without heat. "You remind me of those dashed confounded awful bagpipes of the old 49th Highland Brigade, or was it the 52nd? Fellows in skirts and nothing on beneath 'em. They were next us at Multan in '93 or was it '94? Used to squeal the place down, like a lot of pigs going to market."

"You do not like my playing?" said Mr. Clearwater equably. "Then I will recite to you my latest poem."

"Anything, anything you please," grumbled the Colonel, as he went on polishing his braces. "Not that I care very much for the poets, don't understand 'em, plain English is good enough for me. I remember once, when I was adjutant of the old 87th, a young fellow joined us from Sandhurst. He wore confoundedly long hair. Nice young fellow too—Thompson Thomkins—no, Thomas it was. He died later of enteric, or was it sandfly fever? Well, anyhow, he had dashed confounded awful long hair, and he was a bit of a poet too, used to read Shakespeare, Wordsworth and all the other johnnies. His kit was full of them. One day I said to him in mess: 'You dashed awful young monkey, why don't you get your hair cut? You are bristling with intolerable hair that's what you are.' Upon my word if he didn't answer me back: told me I was quoting Swinburne at him. I'd never even heard of the fellow, unless it was the chap who used to play for Somerset, or was it Gloucester? No, I remember now, it was Sussex."

156

Mr. Deeling stepped forward.

"Hullo, Pills," said the Colonel.

Mr. Deeling drew himself up.

"My name is Deeling," he answered coldly.

"No offence," said the Colonel. "We always used to call the medical office in our battalion Pills."

Mr. Deeling was mollified. He could scarcely resent being addressed as a medical officer.

Mr. Clearwater had by this time produced from his pocket a crumpled piece of paper.

"Listen," he said, "this is the poem I was talking to you about," and waving his flute in the air he began to declaim:

"When death walks down our village street,
His boots are always clean and neat,
For no one ever yet has found
A trace of footsteps on the ground;
Death passes by and makes no sound."

He paused and looked from one to the other.

"It's not very long," said Mr. Deeling cautiously.

"That's only the first stanza," said Mr. Clearwater.

"Good God," said the Colonel, "do you mean to say there's any more of it?"

"That is only the opening of the first canto," said Mr. Clearwater. "In the next twenty stanzas I describe Death walking up the street of a village and pausing outside the house uncertain which he shall enter. No one hears him but one old woman who has been ill for some time. She draws aside the curtain

157

and watches his thin figure pass, and sees him scrab-
ble with bony fingers on the door of one of her
neighbours."

"It will be my masterpiece," continued Mr.
Clearwater, "and it will be very long indeed—almost
as long as the Ring and Book. I will read you some
more," and he again consulted his MS.

Mr. Deeling intervened hastily. "May I ask what
you are doing, Colonel?" he said in a tone slightly
louder than usual.

The Colonel looked up from his polishing.

"That's for your private ear," he said with a signifi-
cant look at Mr. Clearwater.

"I might have known it," said the latter, crumpling
up his paper and cramming it into a trouser pocket.
"My poetry is caviare to the Colonel," and turning his
back on them he walked lightly away.

"Mad, of course," said the Colonel, tapping his
forehead, "mad as Moses."

"Now, Mr. Deeling," he continued, "if we are really
alone . . ."

He looked about him cautiously, while Mr. Deeling
groaned in spirit. The confidences of Colonel Rickaby
were apt to be as long as the idylls of Mr. Clearwater.
He felt, however, that it was his duty to listen.

"I am at your disposal, Colonel," he said. "But I
was proposing to take a little walk. Perhaps you would
have no objection to accompanying me? I do not
propose to go very far, just down the steps into the
meadow and as far as the fourth green, a distance of
three hundred and fifty-seven yards, then back by way
of the second tee, and so to the steps again—exactly

half-a-mile in all."

"Suit me admirably," said the Colonel, and getting to his feet he laid his braces carefully over the back of the seat. Then putting on his coat he fell into step beside Mr. Deeling.

They descended the stone steps to the meadow in silence and, reaching the meadow, they started to walk slowly forward. Mr. Deeling glanced at his companion. The Colonel, to his surprise, was nervous; his rather prominent blue eyes were more protuberant than usual; his face was flushed and he twisted one side of his moustache nervously with his left hand.

"The fact is," said the Colonel suddenly, "I want to ask your advice. Do you know what date it is the day after to-morrow?"

Mr. Deeling thought for a moment.

"It will be the seventh of August," he returned.

"Quite correct," said the Colonel, "the seventh of August it is, and the happiest day of my life."

He paused, and added: "Not lost but gone before."

They walked on two or three paces.

"She was the best wife a man ever had," he continued. "I lost her from cholera in '89 at Hyderabad, or was it Nasipore? Upon my word I forget."

He stopped abruptly, and clenching his right hand beat softly on his forehead, and his face suddenly brightened.

"No, of course not," he said. "It was Jullunder. How could I have forgotten it!"

"The fact is, Pills," he said, turning and laying a hand on Mr. Deeling's shoulder, "my memory is not as good as it was. I keep forgetting things, you know, but I am glad I didn't at any rate forget the day after to-morrow. The happiest day of my life. Poor Agnes."

"I understand," said Mr. Deeling. "You would like to have the usual ceremony."

"Just as usual," said the Colonel, "a few hymns, you know, and a suitable chapter: fade away suddenly like the grass; in the morning it is green and groweth up, but in the evening is cut down, dried up and withered."

Mr. Deeling well remembered the yearly practice. On the seventh of August each year the Colonel was accustomed to hold a small ceremony in the chapel to commemorate the anniversary of his wedding-day, or was it the day on which his wife had died? Mr. Deeling had never been able to decide, for the two occasions were somehow hopelessly entangled. Mr. Deeling had secretly rather deprecated giving way to this recurrent fancy, but he had never ventured to express his views to Dr. Edwardes, and now, of course, that Dr. Edwardes was absent, the ceremony should certainly be performed. To be a party to any change in this respect would be an act of disloyalty to his absent chief.

"Beyond the fact that you have not yet sent out any invitations," continued Mr. Deeling, "I see no reason why the ceremony should not take place the day after to-morrow as usual."

The Colonel paused in his walk and directed an anxious look at his companion.

"You don't think that *he*," and he jerked his head in the direction of the Château, "would object."

"I see no reason," replied Mr. Deeling.

"But haven't you noticed," continued the Colonel. "The chapel is never open now. He keeps it locked," and again he jerked his head in the direction of the castle.

"You mean Dr. Murchison?"

"He keeps it locked. That's why I don't know whether to have the ceremony or not. I've got the invitations ready, but I'd like to know more about it before sending them out. He might not like it, and, of course, if he doesn't like it, he has his reasons."

They had now reached the fourth green, and were beginning to walk back to where the castle loomed ahead of them in the gathering darkness.

"I feel sure," said Mr. Deeling slowly after a pause, carefully weighing each word, "that Dr. Murchison would not wish to depart in this respect from the practice of Dr. Edwardes."

"But he keeps it locked," said the Colonel.

"His motives for such an action," returned Mr. Deeling, "are unknown to me, but I feel sure they are not connected in any way with what you propose. I suggest that you approach him on the subject immediately on your return."

A troubled look came into the eyes of the Colonel.

"No," he said quickly. "I wouldn't like to do that."

He added as though excusing himself:

"Awful bore, you know. Fine man, great man, full of responsibility. Never met anybody like him. Couldn't possibly bother him with a thing like that."

"If you feel any diffidence in approaching Dr. Murchison yourself," said Mr. Deeling, "I shall be

161

happy to act for you. Perhaps, indeed, it would be as well. I can inform him that Dr. Edwardes has always given his consent."

"By George, Pills, that's confoundedly decent of you," said the Colonel. "I call it most friendly and obliging," and he laid a hand heavily on Mr. Deeling's shoulder.

Mr. Deeling's offer certainly had a most gratifying effect. The Colonel was himself again.

"Upon my soul," he said, when they had moved on a few paces, "you've taken quite a weight off my shoulders. Fine fellow, Dr. Murchison, but he's not a man to be bothered. Reminds me of General Carruthers who commanded against the Wazi Wazi in '91 or was it '93? Greatest man I ever met. Brave Carruthers we called him because he was so courageous. Bite your head off as soon as look at you."

"There's only one other thing," went on the Colonel a moment later, "I suppose we can rely on that padre fellow to come up to scratch. He's been rather queer of late."

"I am quite sure that the Rev. Mark Hickett will do all that is necessary," said Mr. Deeling.

They spoke no more on the subject, and the Colonel, by the time they had reached the steps and were climbing the terrace, had begun to bore Mr. Deeling with some interminable history of one of his old campaigns.

A moment later Mr. Deeling stood alone on the terrace. It was very still and oppressive. Night was coming slowly, much too slowly, Mr. Deeling thought, as he moved to the parapet. A breath of air fanned his temples, but it was hot, as though it came from the mouth of a giant. There was to be no relief, then, from the heat that night, and to-morrow would be another burning day.

There was a footfall, and, turning, he found Mr. Clearwater at his elbow.

"Sleep is upon the world," said Mr. Clearwater, looking out over the darkening meadow beneath them. "The mountains are drowsy; the monsters of the sea seek rest; and on the tribe of broad-winged birds sleep has fallen."

II

The night was almost as oppressive as the day, and Constance was unable to sleep. Such weather was really most unusual. And the worst of it was there seemed to be no sign that it would break.

Everyone, she thought, with the exception of Dr. Murchison, was becoming nervously affected by it. There had been that curious fit of Mr. Deeling four days previously. He had apparently recovered, but he looked very white, and Constance felt that a holiday would certainly do him no harm. She intended to say as much to the doctor. Then there was Nurse Webster, obviously in need of a change. Nurse Webster, in fact, had told her only that morning that she had hoped soon to be taking her annual leave, but she had not liked to approach Dr. Murchison on the subject.

Constance, there and then, had gone to Dr. Murchison, who had at once agreed that Nurse Webster should go away in two days time for at least three weeks.

Constance had cheerfully undertaken the extra work. After all, she had only been in the Château a few weeks, and so far she had not been overburdened. If only it were not so hot.

The weather must surely break sometime. Even the weight of the single sheet which covered her was oppressive. She threw it off, and, turning on her back, lay with her hands clasped behind her head, gazing at the ceiling.

Nerves! There must be no nerves in a place like Château Landry. Dr. Murchison had no nerves. He threw himself, heart and soul, without misgiving into everything he did. He was cool and at the same time enthusiastic. She had played tennis with him that afternoon on the red *en-tout-cas* court, under the shadow of the castle wall. He was not a very good player, not as good as Constance, in fact, but what he lacked in skill he made up for in eagerness and agility. She had beaten him in three straight sets, and he had taken his defeat with a smile. She remembered the touch of his hand as he had helped her on with her coat after the game—cool, in spite of the heat. Then he had darted off to have a cold shower-bath, and afterwards to pay his evening visit to Mr. Godstone. She imagined him standing there with the water streaming from his broad shoulders and white skin, dashing away to put on the dark suit of flannels, which he always wore, and entering, a few minutes later, the forbidden door to grapple with the hideous mind of the lunatic within. And to think that for one moment she had believed him to be Godstone! It was incredible, unbelievable, that she should have done so. She would remember it with a pang all her life. The blood came rushing to her cheeks in the darkness.

What was it he had said in the garden. I have seen beauty to-night, and he had talked of roses that were trying to be red under the moon.

But this would never do. To lie thus, thinking of Dr. Murchison. Well, then, shut up the box, put it away and go to sleep.

But sleep was impossible, and a little later she rose, thrust her feet into a pair of heelless slippers, pulled on a dressing gown and made for the door. She would go downstairs to the library and find a book.

Outside the passage was filled with a faint glow coming from the shaded bulbs which hung at rare intervals from the ceiling. The corridor was thickly carpeted, and her feet made no sound as she walked down its length to the head of the stairs leading to the central hall below. At the stairhead she paused, unlocked a little cupboard built in the wall and pressed a switch. This disconnected the system of electric bells which rang in the bedrooms of the warders and of Dr. Edwardes, and gave instant warning if anyone should leave a room after dark and walk downstairs. It was a precaution in use in many mental homes, and one with which Constance was now familiar.

She moved down the great stairway of walnut and

olive wood, and a moment later entered the library. She was carrying a lighted candle, as the stairs and the ground floor of the Château Landry were always left in darkness.

In the library she did not turn on the electric lights, but made use of the candle to give what light she needed. It made but little impression on the darkness as she moved forward; fantastic shadows skipped and ran up the walls of the great room, losing themselves in the upper gloom. But she knew her way. Behind her desk and that of Dr. Murchison there were some low bookshelves filled for the most part with medical books, and works of reference; but there was one shelf set aside for novels, and there was also a table by the hearth at the other end of the room on which was spread a quantity of magazines and reviews.

Constance wanted something light, a novel of adventure. There were quite a number of them, for they were Mr. Deeling's favourite reading. She moved towards the shelves behind the desks, and stooping, held her candle so as to read the titles. There were half a dozen books by John Buchan, Valentine Williams, Oppenheim, and a new one which she did not remember to have seen before, but which Mr. Deeling had been reading, "The Brethren of the Axe," by John Somers. She chose the last, and straightening herself up, turned to depart.

Her eyes, as she did so, fell on the open pages of a book lying on the table of Dr. Murchison.

It was a large quarto volume, apparently of some age. She looked at it a moment with curiosity. The text was in French, in sixteenth century lettering, printed from wood blocks. One page was entirely taken up with a curious illustration. It represented a wizened man dressed in a torn doublet and wearing a hat adorned with cock's feathers. His face was lined and twisted. He wore a straggling beard and one of his legs was of wood. He was seated on a chair made of gnarled boughs, playing on a clavichord, but his notes were composed of the feet of cats held in diminutive stocks, their heads peeping out from where the wires of the instrument would normally be kept. Behind the player of this strange instrument a woman was crouching by a hearth. She had a doleful face and a strange black mark upon her forearm.

Behind the musical instrument stood another man, dressed in a more elaborate doublet and doing something with a sword to an animal of which only a leg was to be seen. On the extreme right of the picture was a bed in which lay a screaming hag, her mouth wide open; her withered arms were crossed, and a crow was perched upon her head. In the foreground was a black sow, and round the musical instrument were grouped half a dozen curious monsters with the heads of dogs or bulls. They held books, displaying notes of music, and they appeared to be singing to the accompaniment of the one-legged man. Above the picture was written: "Le leçon de Grimoire."

Constance, interested by the picture, laid her candle down on the edge of the desk, and began turning the pages of the book in search of further illustrations. Dr. Murchison appeared to be reading a most curious work. She turned three or fours of the thick pages, then something fluttered out from between them and

167

fell to the floor. She stooped to pick it up. It was a typewritten slip and appeared to be part of a catalogue of books. She read some of the titles:

DRAGON ROUGE (Le) ou l'art de commander des Esprits Célestes, Aériens, Terrestres, Infernaux, avec le vrai secret de gagner toutes les fois qu'on met aux loteries, de découvrir les trésors cachés, etc., S.L.1522—(Imprimé au commencement du XIX ᵉsiécle sur l'édition très rare de 1520).

BINSFELDI (Petri)—Tractatus de confessionibus maleficorum et Sagarum—Augustae Treuirorum, 1589.

CAYET (Palma)—Histoire prodigieuse et lamentable de Jean Fauste, grand magicien, avec son testament et sa vie épouvantable—A Cologne, chez les héritiers de Pierre Marteau, 1721, très curieux (rare).

FONTAINE (Jacques). Of the marks of the sorcerers and of the real possession which the Devil takes of the body of man; of the trial of the abominable and detestable sorcerer Louys Gaufridy, etc., dedicated to Her Majesty, the Queen, London, at the Sign of the Archer, St. Paul's Churchyard, 1611 (very rare).

HONORIUS—Grimoire du pape Honorius, avec un recueil des plus rare secrets. Rome, 1670, in-16 fig. (rarissime).

SPRENGER (Jacques) Malleus maleficarum de Lamiis et Strygibus et Sagis, aliisque Magis et Daemoniacis mulieribus, eorumque arte, po-

She looked at the curious picture, an back again at the list of books. They were all to do with magic, the black art, a subject of which she knew nothing. But why should Dr. Murchison be reading them? She did not know, but it suddenly came over her that she had no business to be prying into his affairs. What he chose to read was no concern of hers. Hastily she pushed the typewritten paper between the leaves of the great book, and bent it back slightly so that it might remain open at the page with the picture. But even as she did so, her curiosity proved too strong for her, and she glanced, almost in spite of herself, at the text.

It was a description in old French of the witch's or magician's Sabbath, and appeared to be taken from the deposition of some sorcerer on trial. It was at once grotesque and horrible, and blend of disordered ritual, impious ejaculation and a description of acts so obscene that her hand trembled as she turned the page. But she read steadily to the end.

Then she let fall the pages and closed her eyes. But she could not shut them upon her inward vision. Almost she could hear the cry of the sorcerers, the terrible "Aye Saraye!" as they rushed through the foul air, with their toads and bats, to the trysting place. One sentence kept repeating itself in her mind: "A few minutes later and I saw death vomit forth all the spectres of his empire upon the earth." Master Leonard was there, in his goat form, and there too was

169

the altar with its throne, and all about it the moving shadows of demons and their earthly lovers. Into the rout came shrieking, in white beauty, the miserable queen of the Sabbath, to be seized by the phantoms and greeted with nameless blasphemies as they laid her upon the altar, and the Black Mass began. There they writhed and postured up to the supreme moment of horror when the naked victim herself rose on the altar and added her supreme blasphemy to the rest.

Constance opened her eyes, for a sound had come to her ears. For a moment she listened. Was it Dr. Murchison? That was annoying. She did not wish to be caught reading these books of his surreptitiously. She turned and snatched up the candle and moved rapidly towards the door. Before she was half-way across the room, however, she tripped on the edge of her dressing gown, and was brought to her knees. The candle, loose in its socket, fell to the ground. She was in darkness.

She rose and stood for a moment. This was even more annoying. She would look a perfect fool, standing there in the dark. She pulled her dressing gown tightly about her.

But now there was a glimmer on the wall. She could see vaguely the grey stone with its pointed arch and far up a little lancet window which had caught a single star. And what was that form? The shadow of a huge head with double horns. Beneath it were humped black shoulders. For a moment it was motionless and then it flickered with a vast gesture across the wall.

With a low cry, Constance turned, and in sudden

terror shambled blindly forward. There was a sudden swish of draperies, the sound of a voice, and then, in an instant, the great room was flooded with light.

With a sob of relief, she saw Dr. Murchison, fully dressed, a candle in one hand and the other on the switch of the electric light, standing by the door.

III

The Rev. Mark Hickett was preparing himself for bed. He took off and hung up the long black cassock which he wore in the evening, and removed his high Roman collar and black stock with fingers that trembled slightly.

The revelation for which he waited could not surely be much longer delayed. He had waited for years. Ever since he could remember almost. Perhaps it would come to him that night. He had a passionate conviction that at any moment now his long period of preparation would be rewarded.

He did not know why he felt that conviction. He knew only that during the last months there had been a change. It was as though the whole thing had been taken out of his hands. Even his praying took often an unexpected turn. There was a power that twisted his thoughts so that they could no longer run in the old direction. At first he had resisted this possession, as he had formerly resisted the intrusion into his mind of carnal reflections. But he was quite sure now that only by way of surrender to this new influence would the revelation come. He must yield himself body and soul to the power invisible which was at work by day and by night—a power older than the grace he had hitherto sought in fasting and prayer.

He must overcome his terror of the strange impulses that gave to old thoughts and phrases a new, often a contrary, significance, as white suggested black. Was it for such as he to understand the mystery of good and evil? Always they were hand in hand, and one was an aspect or disguise of the other. He had sought the light. Where was it more likely to be found than where the Darkness awaited its companion? It was not for him to question a dispensation in which all contraries were reconciled.

All that was needed was patience, patience and a humble heart. "I am but a poor crushed manikin," he murmured, using for the thousandth time the words of the old prayer that he had found in a sixteenth century Book of Hours.

He put on his linen night-shirt, white as the robe of catechumen. Then he knelt on the bare floor and raised his hands in prayer. But the old words would not come, the words that he had said so often. That, too, was nothing strange; for now the prayers would never come, or when they came they were never now as they used to be.

For one breathless instant, only four days ago, he had thought that the moment had arrived. There in the hay field, when they had danced together, danced in the sunlight, treading the withered fragrant grass of the valley, he had felt that it was imminent. But at the critical moment, as he had stepped forward, straining towards that cry in the forest, he had been suddenly confused. His mind had swung unaccountably back to the ritual of his old faith. He had fancied himself back in his parish church. There was his pulpit, with its flowers and fruit, and the lectern, with its ears of corn—the first fruits of the garden and the farm.

For that vision and the gesture it had provoked he felt a strange remorse, and since then he had never ceased to pray for yet another chance. Next time he would not thus be taken unawares.

His gaze travelled up the white wall of the bare room to the black crucifix and the white carved figure nailed to it. His heart missed a beat. How had that remained? Was that vigilance, to have left that hanging there?

He rose stiffly from his knees and moved to the wall. He unhooked the crucifix and held it in his hands, looking down at it. He must wait a moment. It would be suggested to him what he ought to do. He had only to listen and obey. Who was it that whispered in his ear? Was it even a whisper? Just a thought that came suddenly from nowhere. He crossed the room with the crucifix and, sitting at his desk, with some little exertion removed the ring by which it had hung upon the nail. He turned it upside down and screwed the ring into the foot of the cross. This done, he rose from his chair and hung the crucifix in its new position head downwards, the figure to the wall.

It swung into place, and the ivory figure scraped against the plaster. He lifted a lean forefinger and tapped the cross once or twice, so that it moved to and fro like a pendulum, scraping each time against the

173

wall.

He moved to the middle of the room. It was very dark outside, dark and very hot. He turned and switched off the light. He was ready. He would never be more ready if he lived to the day of judgement.

Had he not known it would be thus? There came a sudden tap on the door. It swung open behind him, and as he turned he heard a voice which said: "Take up your cloak and come with me."

He moved to the bed; his dressing-gown was lying across it. It was of black wool, with long pendulous sleeves. He put it on and drew the cord tight about his waist. Then he turned to the door and walked straight out, following his invisible guide.

The corridor was in darkness, the little lamps in the ceiling had been put out.

In front of him were soft footfalls and a shadow. He moved slowly down the corridor, and felt the beginning of the stairs beneath his feet. It was dark, and yet he descended without faltering, for this darkness was as noon to a vision entranced.

At the bottom of the great stairs he paused.

"Go to your right," whispered the guide, "and then forward nine paces. Then turn to the left, and when the light gleams, raise your arms."

He moved forward, counting breathlessly.

"Nine," he breathed at last, and turning to the left he stood and waited. He did not know how long he waited, for time had ceased.

Then suddenly the darkness was grey. Gazing straight before him, he raised his arms, as he had been told to do. In front of him, some distance away, was the grey stone wall of the room. On it was a monstrous shadow, the shadow of a head with four horns and humped shoulders beneath it. It wavered a moment, then stood still.

Four horns . . . that was a little queer. . . . Or perhaps it was not so queer. There were gods with many pairs of arms, and once he had seen the picture of a goddess with a hundred breasts.

He stood gazing, and thus he would continue to stand still till the world grew old. But suddenly he was released from the vision. The light went out.

"Go back to your room," said a voice sharply in his ear. "And do not leave it again till you are told."

He turned and stumbled blindly down the passage.

But in his heart there burned an inextinguishable fire.

IV

A moment later Constance found herself in an armchair beside the hearth. She had been carried there by Dr. Murchison.

"Keep quite still," he was saying. "I will go and get you something to drink."

She looked up at him, and contrived the smile.

"No, it's all right," she said, putting her hand to her forehead.

She made to rise from the chair.

"No, sit down," he said.

"But I really am quite all right," protested Constance. "I . . . I couldn't sleep, and I just came down

175

to get a book, and then. . . ." She stopped.

"Yes?" he said.

"Nothing . . . the candle fell out of the candlestick, and I was left in the dark."

"Was that all?"

"It was not altogether that," said Constance. "I thought I heard something."

"How long had you been in the room?" said Dr. Murchison.

"I don't quite know," replied Constance. "It might have been twenty minutes perhaps,"

"And during that time you were choosing something to read?"

"Yes."

He looked at the little shelf of books behind the desk.

"So that was all," said Dr. Murchison.

Constance hesitated.

"Not quite all," she confessed. "I was looking at the book on your desk."

He looked inquiringly towards the open volume.

"I'm sorry," he said, after a short silence. "In our profession one has to face some pretty horrible facts, but that was hardly necessary."

Constance flushed.

"There was a curious picture," she said, "and somehow I began to be interested."

He put a hand on her shoulder.

"It was my fault," he said kindly. "I ought not to have left the book where it was."

"It was horrible," she said in a low voice. "Dr. Murchison, why do you read such things?"

"That book," he said, "is part of the library of Mr. Godstone. I am looking carefully through all his books. I shall have to read them pretty thoroughly if I am ever to understand his case."

He looked at her for some moments without speaking.

"You were frightened by what you read," he said at last.

"Not exactly frightened," she replied.

"What was it then that startled you?" he insisted.

Constance tried to speak, but the words would not come.

"Answer me, please," he said, and the request was almost a command.

"There was a shadow," she began, "a shadow on the wall."

"Oh, come," said Dr. Murchison, as though he were talking to a child. "I can't have you frightened by a shadow."

He walked to the middle of the room, and picked up her candle from the floor. Then he lit it and moved to the door.

"I am going to turn out the lights," he said. "Look at the wall in front of you."

He went to the door and abruptly the lights went out. For a moment she was in complete darkness. Then a series of great shadows moved across the wall in front of her. She realised that they came from the door. For a moment they wheeled in confusion; then they steadied. She caught her breath, for, in front of her, on the grey stone wall, moved once again the great head and the humped shoulders, and even as she looked two horns shot out and completed the illusion. Then with a click the electric lights came on again, and she heard Dr. Murchison walk into the room.

"Was that your shadow?" he asked, and there was a touch of amused contempt in his voice.

"Yes," she admitted. "That was what I saw."

She heard him busying himself with something behind her. There was a tinkling of glass. Then he stood beside her, a tumbler in his hand.

"Your nerves, Miss Sedgwick, seem to be a little frayed. The work here, perhaps, is too much for you."

"Oh, no," said Constance eagerly. "I am perfectly all right, Doctor. I have not been sleeping well, that is all. It's really only that."

He took a step forward, so that he was standing right over her.

"Drink this," he said, holding out the tumbler.

She took it mechanically.

"You are not going to send me away, Doctor?" she said, and on that he smiled suddenly, and put his hands upon her shoulders.

"Not if you do as you are told," he answered. "I've mixed you a sleeping draught. Drink it up, and we will say no more about it."

She drained the tumbler.

"And now," he said, "you must go to bed," and he held out his hands. She took them, and he pulled her to her feet. Side by side they walked across the room. She felt of a sudden curiously weak, but happy. She turned to him in the doorway.

"Good-night," she said. "I'm sorry to have been such a nuisance."

He looked at her and smiled suddenly. Then, before she had a chance to protest, he bent down and picked her up as though she were a child, and strode masterfully up the stairs, along the corridor and into her room, where he laid her upon the bed. For a moment his hand rested on her hair. Then he turned abruptly and left her.

A pleasant drowsiness was stealing over her. She did not trouble to get up and take off her dressing gown. It was still stiflingly hot, but she pulled the sheet up so that it covered her.

It was only on the threshold of sleep that two things crossed her mind. On the first shadow she had seen there had been two pairs of horns, but on the second only one. Also she had not remembered to ask Dr. Murchison what he had said as he had turned on the lights when he found her.

But these thoughts had no power to keep her awake now. She turned slightly on her left side with a little sigh.

A moment later she was asleep.

Chapter IX

I

The Rev. Mark Hickett stirred under the firm dry hand upon his forehead.

"Look at me," came the steady voice.

He sank back a little into the deep armchair in which he was sitting, and gazed, serenely now, into the eyes of Dr. Murchison.

He was no longer afraid. On the contrary, he was happy and at peace.

It seemed to him that Dr. Murchison was smiling at him, but he could only see the doctor's face darkly, as through a mist. He sighed and his thin hands plucked at the padding of the chair.

Then, abruptly, the face of the doctor disappeared altogether. The room, too, had vanished, with its stone walls and the great bookcases and the sheaves of weapons. He was looking through a window and at his feet was a gleaming sea, green and sapphire, and there, in the offing, was the galleon with its painted sails and its crew singing a chanty as they began to heave on the achor.

He would be aboard it soon, to be received by its crew with pikes at the salute, their swarthy faces set in awe beneath their morions of steel as he mounted the companion ladder in his suit of violet and purple, with the great starched ruff.

Already he was rocking in the little pinnace, while the naked backs of the eight oarsmen swung rhythmically to and fro. He was sitting in the stern sheets, playing with the chain of twisted gold about his neck. For a moment the pinnace rose and fell at the foot of the ladder; then the silver trumpets rang out as he climbed on deck. It all happened as he had foreseen. . . .

He was pacing now the quarter-deck, and the galleon was under sail. He held the arm of the grey master gunner, who was very proud to be thus engaged. They talked of the Spanish treasure ship, the *Madre de Dios*, which they had looted two days before homeward bound from the Caribbean, and of the great gold crucifix, studded with emeralds, which was now being melted down in the lazaret.

The look-out in the fore-top screamed down of a sail that he descried. She was a Moorish galley, and her oars were out. They would have to fight for it. She was making for their starboard quarter.

He raised his hand. The ruby on his forefinger flamed in the sun, and the first broadside crashed out beneath him.

The two ships ground together. The air was full of cries and splinters. He was wearing no longer his suit of violet and purple, but golden armour, Milanese plate, chased and scrolled. With his own hand he engaged the Moorish Emir in command of the storming party and ran him through the throat, so that he fell at his feet and rolled to the scuppers, and the deck was crimson.

The smoke of the guns drifted thickly about them till they were smothered in a white pall. He could no longer see the vessels, not even his own yard arm. The mist was whirling . . . without shape or form . . . no, not quite . . . for there was a face within the murk, a strong face that he knew.

He heard a voice say sharply, suddenly:

"What is it, Mr. Deeling?"

The Rev. Mark Hickett sighed and stirred in his chair. In front of him was Dr. Murchison, and, standing at his elbow, was Mr. Deeling, the apothecary.

Mr. Deeling and the doctor were talking, but for a moment he could not understand what they were saying.

But soon the doctor turned to him.

"Mr. Hickett," he said, "it would appear that Colonel Rickaby is anxious that the usual ceremony should be performed to-morrow afternoon. It seems that there is every year a service in memory of his wife."

"I do not know what he means," said Mr. Hickett.

That, of course, was a lie. But he would deny it again if necessary. He would deny it three times, swearing that he did not know.

Mr. Deeling was speaking now.

"I am referring, Mr. Hickett, to the ceremony which you are accustomed to perform for Colonel Rickaby each year, who always, you may remember, desires to commemorate his wife on the seventh of August. I have ventured to suggest that you might be willing to take the service to-morrow at 5-30 p.m."

There was a short silence, during which Mr. Deeling looked inquiringly at the unhappy parson. What was the matter with the poor fool? He had usually looked forward to this annual ceremony, and prepared for it with the greatest unction. He had, in fact, always been asking for services in the chapel. It was rather odd, then, that he should look so blank? There was another thing. The little gold cross on his watch chain, with which he was always playing, was not there any more. That also was rather odd.

The Rev. Mark Hickett passed a thin tongue across his dry lips and shook his head.

"I swear," he said, "that I haven't the least idea of what you are talking about."

Mr. Deeling glanced at Dr. Murchison. The doctor was seated in his consulting chair, the desk in front of him, leaning back slightly, looking steadily at Mr. Hickett.

"Surely," Mr. Deeling protested, "you remember what happened last year and the year before. You take the service always on August the seventh."

"I have never taken it in my life," said Mr. Hickett.

Dr. Murchison leaned forward and spoke with authority.

"That is three times," he said. "You are permitted to remember it now."

The Rev. Mark Hickett looked at the Doctor, incredulous, hesitating, with troubled eyes.

"Very well," he said at last, "if it is permitted."

"You may perform the ceremony, Mr. Hickett,"
said Dr. Murchison. "Do not be afraid. I will take
full responsibility for your acts."

The doctor opened a drawer of the big desk in
front of him.

"We will hold the ceremony," he said, "at half-past
five to-morrow afternoon. Here is the key of the
chapel. You may wish to make your preparations."

The Rev. Mark Hickett rose without a word,
moved across the great room to the door. He walked
as in a dream, holding in his hand the twisted key.

II

Mr. Deeling, that afternoon, was sitting in his
dispensary. In his hand was an envelope, which he
had found upon his desk. That, in itself, was annoying. He had locked the dispensary at 12.15, when he
had completed his morning prescriptions, and he had
not entered it since, but he was prepared to swear
that the envelope had not been there before lunch.
That must mean that either Dr. Murchison or Miss
Sedgwick had during his absence, visited the dispensary to which, of course, they had a duplicate key.
He did not like people to visit his dispensary. It was
his own domain, and Dr. Edwardes had always
respected it. Why, he had even had the courtesy
invariably to knock before he entered. But Dr.
Edwardes was a gentleman.

Mr. Deeling weighed the envelope for a moment in
his hand, and, turning it over, examined it well before
he opened it. It was an ordinary envelope of the

castle stationery, with the words "Château Landry" printed on the flap. He turned it over again. His name was typewritten, he noticed. Then he slid a dry forefinger under the flap, pried it open and pulled out a letter.

This is what he read:

> "Château Landry
> "August 6th, 1927.

"DEAR MR. DEELING,

"I wish to express to you in writing my regret at your unfortunate collapse and subsequent illness which occurred on the second of this month. It brought home to me the fact that you have obviously been compelled considerably to overwork since the departure of Dr. Edwardes. I suppose that to a certain extent that was inevitable. My sudden appearance and many demands upon your time have considerably increased what I have already had occasion to note is almost more than a fair day's work for any one man. I see by reference to your personal file that you have taken no holiday whatever for the last four years. I cannot but admire your devotion, but I feel that you are submitting yourself to a strain that is for the moment beyond your powers, and I am, therefore, writing to inform you that leave for two months is at your disposal, to be taken at your earliest convenience.

"I need not say that I am very sensible of the loss, temporary though it will be, of your services, for I have formed a very high opinion of your capabilities in the short time I have been at

Château Landry. Dr. Sedgwick (who has some knowledge of pharmacy) has, however, very kindly offered to take over that part of your duties which is absolutely essential, and in these circumstances I feel that I am justified in giving you this opportunity to take a rest, of which, as a doctor, I am convinced you stand in need.

"You will, perhaps, allow me to assure you that your full salary will, of course, be paid during your absence, together with a first-class return railway fare to any destination in Europe you may select.

"Believe me, dear Mr. Deeling,

"Very sincerely yours,
"EDWARD MURCHISON."

Mr. Deeling felt behind him for the arm of his chair and sat down. Then, adjusting the pince-nez which he used for reading, he picked up the letter again and read it through carefully from beginning to end once more. By the time he had finished, and laid the letter down, he was boiling with indignation. This was the last straw. He was, it seemed, to be packed off on leave, whether he liked it or not. He was not even to be consulted. He had received a letter in formal terms, and the letter was intended to be final. That in itself had the appearance of a deliberate insult. What right, moreover, had Dr. Murchison to rummage in his personal file and note that he had taken no leave for four years? That was his own affair. Then there was that final paragraph. Did Dr. Murchison think he was a pauper, that he had refrained from taking a holiday because he had been

186

unable to afford it?

This started another train of thought, and, with hands that trembled slightly, Mr. Deeling unlocked a small drawer in his desk, and, taking out a little black book, consulted the list of his investments. It was an extremely satisfactory list, so much so that, when he put it down, he wondered, perhaps, whether he had not allowed himself to be too easily disturbed. Dr. Murchison was genuinely concerned about him, and his letter might be kindly intended.

He looked at the letter again, and again his indignation was aroused.

Miss Sedgwick (or Dr. Sedgwick as she preferred to call herself) was to do his work for him while he was away. He had hardly noticed that before. That was the limit.

"Do my work," said Mr. Deeling, springing up from his chair and moving about his dispensary with a quickness of stride which he had not attained for years. "The patients would be poisoned. *Some knowledge of pharmacy,*' indeed."

He came to a stand by the window and gazed with unseeing eyes upon the terrace. Miss Collett was outside, playing with a large bright rubber ball.

They wanted, for some reason, to get rid of him. He felt it in his bones. There was something curiously wrong at Château Landry. Was it, perhaps, the hyoscin? Possibly, but it did not seem to be a very adequate motive.

He turned back again from the window to his desk. What was he to do? If he replied to that letter with a blunt refusal, Dr. Murchison might insist on his going. That would place him in a very awkward position. He would have to refuse point-blank again, in which case he stood a very good chance of losing his post altogether for insubordination, or else he would be forced to yield to *force majeure* and be sent away to some ridiculous continental spa—Aix, or Dax or Baden Baden. He must think of some better plan. He did not wish to leave Château Landry for two reasons. First it was his home, the only home he knew. He would be lost in the world outside. Secondly, he had a suspicion that, once out of the way, Dr. Murchison would not hesitate to replace him by somebody else, somebody more pliable than he, less likely to oppose, even silently, the innovations which, as the representative of Dr. Edwardes, he so deeply resented.

As he sat scratching the clean white blotting-paper before him with a dry pen (ink would have sullied the virgin whiteness of the pad), there came a knock at his door. Hastily he folded up Dr. Murchison's letter and thrust it into a drawer.

"Come in," he said.

The door opened to admit Nurse Webster, who was closely followed by Warder Jones.

Mr. Deeling slightly raised his geometrical eyebrows.

"Good morning, Mr. Deeling," said Nurse Webster.

"Mornin', sir," said Warder Jones, serious and respectful.

Mr. Deeling looked at them for a moment. Then he made a slight gesture towards two white-painted chairs. He had not thought it necessary to rise at the entry of Nurse Webster. She was only a subordinate.

Obediently they seated themselves. Warder Jones, Mr. Deeling noted, was flushed, like a simple soul confronted with a difficult problem. Nurse Webster, on the other hand, sat bolt upright on her wooden chair, her hands folded professionally in front of her, her honest red face expressionless as a doll's. But it was she who began to speak.

"Mr. Deeling," she said, "Warder Jones has just told me a rather curious story. He seemed a bit doubtful as to what he should do, and I suggested that he should come to you. You may possibly think nothing of it, but, on the other hand, perhaps you will."

Mr. Deeling was surprised. Why had they come to him instead of going at once to Dr. Murchison? He did not, however, think fit to ask them the question. If they had thought him a person of sufficient importance to be consulted, he would be the last to suggest that their conduct was in any degree unusual.

"Well, Jones," he said, "what is it?"

"It's like this, sir," replied the warder. "You know as 'ow by Dr. Murchison's orders I looks after the patient Godstone. 'Don't you let no one else go near that there patient,' says the doctor to me, and I've carried out 'is instructions literal. I'm sure he's had the best of treatment from me, and I'm bound to say, mind you, as 'ow I 'ave 'ad no trouble with 'im whatsoever, barring that time when you and the female doctor, begging her pardon, Miss Sedgwick, came to *h*interview 'im a fortnight ago, when the Colonel broke 'is winder with a golf-ball."

He paused for breath, while Mr. Deeling wondered what would follow this lengthy preamble.

"Now, I'm bound to tell you," continued the warder, "that the doctor's very particular about that there patient. 'E gave me the most minute instructions regarding as to 'ow 'e was to be treated. He was not to be allowed to do anything for hisself, and if he wanted to wash, well then I was to wash 'im, or at any rate stand by and see 'im do it. I was always to walk with 'im if he took any exercise, though 'e 'asn't took none yet. 'Alf the time 'e lies more or less stoopefied."

"Stupefied," said Mr. Deeling. "You mean he has been drugged?"

"Well, sir, that's what I 'ave said to myself. Time and again when I sees him lying there as if 'e was drugged, I says to myself, 'why 'e's drugged,' though I never seen any drugs in his room. In fact, I'm certain sure he couldn't 'ave none, for I looks after the room myself, and there ain't a 'ole nor a corner what I 'ave not dusted a 'undred times, and nowhere to hide 'em, nowhere at all."

"Are you present when Dr. Murchison attends to him?" said Mr. Deeling.

"Sometimes," replied Warder Jones, "but mostly 'e sends me out of the room."

"Go on," said Mr. Deeling.

The warder cleared his throat.

"Well, as I was saying," he continued, "I've always looked after that patient like a child from the very start. There's only one thing that's been what you might call pecooliar. Dr. Murchison, from the very first day, he says to me, he says, 'Don't you ever let that there patient wash 'is feet. It's bad for 'im,' he says. 'I've give 'im a pair of bed-socks and 'e's to keep 'em on, whether 'e's in pyjamas or not. 'E ain't ever to take 'em off,' he says. 'I 'ave told 'im as 'ow it would be bad for 'im if he did, and I think he understands. 'E's got marks on 'is feet,' says the doctor, 'that I don't want 'im to see'."

"Marks on his feet!" said Mr. Deeling.

"Yus," replied Warder Jones, "that's what the doctor said, and I thought it was most pecooliar, because when that patient first came in, unconscious, you know, from that knock on the 'ead that the doctor 'ad to give 'im, I undressed 'im and washed him before putting 'im to bed, and I saw 'is feet, and there weren't no marks on 'em then that I could see. But it was not for me to say anything, so I just said as 'ow I would carry out 'is instructions, and so I done. I 'ave kep' my eye on 'im, and it ain't been very difficult, for, barring that time as the Colonel broke his winder, 'e 'asn't shown much inclination to look at his feet or walk or do anything.

"This morning, 'owever, when I goes to 'im as usual I finds 'im sitting on 'is bed looking sort of wild, so that I thought for a moment 'e was going to be violent. Then I seed it was not violence that 'e 'ad in mind. 'E was more like crying.

" 'Warder,' 'e says to me, 'Warder, 'ow long 'ave I bin a-lying 'ere?' he says.

" 'A matter of four weeks,' I replied.

" 'Good God,' he says, 'is it as long as that! Look 'ere, Warder, I've been insensible most of the time, 'aven't I?'

" 'You 'ave bin quiet like,' I says cautious.

" 'Well,' 'e says, 'I can't remember much about what 'appened, but I know my feet was all right when I come 'ere. Now look at 'em,' and with that, before I could stop 'im, he whips off his bed-socks, and rolling back on the bed, waves 'is two feet in front of my face."

Warder Jones paused, and added solemnly:

"Would you believe it, sir, 'is feet had marks on the soles of 'em."

"What do you mean by marks?" said Mr. Deeling.

"Crosses, they was, like the crosses on a 'ot cross bun. 'I see'd 'em in the mirror this morning,' the patient says to me, sitting up again, 'and I don't like the look of 'em,' he says. 'Well,' says I, 'I'll go and get the doctor to you and I'm sure he'll fix 'em up for you all right.' "

"One moment," said Mr. Deeling, "I suppose you are quite sure that the marks were not on his feet when he first arrived?"

"They were not," said Warder Jones with emphasis. "I could swear to that in a court o' law, and that's what struck me as pecooliar. But that's not my business, and, after all, I'm not a doctor. They may 'ave come there since; they may be symptoms of a pecooliar disease."

"Go on," said Mr. Deeling.

"Well," continued the warder, "when I mentioned the doctor to 'im I thought for a moment as 'ow he was going to become violent again. But when 'e saw the look in my eye he mastered 'isself. 'No, Warder,' he says, 'I'm not going to 'it yer. I'm perfectly sane, as sane as you are, and I seem to remember as 'ow I 'ave told you that more than once. You've never believed me yet, and I don't blame you,' he says, 'for things is pretty black against me,' he says. 'But we've got to get this right,' 'e says, 'or else——' and then he shuddered all over as though he were seeing things, 'orrible things, as lunaticks sometimes does.

"Then he put 'is 'ead in his 'ands, while I kept my eye pretty close on him. Then he lifts 'is 'ead. 'I'll tell you what I'll do,' he says. 'You just give me that there coat.'

"So I went across, and 'anded 'im his coat without a word. It was quite empty, but 'e felt in all the pockets like a terrier after a rat.

"'I thought so,' he said, 'it 'as slipped down between the lining.'

"He put 'is 'and in one of the breast pockets and felt right down, and I saw as 'ow the pocket 'ad got tore and as 'ow 'is 'and was in the lining of the coat itself. After a bit of fishing 'e pulled out a cheque-book, one of them little ones that banks gives to their customers to carry about with 'em. It was all crumpled up and only one cheque left.

"'Now look 'ere, Warder,' says the patient to me, when he had opened the book, 'have you got a founting pen, by any chance?' Well, funnily enough, I 'ad. So, acting on the general instructions of this institootion as to 'ow the patients are to be 'umoured if they offers no violence, I 'anded it to 'im. Then 'e sat back on the bed and 'eld the cheque-book open on 'is knee.

"'Now, Warder,' he says, 'I'm not a rich man, but I've got a bit of money saved up, and I'll fill in this cheque for £100, with your name on it, if you'll do me a service.'

"Well, on that, I looked at 'im and 'e looked at me, and I looked back at 'im, wooden as an image.

193

'Yus,' he says, '£100 or may be guineas.'

" 'It's nothin' serious,' he says, 'and nothin' against your conscience,' he says. 'I only want you to help me get a letter to Dr. Edwardes.'

" 'Dr. Edwardes is away,' I says.

" 'I know that,' 'e replied. 'And I know that this 'ere Dr. Murchison (and 'is mouth twisted a bit as 'e said the name) is taking 'is place, and I don't like 'im,' he says, 'and you know I don't like 'im, and I want to write to Dr. Edwardes about my case. If you'll get me a bit of paper and an envelope, and let me write my letter and post it for me, I'll write you out this cheque for £100.'

"Well, of course, sir, I was took aback. I 'ave seen some queer things 'appen in this chatoo, but no patient 'as tried to bribe me before, and 'e could see as how I was most indignant.

" 'Don't you take on, Warder,' he says, 'I'm not offering you this money as a bribe. It's because of the risk,' he says. 'The circumstances are pecooliar, and I'll be perfectly frank with you. If Dr. Murchison found out you was trying to send a letter from me to Dr. Edwardes, he would sack you on the spot. That's why I'm trying to make it worth your while. If you do this for me, you won't ever regret it. After all,' 'e says, 'who's 'ead of this establishment—Dr. Murchison or Dr. Edwardes?'

" 'Dr. Edwardes,' I says promptly, 'and 'e'll be back soon. Can't you wait till then?' "

" 'No, I can't,' he says, 'that's just what I can't do. We don't know when 'e's going to be back. It may not be for months. Not until it's too late.'

"And again he shuddered and looked past me into

the corner till I felt like turning round to see if any thing was there.

"Then he turned to me.

" 'Now, Warder,' he says, 'are you going to help me, or are you not?'

"Very friendly and honest 'e looked, an' 'e smiled, man to man, not like a lunatick at all.

"So I stood and thought a bit, and at last I said, 'All right. I'll do it for you, but I 'aven't any use for the cheque.'

"On that he gets up from the bed and comes across the room and holds 'is 'and out. 'You're a straight man, Warder,' he says, 'Dr. Edwardes is fortunate to have a man like you to 'elp him.' Of course, I'm only telling you what 'e said."

Warder Jones paused, giving his modesty a moment in which to recover.

"Naturally," he went on, "I shook 'is 'and. I often 'ave to shake 'ands with the patients. They don't mean anything by it. So I went out, locking the door, of course, and got some notepaper and an envelope and came back to 'im. He was still sitting on 'is bed, and at once 'e begins to write, without another word. In five minutes or so 'e 'ad finished, and he folds 'is letter up and addresses the envelope to Dr. Edwardes. Then 'e 'ands me back my founting pen.

" 'You just write the doctor's address on that envelope,' he says, and I did it then and there under his eyes. Then he looks at me most earnestly.

" 'And now, Warder,' he says, 'will you swear by all you 'old most solemn to send that letter off without delay?'

" 'Yus,' I says, and, with that, he shook me once

195

more by the 'and, and then I left 'im.

"Well, of course, I only done it to 'umour 'im, as it is my duty to do, and, of course, I went straight off to Dr. Murchison, but I couldn't find him. Leastways, when I knocked on his door there was no answer. I tried the 'andle, but it was locked. Then Nurse Webster come along and I told 'er what 'ad 'appened, and she suggested as 'ow we should come to you."

"But why," said Mr. Deeling, "why didn't you wait for Dr. Murchison?"

Nurse Webster had sat motionless during the narrative of Warder Jones. She spoke now with a slight compression of the lips.

"As a matter of fact, Mr. Deeling," she said, "we preferred to come to somebody we knew."

Mr. Deeling had a flash of inspiration.

"You don't like Dr. Murchison?" he said.

There was a moment's pause. Nurse Webster and Warder Jones, with faces carefully emptied of expression were looking straight in front of them. It was Nurse Webster who spoke.

"I've nothing against Dr. Murchison," she said. "He treats us most considerately. I don't know what it is, but perhaps I am old-fashioned. I'm used to Dr. Edwardes, and I don't like working with anybody new—man or woman for that matter, and that's a fact."

Mr. Deeling was glowing with satisfaction. Dr. Murchison certainly had a way with the patients, with some of them at least. And that Miss Sedgwick was perfectly crazy about him. But he had apparently failed with the staff.

196

"I think you have both behaved with great propriety," he said, after a pause. "In coming to see me as the senior member of the staff and as, in a sense, the representative of Dr. Edwardes, you have acted wisely and with discretion. If you will leave the letter with me, I will consider the matter and let you know later what I think should be done about it."

He stopped and added:

"I suggest that our conversation and, in fact, the whole incident, should remain entirely between ourselves."

Nurse Webster nodded.

"I quite agree," she said.

Warder Jones, who was obviously prepared to accept her judgment, fumbled for a moment in his breast pocket. He then produced a crumpled envelope and handed it to Mr. Deeling without a word.

"Thank you," said Mr. Deeling.

"I hope that you will take a decision soon, Mr. Deeling," said Nurse Webster, as she rose from her chair. "You will remember that I'm going away for my holiday to-morrow."

"I'll let you know this evening," replied Mr. Deeling.

He rose in front of her, opened the door for her to pass out. He had never done that before, but felt that he owed it to her now.

Nurse Webster and Warder Jones left the room in silence.

Mr. Deeling returned to his desk and sat for a long while, staring at the white envelope which the warder had left with him. Then, apparently, he came to a decision. He unlocked the drawer in which he kept his investment book, put away the envelope and locked the drawer again. Then, taking up his pen, he wrote a short note to Dr. Murchison, politely thanking him for his letter, but begging to decline the offer of two month's leave.

He felt, he said, that it would do him more harm than good to leave Château Landry at the moment. He would, however, undertake to be very careful not to overwork in the future.

He signed the letter, put it in an envelope and placed it on his desk. Then, resting his head on his hands, he bent forward and remained thus for a considerable time, staring in front of him.

III

At a quarter past five the following afternoon the bell of the chapel began to toll. It was an old bell, cast in the sixteenth century, and it bore a curious inscription, *Paco cruentos*, graven on its outer rim. Since the wild ringing in 1792, when the last of the de Landry's had been dragged forth to death by his own peasants, its voice had only rarely been heard. Of late it had hung silent and dusty, only awaking to life on two days in the year—New Year's Eve, when it solemnly rang out the departing year, and on the seventh of August, when it tolled for a few moments immediately prior to the "ceremony," which had been performed now for several years, in commemoration of the late wife of Colonel Rickaby.

The inmates of the Castle began to collect at the entrance to the chapel shortly before half-past five.

Colonel Rickaby came first, very splendidly dressed in an old faded uniform of scarlet, with blue overalls, strapped underneath his black patent leather boots, and gold spurs. Across his chest was a row of medals, and on the left sleeve of his arm a broad black mourning band. He stood in front of the locked door, fussing with a pair of white gloves and with the hilt of his sword.

Next to him stood Miss Truelow, in severest black, her hands folded across a large prayer book bound in limp morocco.

"I hope," she was saying, "that Mr. Clearwater will remember to brush his hair. Last time, you will recollect, he came to church without even a collar. It was most embarrassing."

"Do you think Miss Collett will turn up?" said the Colonel rather nervously. "And will she bring that confounded rubber ball? She's been playing with it all the afternoon. I tried to take it away about ten minutes ago, and she screamed the place down. We can't have her bouncing a rubber ball in there. Most indecorous."

They were joined at that moment by Mr. Curtis. He wore a frock coat and spats, and carried a silk hat in his hand.

"Good afternoon," he said. "What are we waiting for?"

"Stimson," he added suddenly over his shoulder, "why haven't I got a gardenia?"

Miss Collett was the next to appear. She was dressed in a short grey frock, with black cotton stockings and a black bow in her hair. The Colonel was relieved to see that she carried a prayerbook, and that the bright rubber ball had been discarded.

There was a rapid step, and Mr. Clearwater stood before them. He was dressed as usual, but he had taken great pains with his hair. It clung to his head, having evidently been dipped in water to keep it in place. He carried a small book under his arm.

"I have never seen you with a prayer-book before, Mr. Clearwater," observed Miss Truelow.

"Good heavens, madam," said Mr. Clearwater, "it isn't a prayer-book. This is *Yellow Spasms*, my latest work," and he exhibited with pride a slim volume bound in brown cloth boards with a thin line of golden lettering.

"I've tried many poets," he went on. "In fact, I've read them all. But I always come back to my own. They induce in me an exaltation—a species of intoxication. . . ."

"I hope," interrupted the Colonel, "that you will refrain from showing signs of intoxication in church. I rely on you, Clearwater, to behave yourself."

"Good evening," said a voice, and at the sound of it everyone turned. Dr. Murchison was among them. He was wearing a short black coat with striped trousers, and a black tie.

"Let us go in," he said. "Colonel, I think that you, perhaps, should lead the way."

"Excuse me, sir," said the Colonel, "but the door is locked."

"Of course," said Dr. Murchison. "Mr. Hickett has the key. We shall have to wait until he has finished tolling the bell."

> "The bell it tolls
> For dead men's souls."

chanted Mr. Clearwater suddenly,

> "And who can tell
> If heaven or hell
> Holds them in thrall."

"Silence, please, Mr. Clearwater," said Dr. Murchison.

Mr. Clearwater looked at the doctor rebelliously, as though he expected to be indulged and even commended for his indiscretion. Then he laid a finger on his lips and nodded wisely.

"I quite agree, Doctor," he said. "I quite agree."

"Where is Miss Archer?" Miss Truelow abruptly inquired.

"Miss Archer cannot come," replied the doctor. "She is still hardly well enough to leave her bed."

"Most unfortunate," said the Colonel. "This is the first time she has missed the ceremony for years. I always rely on her to lead the hymns."

"I am sorry, Colonel," said the doctor gravely, "but we shall have to do without her for this once."

"And where is dear Miss Sedgwick?" said Miss Collett.

"She also must be excused," said Dr. Murchison. "I have had to send her into the village. There are several people who are sick, and she has gone to help them."

Miss Truelow smiled with pinched lips, and was about to make some comment, when suddenly the bell was silent, and there were footsteps behind the chapel door. There came the sound of a key in the lock, and a moment later it was thrown open.

The Rev. Mark Hickett stood waiting on the threshold. He was dressed in cassock and surplice, and he held a black book in his hand, against which was pressed the key of the chapel. He stood aside to let his small congregation enter. There was a slight pause, and then the Colonel led the way, closely followed by Miss Truelow and Mr. Curtis. The last to enter was Dr. Murchison.

Within the chapel it was cool and dark, for the sun of the late afternoon did not touch any of the lancet windows. The great rose window was a wheel of dying colour.

They filed to right and left, the Colonel and Miss Truelow sitting on one side, Mr. Curtis and Miss Collett on the other, while Mr. Clearwater climbed the small winding stair leading to the organ loft. Dr. Murchison remained at the back of the church.

The Rev. Mark Hickett made his way slowly up the central aisle, paused a moment beneath the chancel arch, and then climbed the three steps leading to the altar. There he turned and faced them.

"We will sing," he said tonelessly, "hymn one hundred and sixty eight. The one hundred and sixty eighth hymn: 'Dark lowers the night above our restless souls.' "

There was a slight pause. Then the Colonel began turning over the pages of his hymn book.

Mr. Clearwater was already playing the preliminary phrase and the four people present rose to their feet.

But something was happening to the Rev. Mark Hickett. He had stood a moment after giving out the hymn, looking over the heads of his congregation towards Dr. Murchison. And now, abruptly, before the hymn could be started, with an uncouth gesture, he raised his hands, gripped the edge of his surplice and tore it in two with a sound of rending.

"No," he said in a voice that cracked, "it is not I that should be standing in this place. I have seen only the shadow of the Master, but there is one here who speaks with the Master himself."

For a moment no one stirred. The Rev. Mark Hickett, his eyes burning and one hand outstretched, was pointing straight at the doctor.

"If you must pray," he continued, "go down on your knees to *him*."

And now they all turned and looked back towards the doctor, Mr. Clearwater leaning from the loft to get a better view.

"We are all believers here," went on the Rev. Mark Hickett, and he spoke now to the doctor himself. "What need is there of any further mystery?"

He paused and then sank swiftly to his knees, his hands extended towards the silent figure at the back of the chapel.

The place was now full of shadows. The sun, which a moment before from the rim of the mountain wall had been shining full on the rose window, had gone down behind the valley and the wheel of the saints in their ruby and sapphire was drained of its glory. In the chapel was a glimmer of white made by the torn surplice of the man on the chancel steps, four motionless figures erect in their places, a pale face that gleamed from beneath the serried pipes of the organ, and, in the thickest of the gloom, darkest of all, the figure to whom all eyes were directed.

The figure stirred. It came down the aisle towards the chancel, as though responding to an invocation. The apostate before the altar sank lower and, as the figure approached and stood at last upon the steps, became a heap of crumpled linen and black cloth at its feet.

There was a sigh and a rustle of garments, and now there were four kneeling shadows in the body of the chapel, blind shadows with bowed heads.

They did not see the man who spoke to them. For a moment, with folded arms, he looked down on them, a smile on his lips, triumph in his eyes.

He stood on the altar steps in his striped trousers and his black coat, as conventional a figure as could well be imagined, but the message he had for them had not been uttered since Gil de Rais had mouthed his secret blasphemies before the slashed corpses of his child victims.

The chapel was dark, when he had finished, and there was a fifth shadow among those who listened from the pews, for Mr. Clearwater had crept down from the loft and was kneeling with the rest. The man at the altar raised his hand.

"You know now," he concluded, "why we are here and whom it is we serve. You have now only to wait until I give you the sign."

The shadows crept to his feet, adoring. He drew back a little as they fawned upon him.

The thin voice of Miss Truelow came from behind her folded hands.

"Master," she began. But he rebuked her.

"You must not call me that. I am but the voice of the Master."

"But there is work to do," and now it was Mr. Curtis who spoke. "Those who do not believe. . . ."

His voice shook, so that he could not continue, but he sprang erect and trembling with passion, seized a brass candlestick from the altar and brandished it above his head.

At once they were all upon their feet, and there was a sudden gleam where the Colonel's sword cut the grey air as he tore it madly from its sheath. Mr. Clearwater fell back, sobbing with terror and desire, and the tall form of Mr. Hickett pointed with arm outstretched towards the door.

"The sun shall not see them again," he cried. "Let none of them escape."

They were all in motion now, except Dr. Murchison, who stood silent among the demons he had raised.

"Miss Archer first," shouted Mr. Curtis. "She would not join us here. She is the worst of the unbelievers."

There was a rush towards the western end of the chapel. A chair fell over with an echoing crash.

"Stop!" cried a voice from the altar steps.

They halted and swung round.

"Not yet," the voice continued. "You will receive from me the sign when it is necessary. Now leave me and go to your rooms."

There was a shuffling in the gloom, a door was

opened and closed. The man on the altar steps was alone.

"It must be soon now," he whispered, "quite soon."

He fell to the ground and lay upon the pavement, his face buried in his hands.

Chapter X

I

On the following day Constance was late for tea. Her visit to the village on the previous afternoon had resulted in arrears of work which had made it necessary for her to pass several weary hours in the little office next door to Mr. Deeling's dispensary, filled with ledgers and a big green safe. For in addition to her other duties she had taken over the accounts of Château Landry.

Tea was served in the rose garden. Most of the inmates of the Château had already finished when she appeared, and were sitting round the large table talking, it seemed, rather more sociably than usual. Miss Collett was the first to catch sight of Constance, and ran to meet her.

"They said you wouldn't come," she said. "They said you would be too proud. But I'm not afraid. I'm not afraid. Will you tell me a story before I go to bed?"

Constance smiled to cover her irritation. She had discovered that Miss Collett got on her nerves more than anybody else. She could scarcely endure the sight of this elderly woman dressed as a small child and talking in the accents of a girl of ten. The worst of it was that she did not appear to have any lucid moments. Her delusion was as fixed and unalterable as the stones of the castle itself.

"Not to-night," she said gently, "I shall be too busy."

Miss Collett looked at her sagely and nodded her grey head.

"I s'pose now you won't ever be able to tell me a story?"

"Why not?" said Constance, falling into step beside her.

"'Cos he wouldn't let you," said Miss Collett.

"Who wouldn't?"

"Why, the great doctor, of course, who is going to save us all."

They were at the large table, the Rev. Mark Hickett, Colonel Rickaby, who was playing chess with Miss Truelow, and Mr. Curtis, who was still devouring macaroons. Mr. Clearwater was sitting a little apart from the others.

The Rev. Mark Hickett rose as she reached the table.

"Miss Sedgwick," he said, "let me get you a cup of tea."

Constance looked at him in surprise. It was the first time he had ever offered to do anything for her; and, as she sat down and he poured out the tea, she found that they were all looking at her with a strange but friendly deference. Even Miss Truelow, from her chessboard, appeared to share it, for, almost timidly, she leaned forward and laid her thin fingers on the sleeve of Constance's dress.

"You are looking tired, my dear," she said, with an ingratiating smile, "and that won't do at all. It's now you should be looking your best."

Constance forced a smile.

"I am not really tired," she answered. "But it is very hot, and I have been working indoors nearly all day."

"Working," said the Colonel, "that won't do at all. Curtis, we shall have to organise a fatigue party. We can't have Miss Sedgwick working herself to a shadow."

"Stimson," said Mr. Curtis, "you will please hold yourself at Miss Sedgwick's disposal until further notice."

He turned to Constance.

"I quite agree with the Colonel," he went on, "if there is anything I can do for you personally, please don't hesitate."

"We must all do what we can," pursued Miss Truelow, bending over the chessboard, and reducing Colonel Rickaby to speechless indignation by the removal of one of his bishops, "for he will expect you to be equal to the occasion."

Constance was about to reply when a soft murmur arose from where Mr. Clearwater was sitting, a little apart from the others:

"Who are these coming to the sacrifice?
To what green altar, O mysterious priest,

Leads't thou that heifer lowing to the skies,
    And all her silken flanks with garlands
drest?"

Mr. Clearwater was looking wistfully away towards the forest and reciting under his breath.

"What I like about this place," said Mr. Curtis suddenly, "is that here we are quite alone. Everything can be done quietly and in order."

"Hold your tongue," said the Rev. Mark Hickett sharply, and he laid a finger on his lips.

Mr. Curtis had the air of a man justly rebuked. He gazed for a moment at the Rev. Mark Hickett, and a look of intelligence passed between them.

"Stimson," he said over his shoulder. "That last observation of mine is not for the minutes."

Mr. Clearwater, haggard and ill-at-ease, turned suddenly to Mr. Curtis.

"Are you quite sure?" he asked.

Mr. Curtis looked at him blankly.

"Sure of what?" he inquired.

"The valley may not be as safe as you think. They may get to us yet, and we must be ready. They must not take us by surprise.

He looked away towards the mountain wall.

"Over the rocks. Over the rocks," he murmured.

Constance glanced at him in dismay. This was the first time he had referred to his special delusion since the day of her arrival.

"Don't you worry, Clearwater," said the Colonel, "We are more than a match for them now. I remember once, against the Wazi Wazi in '87, or was it '89, I got cut off with ten men, or was it eight . . . no, it was six men and a drummer boy. It was Sir Picton-Turnbull's force, or was it Sir Joshua Elford's? Back to back we stood in a narrow defile. One hundred and thirty-seven killed and wounded and not a scratch between the six of us."

"I should feel safe anywhere with the dear Colonel," simpered Miss Truelow. "He is our chosen warrior, our mighty man of valour."

The Rev. Mark Hickett stirred uneasily in his chair.

"Madam," he said, "I would ask you in future to avoid expressions from the Scriptures."

"Why, of course, Mr. Hickett. I quite understand."

Constance, drinking her tea, was struck by their unexpected unanimity. Usually they were intent on their own proceedings and ideas, and paid little heed to one another except to get at cross purposes. She had never known Miss Truelow to be so friendly with Mr. Clearwater.

She became aware that they were all observing her without appearing to do so. She caught, in particular, the eye of Mr. Curtis gazing at her over the edge of his teacup, but his glance shifted uneasily as she looked at him. Indeed, they were all making obvious efforts to appear unconcerned, except Miss Collett, who was gazing at her fixedly, her mouth slightly open and her eyes round with expectation.

Feeling embarrassed, she started a conversation with the Colonel, asking when next he would like a game of golf. But she found it difficult to make progress. The Colonel was so very deferential.

"Entirely at your service, madam," he said. "It's

211

really most good of you to think of it—a very great honour, madam, I assure you."

And now Mr. Curtis was at her elbow. With a low bow he offered her the dish of macaroons.

"Thank you, Mr. Curtis," she said.

"Not at all," said Mr. Curtis, "a privilege, madam, a very great privilege indeed."

Constance, refusing the dish with a smile, stole a further glance at the company. They were all looking at her in that curiously expectant manner which she had already noticed.

Suddenly it became intolerable, and she rose to her feet and faced them.

"Look at me, all of you," she commanded.

They did so with reluctance.

"Tell me," she went on, "why are you all behaving like this?"

"Speak, some of you," she continued after a pause, for they still gazed at her silently.

"Mr. Clearwater, what's the matter with them all this afternoon?"

She had appealed to Mr. Clearwater instinctively as an ally. She never thought of him as being quite as mad as the rest. He looked at her now with an expression which she could not understand, but he glanced away, almost at once, to the Rev. Mark Hickett whose burning eyes were fixed upon him with a menacing regard, and to Mr. Curtis who had the appearance of a dog about to spring.

"Alas, fair lady," he said.

He came swiftly round the table till he stood beside her.

"To-night," he went on, "I shall sit in the moonlight under your window and write a hymn to Persephone: how I gathered flowers with her on the plains of Enna till she was rapt away to become . . ."

He paused suddenly, threw a startled look over his shoulder, and then, falling on one knee, raised the hem of her frock and pressed it to his lips.

"My queen," he murmured, "the queen of us all."

"Upon my word, Clearwater," said the Colonel heartily, "you put it very well. Madam, your humble servant to the death," and he bowed across the chessboard.

"I also perhaps shall be of service," whispered Miss Truelow. "My mother was a lady-in-waiting to the old Queen."

"Me, too, me too," piped Miss Collett. "I will pick some pretty flowers for you every morning and put them in your room."

Mr. Curtis bent to her in confidence.

"Miss Sedgwick," he said, "if you should think of making any little investment, don't hesitate to come to me. I would count it an honour."

"Madam," said the Colonel, "there isn't much that an old soldier can do, but I shall never be far away. Sentry-go, by George, and no one shall pass, not while I live."

They were all crowding about her now. She put her hand to her head. Were they all mad? But, of course, they were. But this was somehow different.

She looked hastily about her, as though looking for a way of escape, and saw, to her infinite relief, Mr. Deeling coming slowly down the path towards them.

213

"Why, here's Mr. Deeling," she said, "and the tea is nearly cold. Miss Collett, do you think you could . . ."

But already Miss Collett had anticipated her request and was running away to the servants.

The others fell back a little and watched Mr. Deeling as he came, with faces which were now expressionless.

Mr. Curtis pulled out a large gold watch from his waistcoat pocket and consulted it. He turned to the Rev. Mark Hickett.

"Still three-quarters of an hour," he muttered. "But perhaps I had better be getting ready."

The Rev. Mark Hickett glanced furtively to right and left.

"I'll come with you, Mr. Curtis," he said.

II

Miss Archer stood for a moment at her window watching the sun sink in majesty behind the rocks.

For days past she had been blind to her surroundings. All had been dark, and her spirit oppressed with a weight of iniquity, so that at times she had felt it almost more than she could bear. But to-day the heaviness had lifted. It had not been removed, but had been, so to speak, drawn up a little and suspended above her, so that it had become at once less menacing and more measurable.

Or she had been as one that lay in a black room for an unknown length of time, and then suddenly, after

214

she had abandoned all hope, someone had passed outside with a lighted candle and the rays had shone beneath the door.

She knew well from what she was suffering. She had read it a thousand times. She had been passing now for weeks through that dark night of the soul of which St. John of the Cross spoke, the state in which all seems lost and life a greater horror than death; when God withdraws himself, and the holy angels hide their faces. She had cried in vain to her patron saints, but no one had heard her, not even St. Theresa, who had felt it all hundreds of years before, and who had told it all so minutely.

And now it was changed. The relief had come just before sundown. She had been lying on her bed, her arms outstretched in the form of a cross, as she had taught herself to do, and suddenly, like some perfume from a garden of spice, peace had entered. She had walked to the window, and there she had seen the sun, and it had seemed to her as though it were a hole pierced in the high wall of heaven to let out the blinding light of the glory within.

She was gazing upon it now, though her eyes saw nothing, till her withered body, battered with the mortifications of forty years, felt light as summer air, frail as an egg-shell, translucent as pearl. No longer, as in her darkest moments, did she feel an old broken woman of sixty, a failure and a fool, a mystic who could not contemplate, one who prayed unheeded prayers, a victim in search of an altar.

She drew a great breath, and began to pray wordlessly as she had been taught, driving, deliberately, her conscious self down into the depths, out of sight and of memory, where it should lie bound, and thus set free her spirit to commune directly with eternal things.

She began one or two pious ejaculations, but left them half unsaid, while her spirit fluttered and struggled, and then suddenly broke free, so that at one moment the world swooped out of sight like a swallow dipping below the horizon, and she was alone—a fervid soul that waited and yearned.

A succession of images drifted across her vision—the coloured pavements of heaven and the great seraphim, with their burnished wings, walking two by two down streets of ivory and topaz. She, too, walked with them towards the garden, where the Mother of God sat in her white robe, among her tall lilies with their golden mouths, and the little angels floated about her, singing among the black cypresses and the rose-coloured clouds. That for the moment was as far as she could go. Not yet could she turn from the garden and mount the hill where dwelt the living radiance, or steep herself in the water of life which she knew to be flowing there. But the time would come. She had only to perfect herself, to cleanse her soul of iniquity, to make pure her heart. She was nearer now than when she had started . . .

She did not hear the key turned in the lock, nor the sudden creak of the door as it opened, nor the footsteps that approached from behind. Even when a cord was flung round her arms, and they were dragged to her side, she scarcely moved to show that she knew what was happening, and she uttered no sound when she was carried out. Her mind was filled with the vision. She had lost all knowledge of earthly things. Time had ceased. She knew nothing of the long road through the forest by which they carried her, or of the hours in the clearing beside the white stone while they were busy about her. She stood in a garden absorbed in a happiness such as she had never known, and it seemed that the Mother of God smiled at her and beckoned, while about her the coloured angels moved in a stately pageant. She could hear thin voices like the murmur of a far-off sea. They were the voices of those who prayed unceasingly to the Mother of God, for the comfort of the afflicted, for the help of Christians.

And then it seemed to her that a hand was laid on her head and the sweet face smiled down at her and told her to go.

And she was filled with fear, and asked whither.

The mouth smiled, and the voice said: "Go, St. Theresa will lead you to my Son."

And at these words her heart leapt, and she cried out for joy, and all the angels about her clapped their hands and said: "At last she is worthy. She is going. She will soon be there."

And it seemed that she walked beside St. Theresa, the friend of Jesus, in her soiled nun's robe, with her white face and her burning eyes. And they left the garden and walked hand in hand up the hill towards the Radiance that was burning on the other side of the crest. . . ."

It was then that she was laid upon the white stone. But now she had left the world far behind. Her eyes

217

were closed, her breathing scarcely perceptible. She was now so near the crest. She trembled, but St. Theresa would not let her falter or turn back. She encouraged her with loving words.

"Soon you shall see Him face to face," she said. "He is not terrible, the Prince of Light."

. . . And at that moment the knife fell, and the blood spurted, and her spirit passed to prove the truth of her vision.

III

Constance awoke with a start. The blood was drumming in her ears, or so it seemed. Then, for a moment she thought she was on board ship with throbbing engines. She even went so far as to sit up gingerly as though she was going to hit her head against the top bunk.

It was stiflingly hot, like a furnace. The bed-clothes were intolerable. She swept them off, then sat up and abruptly realised where she was. She was in her own room in Château Landry, in a wide comfortable bed. And there was the moon peering through the window, his round face almost at the full. Why had she woken up? She had been sleeping so soundly, too; the first time she had slept decently for nights.

Her mind switched back to the events of the evening. Dr. Murchison had not appeared at dinner. A message had come from him to the effect that he was too busy, and would Constance—he had called her Constance in the note—have some sandwiches and whisky put out for him on the table in the study. So she had dined alone with Mr. Deeling, and, indeed, she had been very much alone, for he had not spoken a word, except occasionally when passing her vegetables or salt. He had sat calmly at the other end of the table, his geometrical features in profound repose. Well, if he liked to behave like that, he must. In his dull way he was altogether too odious for words. She was not, however, going to let herself be put out by Mr. Deeling.

His attitude was especially annoying, as now she would need, more than ever, his co-operation, Nurse Webster having gone on leave that afternoon. Constance, watching the broad capable back of the nurse as she climbed into the Citroen to be driven down to Thonon, knew that her departure would mean extra work, and yet, oddly enough, she had felt a sense of relief. She was getting more into the swim of things, beginning to feel that she was of some use in Château Landry.

But what was this drumming in her ears? Was it the height? Surely not, for she must have got used to that by now. There it was again. It was intermittent. She put a finger into her ear and it instantly grew fainter. So the sound was not in her own brain, but came from somewhere outside. She got out of bed and walked with bare feet to the window. It was flung wide and, kneeling on the window seat, she leaned out as far as she could. Yes, there was no doubt of it now. She heard it distinctly, a low monotonous drumming somewhere out in the forest, out in the belt of firs. It was monotonous, and yet not soothing. On the contrary. She felt that, if it went on, she would never sleep again.

She began to count the beats—nine in rapid succession, then a pause. Then eleven more, more slowly, then five, then nine, and then the whole thing over again. What on earth was it? She had never heard it before. She gazed in the direction of the sound. She could see little except the broad meadow bathed in the moonlight, and, beyond it, the black shadow of the firs. Everything was utterly still. There was not a breath of wind and nothing moved. She might have been upon a dead planet, the last living creature of an arid world, except for that throbbing in the heart of the wood.

And then, even as she strained her eyes in a vain effort, the drumming ceased abruptly, as if someone had torn the drum from the drummer, or struck him down from behind, and there was utter silence.

Constance remained at the window, staring. It was not quite still, there was something moving there on the edge of the belt of shadows, something which gradually took form and shape in the moonlight. It was a man, dressed in something long and black, and he moved across the moonlit grass like an unclean shadow.

Once he stopped, and Constance saw the white flash of his face as he lifted it to the sky, but he was too far off for her to see who it was. He paused, stretched out his arms a moment and gave a single cry, meaningless, without any human note in it, like the mechanical noise of a machine. Then he dropped his head and started towards the castle, moving with a long, slow stride. There was something in one of his hands.

Constance turned and left the window abruptly. She threw on a dressing-gown and, thrusting her feet into slippers, opened her door and moved quickly into the passage. Who could be prowling round the castle at this time of night? She would go downstairs and see. She moved along the passage, her dressing-gown rustling about her. She turned a corner and stood in the corridor which ran at right angles to the one off which her room was situated. This was the corridor in which most of the patients had their rooms.

Constance moved down it towards the staircase.

As she passed the door of Mr. Curtis' room she had a sudden shock, for the door stood ajar. She paused, then, making up her mind, seized the handle, and, pushing the door gently open, looked inside.

The room was empty.

She paused again, bewildered for a moment by her discovery. How on earth could Mr. Curtis have got out?

She moved on again towards the staircase, repeating to herself: "I locked all the doors, I know I did. I could swear to it."

She was at the head of the staircase now, peering over the banisters into the blackness, while she fumbled with the switch which controlled the electric alarm bells beneath each stair. To her astonishment she found that someone had switched them off before she had got there. Who could have done that?

She went on again down the stairs into the darkness below, her feet in their soft slippers making no noise on the broad oak boards. Not a creak betrayed her presence. At last she was in the hall. She did not pause, but went straight towards the main door of the castle, feeling her way gingerly, with her hands stretched out in front of her, for it was very dark, and in her haste she had forgotten to bring a candle.

It seemed to her that the hall would never end. What was she doing? She felt like an insect enclosed in a great wooden box, where everything was black. The darkness was solid about her. Nowhere would it ever break. It was like a wall, so that she wondered how it was possible to move so easily through it.

And then it gave way. Just ahead there was a thin slip of light not five yards in front of her. It grew broader, a beam of moonlight, admitting the silver world outside and the peace of the upland meadow surrounding this fever spot of a castle.

The door was opening slowly. Constance came to an abrupt stop. Then, as the door continued to open, she moved instinctively to the side, crouching against the wall.

A figure stood in the patch of moonlight. It was the figure she had seen out in the meadow a few minutes before. It was dressed in a long, black sleeveless robe, and on its head was a cap, fitting close to the skull, covering the ears and the back of the neck and blazoned with signs which she could not read. In its hand was a knife. It stopped a moment in the opening door, then began to move forward stealthily. She could hear its suppressed breathing. It was now right inside, and, as it turned to closed the door behind it, she saw its face in profile. It was Mr. Curtis. His eyes in the light of the moon had a sated, drowsy look.

Then the door was shut, and she was in darkness again. At that moment the heel of one of her slippers, swinging loosely from her foot, tapped once upon the floor. The sound seemed louder than it was, but loud or soft it was enough.

"Is that you, Stimson?" said a voice from where she had last seen Mr. Curtis.

She heard him move in the darkness and the sound of his heavy breathing.

"Stimson, I told you to remain in your room. What are you doing there?

"Answer me, damn you. I know what it is. You've been spying on me, Stimson, and I'm going to cut your treacherous throat for you."

The darkness broke again. There was a slip of silver that widened under her eyes. He was opening the door so that he might see.

The moonlight streamed into the hall again, and he saw her at once, where she crouched, a white figure with dark hair. For a moment she was numb with terror. Then, with a supreme effort, she checked the cry which rose to her lips.

She drew herself up, and, stepping forward, stretched out a hand.

"What are you doing, Mr. Curtis?" she said, trying to assume a note of authority.

Mr. Curtis paused, the knife in his hand upraised, his eyes blazing. Constance, with a violent effort, stilled the quivering of her mouth.

"What are you doing?" she repeated.

He moved towards her.

"You are Stimson," he said. "You're not going to get away in that damn female masquerade."

"I am not Stimson," said Constance, "and you know it very well. I am Miss Sedgwick, and I insist that you should go to your room."

The man took another step. She could almost feel his breath on her face. She threw back her head and gazed into his eyes.

He thrust out his empty fist and touched her.

She shrank from his fingers, and on that something broke loose in him. He flung himself forward at her.

As he did so, however, a hand, white, sinewy and strong gripped him by the shoulder and twisted him half round. Another figure stood in the moonlight, and she saw that it was Dr. Murchison.

Her relief was so intense that her faculties were suddenly relaxed. She leaned for support against the wall, and watched the scene as through a clouded glass. The figures wavered and grew small and large, and the whole castle appeared to be rocking. She did not hear what Dr. Murchison was saying, but she knew now that she was safe, and, sure enough, there at last was Mr. Curtis crawling away, blubbering like a whipped dog.

Then she swayed, and the doctor caught her in his arms. The contact braced her failing spirit. She closed her eyes, but her hands were clinging, and at that moment she felt his mouth upon her own.

"What has he done to you?" she heard him murmur. She opened her eyes again. Her arms were across his shoulder. He was looking down on her, that calm face with the deep eyes that were smiling so tenderly.

"It was nothing," she whispered. "I was only frightened. Thank God, you came."

He bent and kissed her again. Her arms tightened naturally about his neck.

"It's all right now," he said, comforting her.

She began to realise what was happening. She was in his arms. The blood mounted to her face. She struggled to free herself, and he let her go at once.

"What does it mean?" she asked. "I saw someone outside in the meadow. Mr. Curtis's door was open, and the bells on the staircase did not ring."

He laid a hand gently on her shoulder.

"Are you sure that you are all right," he asked anxiously. "You've had a bad shock. You had better go back to bed. I will give you a sleeping-draught."

But she was now determined to show that her weakness had been only momentary. She, too, was a doctor. She would not be treated like a child.

"No," she said. "I'm quite all right now. We must look into this business at once."

"You would do better to go straight to bed," insisted Dr. Murchison.

"We must find out at once what has happened," she urged.

Dr. Murchison smiled.

"Very well," he said. "First we will close the door."

He turned abruptly. Slowly the great door swung forward and the bolts shot home into their sockets.

Light was streaming from a torch in his hand.

"Now," said the doctor, "I will take you upstairs. You are sure you wouldn't rather go to bed?"

"Not till this business is settled," she replied.

"Then go and dress," he answered, taking her instantly at her word, "while I look round at the patients. Meet me at the top of the stairs as soon as you are ready."

She followed him up the broad staircase, and, moving down the corridor, ran into her room and threw on the frock she had been wearing at dinner. Her mind was active again. Something terrible had happened? There had been a breakdown somewhere in the organisation. There would be a hideous scandal, and the life work of Dr. Edwardes might be ruined. She thrust her feet into a pair of shoes and went out again into the corridor.

As she was leaving the room, her eyes fell on the dressing-gown which she had just discarded. On the sleeve, where Mr. Curtis had touched her, was a red smudge.

Dr. Murchison was awaiting her, and his first words were re-assuring.

"The patients are all in their rooms," he said, "and I have given Curtis an injection. He will not trouble us again to-night."

"But how was he able to leave his room," began Constance.

"I think I have found the explanation," said Dr. Murchison grimly. "Come with me."

They walked along in silence, and, turning, moved into the corridor where the patients' rooms were situated. At the end of it, as Constance knew, was the room in which Warder Jones was sleeping. Opposite the warder's door the doctor paused, and threw it open. Then he switched on the electric light.

Warder Jones was lying, half-dressed, across his bed. His face was congested, and he was breathing stertorously.

"Take a good look at him," said the doctor.

She bent above the prostrate man, and was assailed with a reek of whisky. She looked at the doctor.

"Yes," he said, "dead drunk. And his keys are missing."

Even as he spoke, there came the sound of a furious knocking from the other end of the corridor. The doctor pushed her aside and left the room.

Again there came a furious burst of knocking, and a muffled voice cried: "Let me out, I say, let me out at once."

Chapter XI

I

Mr. Deeling had reached a crisis. The events of the previous night had been the last straw. He had woken up early in the night, though now he doubted whether he had ever been asleep. At any rate, he remembered hearing a queer throbbing noise away in the woods. For a long while he had thought that it was his imagination, but, after a time, he had got up to look out of the window, and he had found that his door was locked. He, Mr. Deeling, had been just in time to see two figures standing by the front door, two figures outside the castle at that hour. It had required an immediate investigation.

He had slipped on a coat and trousers and made straight for the door, even forgetting the false teeth which stood in the glass by his bedside. He had tried the handle, and then, to his stupefaction, he had been locked into his own room, like one of the patients. Just as though he was mad like the Rev. Mark Hickett or Mr. Curtis, or anyone of the others. It had taken some time to realise it, which had shown in itself that he could not have been quite well. The fact was that he had undoubtedly had a bad shock in the wood that afternoon, and that it had perhaps impaired the activity of his mind.

But then, as he had stood there bewildered, he had heard someone go past his room, someone who was breathing heavily and who had given a kind of groan or whimper as he passed. This had brought him to his senses, and he had started to beat upon the door with his fists and to shout.

Almost at once the key had turned in the lock, and the door had been thrown violently open. There had stood Dr. Murchison, and, behind him, Miss Sedgwick, still in that ridiculous evening dress of hers—the one with no sleeves which she wore to display her arms. He had, of course, at once stopped shouting and had gazed at the doctor, trying vainly to find words to express his sense of outrage. But the doctor had not allowed him to speak.

"Oh, it's you, Deeling," he had said in a voice that had stung like a whip. "Go back to bed and stop making that silly noise. We've got quite enough on our hands as it is."

On that Dr. Murchison had shut the door and left Mr. Deeling to his devices.

For a moment he had been moved to follow Dr. Murchison into the corridor, but somehow he had shrunk from that cutting voice, and after a time he had got into bed again. The last thing he had remembered was his sudden realisation that the detestable Miss Sedgwick had seen him without his teeth.

Curiously enough he had fallen into a deep sleep almost at once. Exhaustion, he supposed, that was what it was. He was thoroughly exhausted by all three occurrences. He had even overslept himself, for it was now eleven o'clock, and he had only just finished dressing. That in itself was unprecedented.

His mind, at last, was made up. He had taken a decision, and he felt that no other course was open to him. He looked at himself in the glass. Yes, his tie was straight, his black clothes were neatly brushed, and his hair was in order. He would go straight down to Dr. Murchison, and inform him clearly and quietly that his manner on the previous evening had been intolerable, and that he proposed to complain to Dr. Edwardes without delay. Dr. Murchison, of course, would ask for his resignation, but he would refuse to give it. Nothing would induce him to go. By the terms of his engagement six months' notice was required on either side, and, if Dr. Murchison offered him six months' salary instead, he would refuse to accept it. He intended to stay at Château Landry till Dr. Edwardes returned, and Dr. Edwardes would have to choose between them.

But first he must visit the patients. He had already broken more rules since 7.30 a.m. (the hour at which he ought normally to have arisen) than he had ever broken before during the whole eleven years of his existence at Château Landry. He could not continue to do so indefinitely. He must, of course, see Dr. Murchison, but, before doing so, he must carry out his morning inspection of the patients' rooms.

He set about his task with precision and despatch. But his mind kept wandering, running on the eternal subject. Dr. Murchison was intolerable. So, too, was his female assistant. He must protest, and the words must be firm and appropriate.

Then, suddenly, he came to himself. He was standing, absent of mind, in the doorway of a room which was not familiar to him, for he never spied upon the female patients.

Mechanically he put a hand to his head and smoothed the carefully disposed wisps of hair on his cranium.

The room was very bare—a low bed, one wooden chair, a wooden *prie-dieu* and a crucifix in one corner, a washstand with some enamelled tin washing utensils in another, and under the window a long piece of carpet rolled up.

He realised suddenly where he was. This was Miss Archer's room, but where was Miss Archer? The room was empty. There was no possible place where anyone could be concealed. And yet Miss Archer was ill, confined, as he knew, to her bed.

He looked again at the bed. It was rumpled slightly, as though someone had lain upon it. He was turning away when his eye caught something on the wall just above the head of the bed. He turned to examine it. It appeared to be some sort of drawing in reddish brown paint—a five-pointed star. But it was not that which filled him with horror. Next the star was the print of a hand, the four fingers and the thumb, all spread out. And the print was in red.

That was blood, not the slightest doubt of it— blood, a bloody hand on the wall. Only it was dry, not sticky like the blood on the white stone that he had seen in the forest. Frightened? No, he was not frightened. But, on the other hand, this was serious. Miss Archer was not in her room, and there was blood above her pillow.

He turned abruptly and made off quickly down the corridor. Yes, it was serious, very serious indeed. He would have to report this new discovery to Dr. Murchison, who was, after all, the head of the establishment, and must, of course, be informed of this important fact.

He went down the stairs and arrived in the study panting. But the room was empty. He stood for a moment, uncertain what to do. Then a girl's voice floated up through the window.

"No, it's your point, forty-thirty."

He walked to the window and looked out. From where he stood he could see a corner of the castle tennis court, and, as he watched, the slim figure of Constance moved into view, her racquet flashing as she returned a strong backhand. On the other side of the net Mr. Deeling could just see Dr. Murchison.

Mr. Deeling turned and made his way hurriedly from the room. So they were playing tennis, were they—fiddling while Rome was on fire, keeping to their daily programme as though everything was quite as usual.

The doctor, he remembered, preferred to play in the morning.

"You got hotter," he had heard him say, "and you sweated more."

How coarse these doctors were!

He walked across the terrace, taking no notice of Colonel Rickaby, who called to him as he passed, and, descending the steps, turned the corner of the castle and presently found himself by the side of the court. The castle clock was striking mid-day somewhere above him.

"Dr. Murchison," he called.

But there was no reply. The two on the court were hard at it, hammering away at each other from the back line to the accompaniment of a running comment from the doctor.

"Oh, well played. By George, that was a good one."

Mr. Deeling watched in rising anger.

"Dr. Murchison," he called again. But the doctor had at that moment been lured up to the net, and had failed ignominiously to reach a lob on the back line.

"Game *and*," shouted Dr. Murchison, taking no notice of Mr. Deeling. "I'll beat you one of these days, Constance. Upon my word, I will. Wish we had time for another, but that was twelve striking, wasn't it? and I have got the dickens of a lot to do."

He picked up a coat lying on the bench beside the court.

"Dr. Murchison," and Mr. Deeling *fortissimo*, moving to the other end of the bench, "I insist upon seeing you at once. The matter is most. . . ."

The doctor turned and silenced him with a gesture.

"It must wait till I have had my bath," he said shortly, and, without another word he turned his back, and ran lightly to the little wooden hut (pavilion was too lofty a term for it) which had been built next to the tennis court, and where the golf clubs and tennis racquets were kept. It had a shower bath, as Mr. Deeling knew, built in a little shed of corrugated iron.

This was too much. This was not to be borne. He was to wait till Dr. Murchison had taken his bath. Well, he would do nothing of the kind.

Throwing a chest, Mr. Deeling walked purposefully to the wooden hut, threw the door open and went inside. The bath house was at the far end of the room beyond, and as he entered he could hear sounds of splashing. Mr. Deeling crossed the room and dragged aside the mackintosh curtain. Dr. Murchison was stretched at full length in the shallow stone bath which formed the entire floor of the little tin shed. Cold water from a shower was sluicing down on him, and he was rolling under it and running his hands up and down his body with the utmost satisfaction. He did not notice Mr. Deeling, for his head was turned away from him. Nor did he hear Mr. Deeling's apologetic cough.

The doctor ceased rubbing himself, and, lying flat on his back, began to do a series of physical exercises while the water streamed down upon him. Mr. Deeling coughed a second time, but the noise of the water drowned his voice. He watched Dr. Murchison stretch himself out to his full length and bring his legs slowly over his head, over his shoulders, till they touched the ground behind.

Mr. Deeling opened his mouth to call again, but no sound came from his lips. He gave a single start, and then stood rigid, his mouth extended in a silent cry like some grotesque laocoon. For, as the doctor's legs had come over his head, Mr. Deeling had seen his feet. He waited, still as a stone, till the legs came up again once more. Yes, there they were again—*two crosses, one upon each of the soles.*

Mr. Deeling stood a moment, as though unable to move but thinking rapidly. Then, as the full implication of his discovery dawned on him, he turned and ran blindly out of the hut.

II

"I'm sorry, Mr. Deeling, but I really must ask you to come to the point."

It was four o'clock in the afternoon. Constance was sitting in the dispensary on one of the three white-painted chairs which, with the desk, were all the furniture it contained. Mr. Deeling sat on another chair, his thin dry hands spreading along his striped trousers, his face very sallow, crossed unexpectedly here and there with lines which had not been there before.

He had left the bath house just after mid-day. He had found himself some minutes later, he did not remember how, sitting in front of his desk with the door of the dispensary locked behind him. There he had sat, thinking things out, till his brain seemed to be turning like the wheels of an eccentric watch deprived of its hair spring.

Monotonously the thought recurred: Dr. Murchison, the man in charge of Château Landry was the Honble. Geoffrey Godstone, the homicidal maniac. There could not be the least doubt about it. Habit still argued that what he had seen meant nothing much; but his reason assured him that it was proof irresistible. He had seen crosses tattooed on the feet of the man who was masquerading as Dr. Murchison. There were similar crosses on the feet of the patient Godstone. But the crosses on the patient Godstone had been put there some days or perhaps weeks after his arrival at the castle. The evidence of Warder Jones was on that subject conclusive. The real Godstone, with the cunning of a madman, had put them there in order to cover his identity.

His reflections, interrupted by the bell for luncheon, were afterwards resumed; and he was now trying to explain the position to Miss Sedgwick. But Miss Sedgwick apparently either could not, or would not, understand. He must begin again.

"As I have already told you," he repeated, "the Honble. Geoffrey Godstone showed those marks on his feet to Warder Jones, and Warder Jones was positive that the marks were not there when the patient came. Remember that, for it is a most important point. This morning Dr. Murchison refused to speak to me on the tennis court, and I followed him into the bathroom. He was having his bath, and he did not notice that I was there. His feet, Miss Sedgwick, had the same marks on them as those which Warder Jones had observed upon the feet of the Honble. Geoffrey Godstone. Now, do you understand?"

"I cannot say that I do, Mr. Deeling."

Really, she thought, the man was passing all bounds. It looked as though they would have to get rid of him.

"The marks on his feet," Mr. Deeling explained, "were in the form of crosses, and they were tattooed."

"Tattooed crosses," said Constance, with a puzzled frown.

"Tattooed crosses," repeated Mr. Deeling.

He paused and picked up a book which he had brought with him into the dispensary.

"I am now," he said, "going to quote to you a passage from a novel which I read quite recently. It is entitled "The Madonna of the Barricades."

He fumbled in his waistcoat pocket, as he spoke, and produced a pair of steel *pince-nez*. He clamped them on his nose, and, opening a red bound novel at his side, began to read:

"After we had been groping our way for about three-quarters of an hour in the Catacombs we heard the sound of chanting such as one hears in a church. I asked my companion what it was. He replied with a terrific volley of invective that this noise was being made by some of the *canaille* who haunted the Catacombs and were votaries of the Black Mass. . . .

"There were three priests, apparently in vestments, and there were perhaps a hundred worshippers, at least half of them women.

"I am not going to describe all I saw, or all I thought I saw, for the whole effect was dim, and one's observation was distracted by the Gregorian chanting of the Mass—rather good from a musical point of view. Also there was a peculiar strong and stupefying smell of incense. . . .

"I soon signed to my guide to leave, and we crept back from our spyhole. The man was trembling with the emotion of rage. 'Would you believe it, monsieur,' he said in a voice of utmost horror, 'that these men, these priests of the devil have the Cross tattooed upon their feet? I have seen it, and so I know. Therefore, not only do they defile the Body of Christ, but they cannot take a step without trampling upon Him'."

He finished reading, put down the book and looked at Constance. He found that she was gazing at him with an expression of real concern.

"Now do you begin to understand?" he asked.

He looked at her eagerly, anxious that she should share his sense of the extremity of their position. But she did not seem to realise even yet what had happened.

Really, these modern girls were most extraordinary.

"The French diabolists of 1848," he carefully explained, "were accustomed to tattoo a cross on the soles of their feet as an insult to the God they had deliberately rejected. The Honble. Geoffrey Godstone is, as you are aware, a diabolist. You have perhaps examined the papers in his file."

"I have seen the papers," she admitted, "and there is a reference in them to the fact that the patient has these marks on his feet."

She was still looking at him with that odd expression of concern.

"But don't you see what it means?" he continued desperately. "The Honble. Geoffrey Godstone, or, let us say, the patient who goes by that name, complained to Warder Jones a few days ago that someone had tattooed on his feet the mark of the cross. Warder Jones examined his feet and observed the crosses. The warder told me of the incident because he was ready to swear that, when the patient was first brought to the Château Landry, there were no such marks to be seen. Do I make myself clear?"

"You say that Warder Jones was sure that the

patient had no marks on his feet when he arrived?"

"He is ready to swear to it."

"It is unfortunate," she said, "that Warder Jones is no longer here."

"What!" Mr. Deeling exclaimed.

"Warder Jones was dismissed this morning," she informed him. "Last night he was drunk on duty, and he made a very serious mistake. In fact, he neglected to lock up Mr. Curtis, and he locked you up instead."

"Nurse Webster will confirm what I say," began Mr. Deeling.

"Nurse Webster, as you know, is on leave," she pointed out.

She was looking at him kindly almost it seemed, with compassion.

"Is there anything else you would like to tell me, Mr. Deeling?"

"There is one other thing," he replied. "I have just seen Godstone, the patient, I mean. While you were at luncheon I abstracted the keys of his room from the pocket of Dr. Murchison's white overall, which was hanging in the study. This is the first act of that nature which I have ever performed in the course of my life, and I hope and trust that it will be the last. On entering the room of the Honble. Geoffrey Godstone I found him lying in a stupor. I am not a qualified medical man, but I am prepared to swear that he was under the influence of a drug, almost certainly of hyoscin. And I may mention in passing that considerable quantities of that drug have disappeared from my dispensary during the last few weeks without my knowledge. There are only two people besides myself who have access to this room—yourself and Dr. Murchison. I, of course, made a point of examining the feet of the patient as he lay there quite insensible. The marks, Miss Sedgwick, were there."

There was a short silence. It was Constance who spoke.

"Tell me, Mr. Deeling," she said, "what conclusion do you draw from all this?"

"There is only one possible conclusion," said Mr. Deeling. "Your original conjecture was correct. Dr. Murchison is the Honble. Geoffrey Godstone; that is to say the man we know as the doctor is the patient, and the man we know as the patient is the doctor. Château Landry at the present moment is in charge of a homicidal maniac. You've got to realise that, apart from the servants, you and I are the only sane persons in this place."

He leaned forward, stretching out a hand that trembled.

"Miss Sedgwick," he pleaded. "I know that our relations have up to now been far from cordial. But we must put all that aside. We . . . we must co-operate. We are in great danger. For God's sake let us work together."

"Why, of course, Mr. Deeling," said Constance rising and walking towards him.

He looked up at her bewildered.

"Then let us decide at once what we are to do," he said urgently.

"Let us talk of this some other time," she suggested. "You are tired, Mr. Deeling. We have all been working too hard in this terrible heat. What I advise you to do now is to go and lie down."

"Lie down!" exclaimed Mr. Deeling.

Was the woman off her head! Had she no sense of their common peril? And why in the name of heaven was she smiling at him in that idiotic fashion?

Then suddenly it dawned on him. He was being humoured. He had put the case clearly and unanswerably, and the woman merely thought that he was overwrought, that his brain was turning, in a word that he was mad.

He sprang to his feet, flushing helplessly.

"Good God," he shouted, "why are you smiling at me like that? Do you think I'm mad like all the rest of them. Answer me, Miss Sedgwick. Don't stand there like a doctor leering at a patient. I won't have it. Do you hear me? You think I am mad, don't you? You think I am mad, damn you."

He took another step towards her.

"You'll be the death of us both," he went on, his voice rising almost to a scream. "We shall all die, I tell you. We shall all of us perish miserably like birds upon a tree. The man is a devil-worshipper. He has done the most terrible things. He . . . "

A sudden knock on the door brought him to an abrupt stop. Constance stepped to the door at once and opened it.

Dr. Murchison stood on the threshold.

"Excuse me," he said, "if I am interrupting. But I thought I heard somebody shouting. Can I be of any help? What is it Mr. Deeling?"

Mr. Deeling looked speechlessly at the doctor.

"Mr. Deeling is not very well," began Constance, but she was not allowed to finish her sentence.

Mr. Deeling, utterly distraught, pointed full at the doctor.

241

"You are not Dr. Murchison," he said. "You have deceived us all. You are the Honble. Geoffrey Godstone. I have seen the marks on your feet. I can prove what I say. I saw them this morning in the bathroom."

Constance moved swiftly to the doctor, who put his arm across her shoulders.

"Mr. Deeling," said the doctor, "I believe we had some conversation on this subject before. On that occasion it was Miss Sedgwick who doubted me."

He paused and looked down at Constance beside him.

"You do not believe him now?" he said softly.

"Of course not."

"You believe in me utterly?"

"Of course," she said again.

"And yet Mr. Deeling is right," said the doctor gently. "I am, as he says, Geoffrey Godstone."

For a moment the silence closed over them like water over a stone.

"Well," said the doctor, looking from one to the other, "what are we going to do about it?"

III

Mr. Deeling's face turned from red to white.

"You confess it," he muttered.

The doctor turned upon him abruptly.

"Go to your room, Deeling, and stay there till I come to you."

"But I . . . I . . ." began Mr. Deeling, looking at Constance.

"You had better leave us, Mr. Deeling," said Constance.

The doctor moved aside to let him pass. Mr. Deeling shuffled along the wall like a crab, and scrabbled at the handle of the door.

"This is terrible, this is disastrous, this is the end," he muttered.

The door closed gently behind him. Constance and the doctor were alone.

"And now, Constance," he said, glancing towards her.

She looked at him steadily.

"Doctor," she said professionally, "do you think that was really the best thing to do?"

Dr. Murchison made no sign that he had heard. He was staring straight in front of him, as though lost in reflection.

"I think you behaved very cruelly just now," Constance went on, "pretending to be Mr. Godstone. You frightened poor Mr. Deeling out of his wits. I am sure it's bad for him after the shock he had the other day."

He turned to her suddenly.

"There was no pretence," he said, "I was speaking the truth."

She looked at him a moment with wide eyes.

"I don't understand," she faltered.

"It's quite simple," he returned. "I am Geoffrey Godstone, the man who was sent to this place in the charge of Dr. Murchison six weeks ago."

"But that is impossible. You are making fun of me. It . . . it isn't sensible."

"Not so long ago you were ready to believe it."

Constance flushed.

"I hoped you had forgotten that silly business. I

suppose this is your revenge. Very well. It's one up to you. And now we'll go and put things right with poor Mr. Deeling. He really *did* believe. . . ."

"Come here, Constance," the doctor interrupted.

After a moment's hesitation she moved towards him. He put his hands on her shoulders.

"Look me in the face," he said.

Obediently she raised her eyes.

"I solemnly assure you that what I said is truth. My name is Geoffrey Godstone. I am the second son of Lord Bramber."

"But . . . but you are as sane as I am," she returned.

"Sane?" he echoed. "What do you mean by that? I am sane to myself. I have been sane to you. Or do you prefer the sanity of that poor fool who was with us a moment ago?"

A look came into his eyes which she had not seen before.

"But if you are Godstone," she said, "you . . . you . . ."

She broke off.

"Yes?" he encouraged her, still in the same gentle voice.

"Oh, let me go," she said with a sudden jerk of her shoulders backwards. But his grip only tightened.

"You are beginning to realise it now," he said. "I am Godstone, and I am not like other men. But I am still the man who walked with you in the garden, who came to you when you were frightened by a shadow on the wall, and carried you to your room like a child. I am sane, sane I tell you. But I am different. I have a mission to fulfil. I have been chosen out of all the world. And you have been sent to help me. You, too, have been chosen."

He pulled her slowly towards him. His hands slipped from her shoulders and crept about her, pressing her closer. And suddenly she began to fight him desperately, striking at his chest and broad shoulders, struggling to get free.

"Let me go. Let me go," she panted.

He released her, and she staggered back into Mr. Deeling's vacant chair.

"You believe me now," he said at last. "Answer me, Constance."

"I believe you," she replied with a sob.

"Will you believe me, too," he went on, "when I say that I love you?"

She made no answer.

"I love you," he repeated.

He moved towards her and put a hand again upon her shoulder. She sprang from the chair with a cry and rushed blindly to the door. She fumbled with the handle. Before she could get it open he was upon her again. He drew her away, not roughly, but with a strength against which she was powerless.

"Sit down," he said. "I shall not molest you."

She moved as far away from him as possible and sat down by the window. She was trembling from head to foot, sobs rose in her throat every now and again which she could not control. She must think. She must keep her head. What, oh, what did one do?

"Now," he went on, "there is a question of love between us, isn't there? You will not deny that if, as Dr. Murchison, I had asked you to marry me, you would have done so. Wouldn't you?"

"Wouldn't you?" he repeated.

"You must be mad," said Constance suddenly, "to think that I could ever. . . ."

She stopped.

He smiled.

"Yes," he said, "it's not much use telling a mad-man that he must be mad, is it? This, my dear, is a situation to which the usual phrases cannot apply. As I have told you already I am not an ordinary man."

But she was not listening to him now. There was a bell somewhere, if she could only remember where, which rang in the servants' quarters. She had merely to press it and help would come.

"I did not try at first to win your love," he continued. "Our relationship has been a sort of accident. But it fitted in with my purpose. I thought it might make matters easier for you. We have a mission to fulfil. Perhaps you have begun to guess what it is."

She had risen to her feet and was walking as naturally as she could to the desk. The bell was in the under part of the kneehole. She had only to sit in the chair and she could reach it easily.

"I gave you my case to read," he went on. "I did that deliberately. You must know me for what I am."

"No," he broke off suddenly, "I should not ring that bell if I were you. No one will hear it. Warder Jones, as you know, was dismissed this morning, and the other warder has been called away by a telegram to the bedside of a sick mother. We are quite alone in Château Landry. Here I am, king in this little kingdom, lord of this little pasture set high in the hills."

His eyes were kindling as he spoke, and he began to walk restlessly about the room.

"They are all devoted to me here except the poor fool who was with us a moment ago. I am free now to do the work for which I was chosen. The valley is shut. There is no escape and this time I shall not fail."

He came abruptly to a standstill in the middle of the room. His excitement had mounted rapidly. His words came faster. He became, under her eyes, a man possessed.

"All is now ready for the master, who has chosen me out of all the world, the black bread and the unsalted spices, the place unhallowed with a bloody sacrifice, the crowns of vervein, the ambergris and the storax, the blood of the mole and the mouse with wings and the goat. For many nights the ancient rites have been performed. The white stone is made ready. The circle shall be drawn and the pentacle within the circle. The fire of alderwood shall be lighted, and I shall call upon him by the key of Solomon and the great name. He will enter me. And in the time appointed he will take my flesh. He has chosen me for his great purpose. After the sacrifice, fulfilment. But first the sacrifice. . . . You have seen the record of what I have done. Do you understand? Yes, I see the horror in your eyes. Everything is ready. All that is fair shall be foul. The blood of the innocent shall cry in vain."

He paused suddenly and, moving swiftly to Constance, seized her hands and looked into her eyes.

"All these things—you shall see them yourself. For yours is the glory and the shame. You are a partner in the mystery."

He went rigid as she gazed at him wide-eyed with horror, and there was foam on his lips.

"But not yet . . . not yet," he muttered thickly and suddenly dropping her hands he turned and ran blindly from the room.

Chapter XII

I

She stood a moment facing the door which had closed behind him. Then impulsively she started forward and put her hand on the doorknob. But at once she drew back. Where was she going? She could not act without a plan, and she had no plan.

She must not lose her head. She must force herself to think calmly and collectedly.

She turned and went to the window.

There was the familiar terrace, the meadow beyond, drowsy with heat, the menacing circle of firs and the final barrier of rock. The scene was clear, but somehow colourless. All those things continued to exist, but they were flat, like a Japanese picture. Her mind was stunned, and the things about her seemed empty of life or reality.

Then, stabbing its way through the confusion of her brain, shot a memory of what she had read in the file of Godstone, the man who now had charge of Château Landry. Godstone was the lunatic who believed in the devil, the man who had committed, according to the sworn testimony of his distracted friends, at least two assaults so horrible, so devoid of any mere human passion, that in panic they had sought any means to isolate him from the world. One sentence in one of the letters sprang to her mind, spinning round like the written prayer on a wheel: "*It was only after three hours unceasing work that we saved the child's life; when we found him we thought he had gone.*"

And that was the man who was loose in Château Landry. Not only loose, but in power; who had been in power for weeks. During all that time he had behaved as sanely and as conscientiously as the most exacting critic of the medical profession could require. His indeed had been a terrible sanity, for he had been at once menacingly efficient and filled with dark pity for the unhappy patients. And yet—yet he was worse than all of them, incredibly worse, worse even than Mr. Curtis.

For a moment Constance knew despair. Fear came at her like a great wave. Her only thought was to escape, to rush blindly from the castle, out of that valley with its dreadful air of false security, into the busy world of sane men and women moving on its accustomed round only a few miles away.

Over the rocks. Over the rocks. For Mr. Clearwater that was a phrase of terror. Might it not for her be a way of escape. The ascent of the steep mountain must be terribly dangerous—and yet, what was that peril compared with that in which she stood. Surely there was a path, a path that wound through those yellow

250

rocks, lost here and there in patches of snow that not even the August sun could melt, leading down, when the summit and the danger were past, to the plains, to the great lake, to the homes of happy men.

But in that moment of abject fear she came to herself. This was sheer panic. She must put such thoughts as those out of her mind. They were craven, a final defeat of the spirit. She had not yet even considered her responsibilities. She was now in charge. Could she, if she ran away, or tried to run away, ever lift up her head again. Her responsibilities were frightful. But she must face them somehow. She must think. She must have a plan.

The first thing, obviously, was to communicate with Dr. Edwardes. He must be warned immediately of what had happened, and urged to return at once. But how was this to be done? Godstone was sure to restrict her liberty now that he had revealed himself; even if he did not—even if he left her, as before, free to move about the castle and among the patients—she could not leave the valley or hope to reach even the village below the gates. In her mind's eye she could see the great fence gleaming in the sun, its meshes of fine steel, close-woven, impenetrable, and the white ribbon of road that ran up to it, and the lodge that guarded the single gate, the single gate that could only be opened by working the locked lever in Dr. Edwardes' room, the room that now was Godstone's.

But it had to be done somehow. For the moment, at any rate, she was free.

She sat down at Mr. Deeling's desk, found pen and paper and began to write. Once the pen was in her

251

hands her faculties returned. She found herself thinking clearly, lucidly, almost calmly. She stated the facts, concisely, and asked for immediate help. In ten minutes she had finished.

The letter was written, but how was she to send it? She began to turn over possible plans.

Her mind turned suddenly to the real Dr. Murchison, the man who had been confined as Godstone all these weeks, who had never left his room. She remembered with a pang the desperate appeal he had made to her. For a moment she had believed him. Why had she gone back to Godstone to be so easily deceived? In five minutes she had been apologising to the madman for ever having doubted his sanity. She must have been infatuated with the man. He had fooled her to the top of her bent. Not only that. He had made love to her. That was the bitterest thought of all. This madman, whom she had admired from the very first for the splendour of his mind, the tenacity of his purpose, for the beauty of his soul, had made love to her. He had kissed her lips. She had been ready to pledge herself to a madman, to one who, when the fit was on him, did the deeds and uttered the blasphemies which had appalled her merely to read of in the cold, exact language of his medical file. Horrors of horrors! But now again her head went up. This would never do. She was giving way again. She was plunging once more into the abyss into which she had sunk a few moments ago. She thrust the letter to Dr. Edwardes into the pocket of the silk coat she was wearing, and began to think again.

The man in the cell was Murchison, Murchison

who ought to have been her chief during these last weeks, the young doctor sent out from England to take charge of Château Landry. He must be set free at all costs. He would be her only real ally, for Mr. Deeling was useless. Presumably, he was now locked up in his room in a state of drivelling panic. Murchison and Deeling were, besides herself, the only sane inmates of Château Landry, except, of course, for the servants who were peasants from the village. She felt instinctively she could place no reliance on them. All the people from the village hated and feared Château Landry. She felt sure that at the first hint of anything unusual they would leave it in a body, and that nothing would induce them to meddle in any matter concerning it. She might have to appeal to them, but she was almost sure in advance that there could be no possible help from that quarter.

If only Warder Jones had remained. There, again, she had been hopelessly fooled. He had been dismissed for being drunk on duty, and she had not even inquired into the matter. She had simply accepted the decision of Godstone—for she must not call him Murchison any more. Yet she was familiar with the warder's record, an unblemished record for fifteen years, and he had sturdily denied having touched a drop of whisky, and had been quite unable to account for the fact that he had been found drunk. He had not been drunk at all; he had been drugged; and she, a doctor, had not suspected it. Godstone had drugged him, and then poured whisky over him so as to have an excuse for getting him out of the way. Nurse Webster, too, had gone. He was getting rid of all the sane persons, one by one. He was working up to the great climax of which he had spoken, the climax in which she was to play a part. But, again, she must not think of that.

She forced her mind back to the question of the drugs. Warder Jones had been drugged, and of course, Murchison, the real Murchison, he had been kept under drugs on and off for days together. There at last was the explanation of the large quantities of hyoscin that were being used.

She went to the drug cupboard, and taking the key from her pocket, unlocked it. There was the bottle. She picked it out and held it up to the light. It was rather more than half-full. One thing, at any rate, she could do. She moved to the zinc table where Mr. Deeling made up his prescriptions, and carefully poured the hyoscin down the sink. Then she washed out the bottle and filled it with distilled water, taking care that the amount she put in should exactly equal the amount of the drug she had poured out. Then she replaced the bottle.

She glanced along the shelves and her eye fell on a small blue phial containing a concentrated solution of laudanum. She took it down from the cupboard and slipped it into her pocket. She stood a moment thinking. That way of escape was always open. Then, appalled by her thoughts, she made to return the bottle to the shelf.

But no—she would keep it, after all. She locked the cupboard.

Now she must go and find Mr. Deeling. They must act together now. She must secure his help, whatever that was worth.

She decided to go through the glass window and by way of the terrace. She moved to it, and was about to pass through when she heard the sound of wheels on the gravel of the terrace to the right, behind the corner of the castle. A moment later, there was the screech of a klaxon, and the Citroen—the car which had brought her to Château Landry—came suddenly into view. It was being driven at great speed and was full of people, whom Constance did not immediately recognise. It shot past her, swaying slightly as it bucketed over the gravel, and skidded round the sharp bend where the road went down the castle mound to the village.

It was gone in a flash, its klaxon shrieking continuously, so that it seemed like a panic-stricken monster fleeing from an unknown doom.

Abruptly she realised what had happened. Those people in the Citroen, they were the servants. They had heard or seen something, and they were escaping while there was yet time.

She stepped from the window on to the terrace, and, as she did so, a figure, dusty, red in the face, gasping for breath, ran almost into her. It was Mr. Deeling. He gave no sign of recognition, but pushed her roughly aside, and stumbled on desperately down the road crying in a hoarse voice:

"Stop. For God's sake, stop. Take me with you. You can't leave me behind."

II

"Mr. Deeling," said Constance sharply.

He turned a face working with fear and flushed with running.

"Mr. Deeling," she said again. "Pull yourself together, for goodness sake. It is no use running after them like that."

He stood before her, panting, his hands fluttering by his side like two broken birds, as unlike the precise Mr. Deeling of daily life as could well be imagined.

"You are right," he said at last, passing a handkerchief across his forehead. "I cannot catch them now."

He was silent a moment, looking down the drive. Then, losing all control again, he raised his clenched fist.

"The cowards," he shouted, "the cowards, to leave behind them an old man like me."

Constance took him by the arm and led him towards the window of the dispensary. As she laid her hand on the edge of the glass door, to push it wide open, he shied violently to one side.

"No, no," he said, "not in there. I won't go into that room again."

He spoke in little jerks, but already he was recovering himself. His eyes rested for a moment on his patent leather shoes.

"Dear me, what a state they are in," he muttered.

Constance laid her hand again on his arm.

"Let us go to the rose garden, Mr. Deeling," she suggested.

He moved a little to one side.

"I am quite capable of walking without assistance," he answered, with a faint return to his formal manner, and without another word he moved past her and led the way across the terrace to where the garden showed crimson and white and green in the afternoon sun.

He sat down on the stone seat at the farther end where Mr. Clearwater had a few days previously recited his poem. Constance did not immediately follow Mr. Deeling's example, but stood looking down at him. She felt as yet no pity, nothing but an angry contempt.

"Now, Mr. Deeling," she said. "Kindly tell me exactly what you have been doing. Why have the servants suddenly decamped like this in a body? I suppose you have been talking to them and frightened them away."

He did not answer for a moment, but sat silent, his thin elbows propped on his long thighs, looking steadily in front of him. His face was again that geometrical mask which, until a few days before, she had thought impenetrable.

"Of course, I told the servants," he said at last. "It was my duty to warn them. It was not right to leave them in ignorance."

"And, of course, they have run away."

"I am not responsible for that," he answered doggedly.

"And you, it seemed, were doing your best to follow them."

There was a pause. He opened his mouth once or twice but no words came.

He looks like an underfed carp just out of the water, she thought.

"How can I possibly remain?" he said at last. "You

257

don't seem to realise what it means."

He fumbled for his handkerchief and passed it across his mouth. Then suddenly he broke out.

"The lying, selfish cowards," he said. "They have left me in the lurch. . . . Sneaking off like that . . . "I was not gone for more than five minutes . . . just time to put a few things together. . . . Then I heard the car, and I knew they were going to leave me. . . . So I ran down the stairs. I shouted at them, but they would not stop. . . ."

"But there is the gate," said Constance. "It is sure to be closed, and can only be opened from the lever on Dr. Edwardes' desk."

"We thought of that," said Mr. Deeling. "The gate is controlled from the castle, but it can also be opened from the lodge, if it isn't disconnected. He hasn't disconnected it yet, but he can do so if he likes at any moment. The gate will be opened all right. We sent a boy down to the lodge on a bicycle."

He did not seem to be aware that he was confessing his complicity with the deserters, and, before Constance could comment on his admission, he started to his feet and moved a few steps to the parapet. Suddenly he pointed, and Constance looked in the direction of his hand.

She could just see the end of the white road where the little lodge was situated. Something winked and flashed at rare intervals along the end of the valley. That must be the sun striking the steel fence. Even as she looked, she saw something moving far away. That could only be the motor car. It ran past the lodge, and there was a flash of white. The gate had opened; the car had passed through.

"What did I tell you," said Mr. Deeling.

She looked him up and down.

"Why don't you follow them?" she asked. "Presumably the gate is still open."

"It will never be opened again," he said.

"What do you mean?"

"That madman is in the library now. I saw him as I ran past the windows. There was a smile on his face. He, too, had heard the motor car. He knew what was happening."

"Then he could have disconnected the lodge and prevented them from getting away."

Mr. Deeling looked at her with a dull contempt.

"Why should he do that?" he asked. "Do you think he wants a lot of servants here now. He wants to be quite free. He is only too thankful that they have cleared out."

"Do they know exactly what has happened?"

"They know enough."

"Then, in that case," said Constance quietly, "I see no cause for alarm. They will tell the people in the village. We have only to keep our heads and play for a little time."

Mr. Deeling laughed shortly.

"The village will not raise a finger," he said.

"But that, surely, is absurd," she protested.

"I've been here now for eleven years," said Mr. Deeling, "eleven years and six months to be exact, and I can tell you at once that it is useless to look for help in that quarter. They'll be crossing themselves tonight and waiting for the castle to go up in smoke.

They think we are all of us in league with the devil. Those who come here are the bravest of them, and even they only came for the big wages they get. They believe in all sorts of queer things. They hate us. The village priest preaches against us at least once a month. Once he offered to help Dr. Edwardes by performing some sort of ceremony over the patients— to drive out the evil spirits, he said. They will do nothing to help us, nothing at all."

Mr. Deeling was recovering his self-control. He was almost, except in appearance, his normal self. Even the little didactic inflections had come back into his voice.

"Very well," said Constance. "That means that you and I are now the only sane persons in this valley. We have got to do something, and you have got to help me, Mr. Deeling."

She paused and waited for him to speak. He had dropped his head on his hands again. Now he raised it and looked at her.

"It is now too late," he said, and she saw that his lips were trembling. "You should have believed me at once, this afternoon. Then we might have got away. Now it is impossible. God only knows what frightful thing is going to happen."

"Nothing is going to happen," she said bravely. "We have got somehow to control this man."

"Are you armed?" she added.

Mr. Deeling shook his head.

"I often carry a pistol. It was in my room yesterday, but when I looked for it just now it was not there. He has taken it away, and I suppose you haven't got one yourself."

"No," she answered.

"And your keys," he went on. "We might be able to lock him into his room. But I expect he's taken them away by now.

She looked at him for a moment.

"I will go and see," she said. "Wait here for me, Mr. Deeling."

For a moment he seemed about to stop her going, as though he feared to be alone.

Her footsteps died away on the gravel, as she moved quickly to the castle. Then there was silence.

He was so tired that his brain just would not work. He did not know what was coming next. He could not even imagine what it would be. He had no imagination. He was proud of having none. And yet—something had happened in the wood that dreadful day. What was that infernal buzzing? It was a wasp.

"Go away," said Mr. Deeling irritably, waving his hands.

But it would not go away; it kept on buzzing round his head. He got violently to his feet and waved his hands again about his ears.

"You were right, Mr. Deeling," said the voice of Constance, "the keys are no longer in my room."

"These wasps are really intolerable," said Mr. Deeling. "There must be a nest of them somewhere. I must speak to Mr. Curtis. He once smoked out a wasps' nest."

"The keys are not in my room," repeated Constance.

Mr. Deeling turned and looked at her.

"Then how are you going to shut him up?" he said. "What are you going to do?"

"You must do something," he went on accusingly. "You are in charge of Château Landry. It's you that have got us into this awful mess. I am not going to have my throat cut because of you, like Miss Archer. *You* are responsible, do you hear?"

"Miss Archer," said Constance, "what do you mean by that?"

"I tell you, Miss Archer has been murdered," he said. "I saw the bloodstains on the wall above her head. That's what I was going to tell the doctor about before I found out who he really was."

"She's dead I tell you," he repeated with rising excitement. "They've put some horrible mark above her bed—a star in blood—blood do you hear? They will be doing the same to me soon."

He shook violently from head to foot.

"Keep calm, Mr. Deeling," said Constance, but she said it mechanically. Her mind had returned to Mr. Godstone's file—something about smearing charms with the blood of the victim on the walls of the place he had last occupied.

She felt suddenly sick. There was silence between them.

"You are quite right," said Mr. Deeling at last, swallowing in his throat. "I will be calm. I . . . I'm a little overwrought, but I'm better now. Yes, I will do anything you say. Only don't abandon me. Don't leave me alone."

He made a weak gesture.

"I refuse to be left alone," he concluded.

"I'm not going to leave you alone," said Constance, as if she were talking to a frightened child.

"Now, let us think clearly," she continued. "There is only one immediate thing to be done. We must try to set free Dr. Murchison."

He looked at her bewildered.

"I mean, of course, the real Dr. Murchison—the man Godstone has been keeping shut up all these weeks."

"But he is always drugged," said Mr. Deeling.

"I know that," replied Constance, "but I have poured away the hyoscin in your dispensary, so that unless Godstone has got a private store of his own, he won't be able to drug Dr. Murchison any more. I filled the bottle up with distilled water. He may not notice the difference. Anyway, it is our only hope. If we can get the real Dr. Murchison out, the three of us ought to be able to do something."

"You poured away my hyoscin," said Mr. Deeling. "I must make a note of that, and you must please tell me the quantity. It will throw out all my accounts."

Constance gazed at him.

"Never mind that now," she said. "We've got to decide how we are going to get at Dr. Murchison. Somehow I shall have to recover my keys. Perhaps I could persuade Godstone. . . ."

"Yes," broke in Mr. Deeling eagerly. "That is the way. Talk to Godstone. Persuade him. He will do anything for you. Why, I've seen you together in the garden. Perhaps, if you were really nice to him . . . you may be able to save us both in that way. And, in any case, he will not kill you. . . . No, he will not kill you. He has other views. . . . Of that I am quite sure. . . ."

"I must, in any case, try to get the keys," she said, more to herself than to him.

Mr. Deeling did not appear to hear what she said. An expression of idiotic dismay suddenly came over his face.

"Good God," he whispered. "Only to think of it."

"Why, what's the matter now?" said Constance, looking at him in amazement.

"The letter," he exclaimed. "Dr. Murchison's letter! It would have saved our lives."

"What letter?"

"Warder Jones gave it to me only the other day. From Dr. Murchison to Dr. Edwardes. And I had forgotten all about it. It's lying still in my drawer, and we cannot send it now."

III

Mr. Deeling turned and left her. Constance imagined he must be going to see whether the letter to which he had referred was still in his possession.

She was alone again, with nothing as yet decided. Her one ally was a man of straw. Poor Mr. Deeling! It was not altogether his fault. He was part of a machine, a small cog that could be relied upon to turn correctly, as moved by the larger cogs, above and beneath. The machine had gone wrong, and the small cog was out of action.

What was the use of sitting there thinking about

cogs and machines. Miss Archer had been murdered
. . . murdered, by order, perhaps by the act, of the
man with whom a few hours ago she had been playing
tennis. He had played with his head and heart on the
game, and yet he had known of that smear above Miss
Archer's bed—put it there, for all Constance knew. It
must have happened last night out in the forest. . . .
She had heard a drum, and Mr. Curtis had come
back. . . . He had touched her dressing-gown, and
she had found a smudge where his hand had rested.

Again the sick feeling rose. She must not think of
these horrors, but consider only how to get at the real
Dr. Murchison. She must contrive somehow to set
him free. She pinned her whole faith on Dr. Murchison. He would know what to do. But how was she to
get at him? And, if by a miracle she did get at him,
what was to happen then? They could not leave the
valley. If ever they were to open that gate in the fence,
someone would have to remain at the doctor's desk to
control the lever. She had seen the lever more than
once. To open the gate it had to be held in position by
a human hand. It had to be switched over and the
thumb pressed firmly on the knob at the end of the
handle. It could not be tied or otherwise kept in
position. Someone would have to hold it while they
escaped. And who was that someone to be? They
must all three get away, Dr. Murchison, Mr. Deeling
and herself—for the one who was left behind would be
torn in pieces.

Of course, if anyone must stay it must be herself.
She was in charge, and she alone might perhaps have
some influence with Godstone. He had loved her. He

was a madman, but not, perhaps, inaccessible to persuasion. Should she stay behind and plead with him so that the others might get away? Could she hold the affection of a madman against the full force and strength of his mania:

A line of poetry floated into her mind:

"For each man kills the thing he loves."

If only she could divine his thoughts for one moment! As she sat, in shadow now, for the sun was over the highest of the peaks to the west and the light was fading, she began to remember the words Godstone had used earlier in the afternoon, his strange, incomprehensible ravings: the circle and the pentacle, and the weird beasts, the mole, the goat, the bat, incense and wine. She felt that those allusions were not merely aimless. Then to what dreadful ceremonial did they refer? He had used the word "sacrifice." She gripped the arm of the stone bench. A sacrifice, with herself, perhaps, for the victim. He would kill the thing he loved, as a supreme sacrifice to the Lord of Evil who was his master.

It was senseless to sit there and think. She was, it seemed, to be butchered. But, at any rate, she would make a fight for it. She was not bound yet. Not yet was the knife at her throat. If only that lever could be controlled for half an hour!

She heard a step on the path beside her, and looking up saw Mr. Clearwater. He was carrying a bunch of roses. He looked at her in a respectful, almost timid way.

"Gracious lady," he said, "behold a few poor flowers, pale and unworthy, together with this little roundel, which I have composed in your honour."

And forthwith he began to recite, waving his white hands gracefully up and down, and pointing his feet like an eighteenth century dancing-master.

> "Your eyes are set" (he said)
> "In sweet surprise.
> You laugh and yet,
> Your eyes,
> When laughter dies,
> With tears are wet."

He paused and looked at her.

> "All paradise
> Is here. Ah, let
> Me kiss, where lies
> Love in a net—
> Your eyes."

"But that, of course, is not for me," he went on hurriedly. "For me it is permitted to kiss no more than the hem of your robe."

Before she could say or do anything, he had fallen on his knees and was kissing the edge of her skirt.

" 'If I were rich, I would kiss her feet, and thereabouts where the gold hems meet,' " he whispered, "but, alas, I am very poor."

"I am a fool, you know," he went on, sitting crosslegged on the ground and looking up at her. "I am a fool, and sometimes I think I must be mad. Not often. But when the moon is at the full I have strange fancies. I dreamt last night that I put out to sea in a boat made of emeralds, but they were so heavy that the edge of the boat was level with the brine, and it sank like a stone just outside the harbour mouth."

He paused and looked at her wistfully.

She raised the roses he had given her to her face.

"Thank you, Mr. Clearwater," she said gently, "for your poem and these roses. They are beautiful."

His white face flushed.

"My lady is gracious," he said. "How else is it possible to serve you?"

She looked down at his upturned face.

"Serve me?" she asked. "Would you really serve me, Mr. Clearwater?"

"I would die for you," he answered.

It was simply said, without flourish or exaggeration. There he was, squatting at her feet, a ridiculous lanky figure, with his stained shirt open at the throat, and his old grey flannel trousers. But his eyes were alight with something that was not altogether madness.

"I wonder," she said, "if I can really trust you."

"What is it?" he asked. "Tell me at once, dear lady."

"I want you to go to the doctor's study," she said slowly, "the great library, you know, where I work so much during the day. When you are there, I want you to sit down at the doctor's desk—"

She got no further. Mr. Clearwater was gazing at her with a fixed intensity, and at the first mention of the Doctor, he had put his hand upon her knee. He was tense and very still, as though all his faculties had been called to attention.

"This thing you want me to do," he interrupted. "Is it . . . is it against him?"

"It is for *me*," she answered. "And you can do it very easily. You will do it, won't you, if I ask you to help me?"

He looked away from her, dejected and unhappy.

"Don't ask me, please. You mustn't ask me to do anything against him. Besides, it would be useless. He sees everything, you know."

"You needn't worry about the doctor," she urged. "He won't be there. I will see to that."

He fidgeted a moment, and then suddenly he looked at her again.

"What do you want me to do?"

"You will find a drawer in the desk," she said slowly. "It is on the right hand, the second drawer. You will open it with a key which I shall give you. Inside you will find a little lever of black ebony. I want you to press that lever down and forwards, as far as it will go, and to hold it with your hand and keep it in that position, with your thumb on the knob on the handle, till . . . till you have counted up to five thousand."

He did not seem surprised at her strange request.

"Up to five thousand," he repeated gravely. "I push the lever forward and down as far as it will go, and keep my thumb on the knob. And I mustn't take my hand away. If I took my hand away the lever would spring back, and then it would all be to do again."

He paused a moment, and again looking away from her, he added with an abrupt change of tone.

"Suppose I cannot do it. If he does not wish me to do it, he will surely prevent it."

"If you refuse to help me," said Constance steadily, "I shall be in danger. We shall all be in very great danger."

"Danger," he said. He sprang to his feet, and looked wildly away to the mountain.

"I know what you mean," he went on. "They will come down over the rocks. They will come swarming down . . . in hundreds and thousands . . . with their swords flashing and their eyes of flame. Over the rocks . . . over the rocks. Is that what you mean?"

"Yes," said Constance quietly, with compressed lips, "that is what I mean. You see now, don't you, that you must do what I ask?"

She was outraging every professional sense, playing deliberately upon his mania. But it was necessary. There was no other way to hold him.

She heard footsteps suddenly at the end of the garden path. A group was walking towards them. Mr. Clearwater heard them as soon as she did. He bent to her while they were yet some distance off.

"I'll do it," he said in a rapid undertone. "I am to press the lever forward and down, and count up to five million. Is that right?"

"Up to five thousand," said Constance in the same tone. "I will tell you later when I want you to do it."

She turned to meet the newcomers.

"Good-afternoon, Colonel," she said. "Have you been playing golf?"

"I've just been practising a bit with a putter," said Colonel Rickaby. "But that confounded fellow, Hickett, wouldn't let me go on. 'You do your job of work,' he said to me, 'or I won't be answerable for the consequences.' So I went along to give old Curtis a hand. Confound him, where is he? Curtis! Where the deuce has he got to?"

"I'm here, Colonel. I've been washing my hands," said Mr. Curtis, appearing suddenly from behind a rose tree.

"Stimson," he called over his shoulder, "be very careful with that mole. See that it doesn't get hurt at all. We aren't going to kill it yet."

He turned back to Constance.

"It's the mole, you know," he explained.

"Dashed awful business it was," mumbled the Colonel. "Thought we should get to Australia before we'd finished. And bless my soul, if that fellow Hickett, while we were digging it out, didn't go chasing through the woods after bats."

"Bats?" said Constance.

"Bats," repeated the Colonel, "great big bats with leathery wings. He was out after 'em most of last night. Never shot a bat in my life. It isn't sporting. You can't pot 'em unless they're sitting."

A shrill sound of lamentation arose from the end of the garden, and Miss Truelow appeared, her arm round Miss Collett, who was weeping bitterly. They were closely followed by the Rev. Mark Hickett.

"Now, Miss Collett," he was saying, "there's nothing whatever to cry about."

"Oh, my dear Miss Sedgwick," she wailed. "They

271

have killed my poor little black kitten and cut his head off."

The Rev. Mark Hickett cast up his eyes.

"Out of evil comes good," he said. "Death is swallowed up in victory. . . . No. . . . I must remember not to use phrases like that. Curtis, kindly warn me if you hear me saying things of that nature."

"Certainly, sir," replied Mr. Curtis hastily.

"Stimson," he added, "please make a note of that. No phrases of that kind to be used in this house."

"We shall be all quite ready for the wedding soon," said Miss Truelow to Constance.

"Why," said Constance, "is somebody going to be married?"

"You must let me be bridesmaid," went on Miss Truelow. "I have frequently been a bridesmaid at weddings in St. George's, Hanover Square. I shall know exactly what to do. I hope you don't object."

"I . . . I don't quite understand," said Constance.

"What a shy little person it is, to be sure," said Miss Truelow. "But we are not quite blind, you know."

She wagged a roguish finger at Constance.

"You were going to keep it as a surprise," she went on. "Isn't that so? But we know all about it now, even the happy day. Why, it's to be in two days' time."

"Two days' time," said a voice thickly.

Constance started.

Mr. Deeling was standing in the path, swaying slightly.

"Two . . . days' . . . time," he repeated solemnly.

"What's this? What are *you* doing here," said the

272

Colonel.

"The man is intoxicated," observed Miss Truelow.

Mr. Deeling took no notice of the interruption.

"Two days' time," he said again. "Without benefit of clergy, as Kipling says. Fine fellow, Kipling. Fine fellow, Murchison . . . Godstone . . . whoever he is. All fine fellows . . . fine fellows."

Mr. Deeling turned in the path and lurched away in the direction from which he had come.

Chapter XIII

I

Dr. Murchison was lying on his bed, gazing at the ceiling.

It was about six o'clock in the evening, and the room was in shadow, for it faced north, and only the morning sunshine penetrated the narrow-barred window broken by the golf-ball of Colonel Rickaby, which was its sole communication with the outer air. The room was furnished with a sort of bare comfort, efficient but quite impersonal. There were two padded chairs and a table with rounded corners and legs. The walls of the room were also padded with grey felt.

He lay back breathing quietly, an acrid taste in his mouth. For the moment he could only realise his physical condition. His mind was not yet at work. Half-phrases, catchwords of the old life, from which he had so long been shut off, came and went. "The morning after the night before." But that was silly, for it was evening, six o'clock in the evening. Or was it early morning? He did not know. He had lost all count of time.

His eyes wandered over the ceiling above him. There was a discoloured patch in the plaster over his head. How often had he gazed at that patch since he had been shut up. Sometimes it appeared like some great animal, a mis-shapen elephant or a whale; sometimes like the topsail of a galleon driving before a storm; and, sometimes, merely a damp patch. It had become associated in his mind with all kinds of fantastic thoughts since that first moment when, awakening from unconsciousness, he had remembered the details of that disastrous journey from Thonon—the burst tyre, the sudden outbreak of Godstone, the scream of the chauffeur as he had rolled over the precipice, and the crackling of boughs as the unhappy man had bounced through some dry bushes to his death. After that it had been a blank. For at that moment he had, he supposed, been struck on the head.

He passed his tongue across his dry lips. He felt better to-day. His head was clear. The patch on the ceiling was a patch and nothing more. He had not often felt so well. How long had he been lying there? How many days was it since he had spoken to that woman. He had told her that he was Murchison, and she had not believed him. Obviously, she had not believed him, or he would not still be there.

And then there was that terrible day when he had seen the marks on his feet. Had Warder Jones kept his word about that letter? He did not know. He had no means of telling. No one had come in answer to it. It could not yet have reached Dr. Edwardes.

If only he had some means whereby to measure time. He had been drugged, of course, drugged on-and-off for days. He raised his arm, and, pulling back the sleeve of his pyjamas, looked at the tiny punctures in the skin where the hypodermic needle had been pressed home. He had spent his days in the realm of dreams, not the quiet fancies of a happy man, but peopled with phantoms, armed and bickering, that had fought and torn each other under the shadow of topless cliffs by the margin of a poisoned sea.

The worst of it was, of course, that Godstone had been trained as a doctor, so that he knew just the proper dose to give, just enough to keep his subject under, semi-conscious for days together, no trouble to anyone, a sack of clay, dumped on a bed in a forgotten attic.

That was all he had been. And, meanwhile, the madman was supreme in the castle. What was he doing? What unknown horrors had been perpetrated?

He sat up weakly, pressing his hands to his head. For the hundredth time he was tortured by the same thought: that madman was in control. And he himself was helpless.

How cunning Godstone had been, to all appearance sane and always charming! During that journey from London, he had revealed a breadth of view, scholarship and high courage that had won his esteem. He had talked quite openly about his madness, saying that he knew he was like that, and prayed daily to be cured. Would he, Murchison, help him? And all the time the madman had been awaiting his chance.

Then, just before Château Landry had come into sight, there had been that awful disaster.

Murchison groaned. He sank back again on the bed, and, as he did so, the door was opened and then was quietly closed.

He looked round. Yes, there he was again, his torment, in the white overall, and in his right hand the hypodermic needle with the plunger drawn back.

Murchison could not repress a shudder. It swept over him like wind over a cornfield.

"So you are awake," came the hated voice. "Are you hungry?"

"No, damn you, no," said Dr. Murchison, propping himself up on one elbow.

He tried to rise, but he felt his strength beginning to ebb. The room was swaying like a ship's cabin. He sank back a second time on the pillow. It was useless trying to resist. There was Godstone in the white overall, cool and collected, with his smile. And there was himself, lying on a touzled bed in his suit of drab pyjamas, with disordered hair, a beard on his chin and lips, for they had not shaved him since his arrival. To look at them, who would doubt which was the madman, and which the doctor. Was he really the sane man of the two? But, of course, he was. He knew quite well that he was Murchison, Murchison, M.D., who had done so well at Bart's, and had been offered this excellent job, a thousand a year and all found, a thousand a year and free of income tax.

There was a madman bending over him, rolling up his pyjama sleeve, and the needle was poised.

Murchison drew in his breath sharply as he felt the point enter beneath his skin. His eyes, which had been closed, opened and met those of Godstone, in which there lurked a trace of mockery as he pressed home the plunger.

"I have given you a stronger dose this evening," said Godstone, as he withdrew the needle. "I shall want you to keep very quiet for the next two days."

Murchison did not answer, but without another word, watched Godstone leave the room. The key turned in the lock, and the footsteps died away almost immediately in the corridor.

He lay quite still, waiting. He knew what was going to happen only too well. Just at first there would be no change. Then he would begin to feel lighter, as though his head had been pumped full of gas, and, at the same time, the walls of the room would expand and contract as though they were made of elastic. And then would come a soft murmuring, and he would begin to rise and float, and everything would disappear. And he would go on floating through darkness, streaked now and then with coloured lights—until the dreams began.

He continued to wait, with closed eyes. But nothing happened. After an appreciable time he opened them. Everything seemed normal, the patch above his head was just the same, the grey walls as solid as in his waking moments. He could even hear a bird singing somewhere outside. This was astonishing. It must be quite ten minutes since Godstone had left the room. And yet he was feeling stronger. He took his right wrist in his left hand and felt his pulse, counting the beats with great intentness. It was weak, but, as far as he could tell, it was normal. Had the drug not acted, or was he immune from the quantity he had taken? His medical training told him that was absurd. What had happened?

Then, suddenly, he heard a tapping from the direction of the window. At first, he took no notice, but continued to count his pulse beats—seven, eight, nine, ten, eleven—they corresponded with the taps on the window-pane. He looked up. Something white was touching it; and, even as he watched, there was the tapping again.

What on earth was it? He sat up and dropped his feet to the ground. Then, with a great effort, he stood upright, and walked slowly, with hands outstretched, like a child learning to walk for the first time, towards the window. Tap, tap, tap. He could now see what it was, a bit of paper folded.

But how could a piece of paper make a noise like that? With a great effort, his hands touched the sill and remained there. The sill was above his head, and he had to reach up to it. He leaned his head back as far as it would go and looked up. Yes, he was right. It was a piece of folded paper, stuck in the end of a stick. A wild hope seized him. He put up a trembling hand, and, pushing it between the bars, snatched at the paper. The stick was instantly withdrawn.

With shaking fingers he opened the note and read:

"Courage. I know who you are. I am going to

try to release you to-night. Pretend that you are under the influence of hyoscin. Destroy this.

"CONSTANCE SEDGWICK."

II

The white stone, set in the little clearing guarded by the dark firs, shone in the moonlight. There were four figures about it, busy upon its sides and surface. They held in their hands bunches of a dark green plant.

They rubbed and beat the stone till the air was heavy with the smell of bruised herbs. And then one of them began to bind a garland about the stone.

None of them spoke a word. The remaining three stood by, and watched.

Then one of the watchers drew back a little, and the other two knelt down beside the stone. There came the sound of flint on steel. A little pale blue flame fluttered for a moment.

"The spot by morning must be bare and clean. Nothing green or living must remain upon it," said one the the three who watched.

"It shall be as you say, master," said a voice.

The blue flame fluttered along the grass above the stone. The grass crackled sharply, for it was very dry. The flame ran along the ground and began to eat it up, purring like a cat.

The thin blue smoke which rose from the burning grass obscured the stone and the figure weaving a green chaplet round its white sides.

III

Constance stood at the door of her room listening. It was a little past midnight and her preparations were complete.

Following the drunken appearance of Mr. Deeling in the rose garden, she had fled blindly to her room, and there, realising the full implication of his words, she had for one terrible half-hour given way altogether.

But she had soon recovered, and, from sheer panic and a world crawling with horrors, she had suddenly passed into a period of utter calm. It was as though she had arrived at the very centre of a typhoon where all was deathly still and where a false peace and security reigned. About her on every side whirled the destroying elements, lust and cruelty and madness. But for the moment she was safe.

Presently she had risen, bathed her face and hands in cold water, and had begun to pace her room, thinking desperately, working out her plan. She did not wait to sum up coldly the *pros* and *cons* of it. If she did that her resolution might fail, and she would fall back again into despair.

She had begun at once to act.

First she had written a short note to the real Dr. Murchison. She had then left the castle, keeping an eye alternately on the windows and the meadow, for at all costs she must not be seen. She had gone straight to the shed at the foot of the castle mound in which were kept spades and other garden implements, including, she remembered, several long poles. She had reached the shed, apparently unobserved, and she had chosen one suited to her purpose. She had split the thin end, stuck the note into the cleft, and moved off again round the castle in the direction of the last green of the golf course. Just opposite it, twelve feet or so up in the wall of the oldest tower, was the room in which Dr. Murchison was confined, the room whose solitary window had been smashed by Colonel Rickaby's ball.

She had crept along in the shadow of the wall, trailing her pole like some child, as she said to herself, playing at knight errantry. Presently she had reached the window and lifting the pole tapped on it, for how long she had not known. It had seemed an eternity, and, as she tapped, holding the pole to the full extent of her arms, for it was only just long enough, she had prayed wildly that her trick with the hyoscin had passed unnoticed. Otherwise there was nothing to be done.

And then, just as she had given up hope, she had felt the end of the stick quiver, and, looking up, had seen a hand clutch it for a moment, pull the note out of the cleft and disappear. With a sigh of relief she had thrown the pole down in the long grass beneath the wall and returned to the castle.

There she had passed a curious evening. Neither Dr. Murchison nor Mr. Deeling had given any sign of life, but at the usual hour the gong had sounded for dinner and she had gone to the dining-room to find a single place laid for her, with Miss Truelow in attendance.

At any other time Constance would have felt inclined to laugh at her appearance. In addition to the severe black which she affected, Miss Truelow had put on a white apron trimmed with lace and a white cap, her resemblance to the ordinary, respectable parlour-maid grotesquely impaired by the large diamond rings which never left her fingers.

She had greeted Constance with effusion.

"Miss Collett has cooked your dinner," she had said, "and I am to have the privilege of waiting."

Constance had protested without success, and finally she had obediently sat down and made a pretense of eating, though the roof of her mouth had been dry and her pulses throbbing.

The meal had been excellent, especially the mushroom omelette, but Constance had felt she would never be able to eat such a dish again. Her wine had been poured out for her by Mr. Curtis, who had assumed evening dress for the occasion, and looked the kind of butler to be seen in amateur theatricals.

After dinner she had gone straight to her room, had made her few preparations, set her alarm clock for half-past eleven, and then deliberately taken off her frock, lain down on the bed and tried to sleep, though, of course, in vain.

It had been utterly quiet in the castle, though once or twice she had heard footsteps and whispers in the corridor outside. At half-past eleven had come the relief of action. She had stopped the alarm clock before it had begun to ring, and had then risen from her bed and put on a short skirt, with a black silk jumper. Over this she had put on her dressing-gown, into the pockets of which she had thrust a pair of low heeled brogues, which she used for golf, and an electric torch.

And now she was standing by the door in her stockinged feet, listening. There was no sound from outside. She glanced again at her wrist-watch where the moonlight struck it, for the moon was nearly at the full. Then, advancing resolutely, she turned the key and softly opened her door. She stepped through into the passage, pulling the door to behind her, but, even as she did so, there came a hoarse voice from the darkness:

"Halt, who goes there?"

She gave a little gasp of surprise.

"Is that you, Colonel?" she said. "What are you doing outside my door at this time of night?"

There was a chink of spurs in the shadows, and into the thin patch of moonlight, filtering through between the door and the jamb, stepped Colonel Rickaby. On his feet were top boots with spurs and khaki riding-breeches, into which was tucked a wide night-shirt, with open throat. He wore a woollen cap on his head and carried a drawn sword in his hand.

He drew himself up with another chink of spurs, and gave her a smart salute, his sword whistling down within a few inches of her face.

"Sorry, madam," he said, "but orders are orders. No one is to leave the castle to-night."

"But who ordered you to stand here?" said Constance in the same tone. She was thankful to be wearing her dressing-gown over her clothes, so that he could not see she was fully dressed.

"The . . . the officer commanding," said the Colonel with slight hesitation. "Sentry go, by George. I'm to march up and down here until I am relieved by that fool Hickett, who knows nothing about the job, of course; can't even remember the countersign."

Constance thought rapidly. She must at all costs get rid of this tiresome old man.

"It's very good of you, Colonel," she said. "But I am tired, and it is difficult to sleep, you know, with somebody walking up and down just outside the room."

" 'Pon my word, Madam, I never thought of that. It's these dashed confounded spurs. I'll take them off."

"It's not only the spurs," objected Constance.

"I'll take off my boots as well," said the Colonel. "I am used to hardships, Madam. When I was campaigning against the Wazi Wazi in '89 or was it '91. . . ."

And he started off on one of his interminable reminiscences.

She laid a hand on his arm.

"Colonel," she said, "I much appreciate what you are doing for me. In fact, I am most intensely grateful for your kind care."

"By George, Madam, it's most good of you to say so. It does me very great honour, I assure you,

Madam. Biggest compliment I have ever had paid to me in my life."

"Listen to me, Colonel," she said persuasively. "Orders are orders, and you are an old soldier and could not dream of neglecting them. But wouldn't it be possible for you to transfer your beat . . . "

"Guard, Madam. Not beat. I'm not a dashed awful confounded policeman."

"Wouldn't it be possible for you to transfer it, say to the ground outside my window? I should not hear you from there, and you could keep guard below just as easily. Nothing can possibly happen to me in this corridor, especially if I lock my door."

The Colonel reflected for a moment.

"Will you give me your word, Madam," he said at last, "that you will lock your door?"

Constance hesitated.

"You will pardon my insisting," went on the Colonel, "but orders are orders, you know. I would ask you, Madam, with all respect, to be good enough to lock your door and throw the key of it through the window. I am sorry to make this request, but I am sure you will understand."

"Very well, Colonel. I'll lock my door and the moment I see you down below I will throw you the key."

"In that case, Madam," said the Colonel, "I shall be most happy to meet your wishes. And I have the honour to bid you good-night."

He stepped back two paces, and turning from her chinked away down the corridor.

Constance went quickly back to her room, closed the door, locked it and went to an old chest of drawers that stood near her bed. There was a key in the bottom drawer. She pulled it out and compared it with the one which she had in her hand. Then she stood by the window waiting. A door closed somewhere and presently the Colonel appeared below in the moonlight. He had put on a short thick coat, a kind of peajacket and his drawn sword glittered in his hand.

He approached the wall beneath her window and looked up. She threw down the key of the chest of drawers into his outstretched hand.

"Good-night, Colonel," she said, and heard his gruff answer as she drew back from the window.

She wasted no more time, but unlocked her bedroom door, slipped into the corridor, relocked it again, and thrust the key into the pocket of her dressing-gown.

And now the hardest part of her task was before her. Silently, for her stockinged feet made no sound on the carpet, she moved down the corridor until she was opposite Godstone's room. Was the door locked? With infinite caution she gripped the handle. It turned slowly. Thank God, it was open.

Her mouth was tight shut, and her pulses beating as she pushed the door slowly open inch by inch until she could slip inside.

Then, bending down, she pulled one of her shoes from her pocket, and put it beside the door to prevent it closing again. She moved two paces forward and stood listening. She had only been in that room once before for a moment to get some tennis balls. But she remembered the position of the bed. It was along the wall to her left. She turned her head and looked at it. She could discern the tumbled bedclothes, white in the darkness. Everything else was in shadow. Foot by foot she crept nearer the bed. At last she could see a chair at its foot on which clothes was lying. There was a coat, hung across the back of it. She moved to it and, holding her breath, began to feel rapidly in the pockets, gazing steadily at the bed as she did so. Suddenly she gave a sigh of relief. The bed was empty.

Speed was essential now. Godstone was not there. But where then could he be?

There was nothing in the coat, and she turned to the trousers. There in the hip pocket she found what she sought, a bundle of keys which jingled slightly as she took them. She held them up in the moonlight. Yes, there were the keys she wanted. She moved swiftly to the door, picked up her shoe, closed the door, and moved away down the corridor, her heart beating fast.

She went down the staircase, pausing at the top to disconnect the electric bells, and so reached the ground floor corridor where Dr. Murchison was shut up apart from the rest.

She paused, this time outside the room of Dr. Murchison. She inserted one of the keys and turned the lock, pushing the door wide open.

"Who's that?" said a voice.

"Constance Sedgwick," she replied.

"Thank God," said the voice again.

She could see him now, lying on the bed fully dressed.

"Quick," she said. "We have no time to lose. Godstone is not in his room, and I don't know where he is. He may be here at any moment."

He rose slowly from the bed.

"I am ready," he said. "What are we going to do?"

"We are going to get away," she said. "It is the only thing. Except for you and me, there is only one other sane person in this place, and when I saw him last he was drunk."

"Drunk," he repeated mechanically.

"Yes," she said. "Mr. Deeling is drunk."

"Who is Mr. Deeling?"

"I will tell you that later," she said urgently. "Follow me now, and don't make any noise."

He turned obediently and followed her out of the room. She locked the door and touched him on the shoulder.

"Down the corridor," she said, her lips to his ear. "Keep your hand on the wall. The staircase is at the end. Wait at the foot of it."

"I am in your hands," he whispered, moving off as she directed. She noticed with concern that he could hardly stand.

Her next move was to find Mr. Deeling. As she went back along the corridor and up the stairs, she wondered what she would do if she found him incapable. Would she leave him behind? In that case he might be torn to pieces. Was it worth while trying to save him? The man was worthless, a machine thrown out of gear. And then suddenly she felt a rush of pity. Poor fellow, it was not altogether his fault. When one lived as he did, it was so easy to be thrown out of gear. But still—drunk, the final resort of a feeble mind.

She reached his door and tried the handle. It was, as she expected, locked. She tapped on the door, but there was no answer. She tapped again louder, and all the time there was a lump like ice on chest and her mouth was dry with fear. Supposing she roused others than Mr. Deeling by her knocking. Where was Godstone?

At the fifth or sixth tap there was a movement in the room. Footsteps approached the door, and she heard a quavering voice:

"Go away," it said, "go away. I will kill the first man that enters. I am armed, I tell you, heavily armed."

"Mr. Deeling," said Constance as loudly as she dared, "Mr. Deeling, open the door at once, it is I, Constance Sedgwick."

"How do I know that," replied Mr. Deeling from the other side of the door.

Constance fought down her irritation.

"Very well," she said sharply, "stay where you are."

She took a step or two to the left, loud enough to be heard by Mr. Deeling. Instantly the door began to shake.

"No, no," said the voice. "Don't go away. Don't leave me."

She heard the key turn in the lock. The door was thrust a few inches open, and Mr. Deeling's face appeared behind it. His mouth was fallen in like that of an old man. His scanty locks, of which he took such care, lay disordered on his big forehead. He was in pyjamas and a dressing-gown, and his right hand was brandishing a hair brush.

"Quick, Mr. Deeling," said Constance. "We are going to get away. I have got the keys. Don't make a sound, as you love your life. Get on your clothes. You must be ready in three minutes."

His mouth worked, his eyes seemed to be starting out of his head. But he nodded and turned away.

"Wait outside, you can't wait for me here," he said over his shoulder. "That would be most unseemly."

"I shall be back in a minute," said Constance, "and when I return you must be ready, Mr. Deeling."

She left him and moved on again, till presently she reached the corridor in which most of the patients had their rooms. She must now find Mr. Clearwater. She approached his door, and moved back the shutter of the spy hole. It was dark inside, save for a triangular patch of moonlight by the window.

She opened the door with her pass key, and stepped in softly. Mr. Clearwater was lying on his side asleep. She flashed her electric torch on him. He was smiling in his sleep, but the smile turned to an expression of fear as she touched him on the shoulder. He sprang up, his mouth open to cry out. She laid her hand upon it.

"It's all right, Mr. Clearwater, it is Miss Sedgwick," she said.

For the moment he looked at her bewildered, then

he sprang from the bed and knelt down in front of her.

"Lady," he murmured, "that you should come, that you should find me worthy."

She stretched out her hand to him.

"Now, Mr. Clearwater," she said, "I want you to put on your dressing-gown and come down with me to the study. You know what I want you to do. I will show you the desk and the drawer where the lever is kept. You will hold it down, won't you, as we arranged in the garden?"

He was looking up at her with a devoted, hopeless expression in his eyes.

"I remember," he said. "But this, dear lady, is the end. I know it. He will never allow me to do this thing. But I have promised to serve you even to death."

"Nonsense," said Constance, rebuking her own uneasy fear. "He will never know. You will just have to stay there only for a little while. You need not even turn on the light. Then, when you have counted up to five thousand, you can go straight back to bed."

Mr. Clearwater did not answer. He had risen and was now wrapping about himself a long dressing-gown of quilted silk, fantastically embroidered in green and orange. He was very proud of this dressing-gown.

When he was ready, she took him by the hand.

"Not a sound," she whispered. "We must not wake up any of the others."

He nodded, and together they moved down the corridor till they stood once more outside the door of

Mr. Deeling.

Constance tapped once and the door was instantly opened. Mr. Deeling stood there. He was dressed now in a morning coat and striped trousers. He had a silk hat in his hand and a pair of grey gloves.

Constance gazed at him in astonishment.

"Saved from the wreck," he muttered. "I can carry nothing away with me, but this is my best suit."

Constance did not answer. The clothes might be incongruous, but at least they were black and would in the darkness be invisible.

They moved, all three of them, down the corridor, Mr. Deeling walking in front, closely followed by Constance, who held Mr. Clearwater firmly by the hand like a child.

All went well till they reached the foot of the stairs when suddenly there came the sound of a scuffle in front, then a sharp cry from Mr. Deeling.

"Help," he called. "There is somebody here."

"Silence, you fool," said Constance sharply. "That is Dr. Murchison."

"Dr. Murchison," said Mr. Deeling, his voice rising almost to a scream. "This is a trap. He is going to kill us all."

"Silence, Mr. Deeling," Constance said savagely. "That is the real Dr. Murchison. You had better be silent, for if there is any killing to be done I will see that you are the first victim."

She could now just see Dr. Murchison. He was on his hands and knees, but already scrambling to his feet.

"This is Mr. Deeling," she said hurriedly. "He is rather overwrought."

"I've noticed that," said Dr. Murchison dryly.

Mr. Deeling had collapsed beside the wall and was sobbing quietly to himself.

"Listen, Mr. Deeling," said Constance. "If you make another sound we shall leave you here to perish miserably."

"No," he said, "no, I will pull myself together. Let us get away from this dreadful place."

"I am sorry," said Dr. Murchison's voice. "He tripped over me. I found I could not get to the stairs walking. I am rather weak still, and I had to crawl. You'd better leave me behind."

"Nonsense," she protested. "We'll get you out all right."

They listened a moment, but heard nothing. All, it seemed, was well.

The four of them groped their way slowly forward, Mr. Clearwater still holding her hand. He, at any rate, could be trusted, for he had not uttered a sound since he had left his room.

He and Constance were now in front. She could hear the heavy breathing of Mr. Deeling behind her. He was apparently supporting the doctor.

They reached the library door without accident, and Constance, asking the two men to wait, pushed open the great door, for it was not locked, and led Mr. Clearwater straight to the desk, flashing her torch upon it for a moment.

"Now, Mr. Clearwater," she said, "you must remain here."

She pushed him into the doctor's chair. He was trembling, she noticed, but still he said nothing. Constance fumbled with her keys and unlocked the drawers.

Yes, there it was, the little black ebony lever.

"Give me your hand, Mr. Clearwater," she said.

He obeyed, and she put it on the lever and pressed it forward.

"Hold it down, and don't take your thumb from the button for an instant," she said. "Now you can begin to count, up to five thousand, remember, and then you may go back to bed. You won't let go the lever or stop pressing the button till then, will you? Promise me."

"I promise," he said.

She turned to leave him, a seated shadow in the darkness, wrapped in his fantastic dressing-gown. Her hand was caught as she moved away, and she felt the warm pressure of his lips upon the back of it. Then she moved swiftly from the room.

"Up to five thousand," muttered Mr. Deeling. "Will it be enough?"

Two minutes later they were all three of them outside on the terrace. Constance had opened a side door near the dispensary and locked it again behind them. So far they were safe. The Colonel was marching up and down on the further side of the castle.

"We must keep in the shadow," she said, speaking for the first time above a whisper, "and we must make haste, for we have only just enough time to reach the

295

gate."

"I will do my best," said Dr. Murchison, "but I am afraid I am not very strong."

He swayed as he spoke. She caught him by the arm. He leant heavily on her, and they stumbled off, preceded by the grotesque figure of Mr. Deeling in his silk hat and his flapping coat.

They passed down the stone stairs leading to the meadow, and paused again in the shadow of the castle. Where, she wondered, was Godstone.

"Come on, come on," said Mr. Deeling in a frenzy of excitement. "Don't stand waiting there."

Constance explained rapidly as they moved forward what Mr. Clearwater was doing.

"Let's hope he is counting slowly," said Dr. Murchison. "Couldn't you have tied the lever down. Then Clearwater would not have been necessary."

"No," replied Constance. "That was impossible. There's a button on it which has to be pressed right in with the thumb. Otherwise contact isn't established. It's a patent idea of Dr. Edwardes. The gate can only remain open as long as the thumb presses the spring. And you've got to press pretty hard."

"I see," said Murchison shortly.

They stumbled on again, keeping to the edge of the wood. They had to pause twice on the way, owing to the weakness of the doctor.

"2,777, 2,778, 2,779," muttered Mr. Deeling. "How fast do you think he is counting?"

They had barely a half-a-mile to go in all, but it was impossible to move at more than a slow walk. The doctor's breath came in gasps, he seemed on the edge of fainting.

"Fool," thought Constance, "fool, why didn't I bring some brandy."

"Mr. Deeling," she called, "have you any brandy with you?"

"3,267, 3,268, 3,269," said Mr. Deeling.

"Quick," he added, "but not through the wood, I won't go near the wood. It's hell in there."

"You must have had a pleasant time with that fellow," gasped Dr. Murchison, as they stumbled on again.

The going became more difficult, for they were now in the part of the meadow which had not been cut. The hay was tall, coming above their waists. The doctor fell three times. At the third fall, he lay still, making no effort to rise.

"3,725, 3,726, 3,728," mumbled Mr. Deeling.

"Go on," said the doctor, "go on and leave me."

Constance shook her head. Bending down she put her hand on his shoulders and dragged him to his feet.

"No," she said, "come, Mr. Deeling, give me a hand. The gate is in sight. Give me a hand, Mr. Deeling."

But Mr. Deeling at the prospect of freedom lost all control.

"The gate is open," he screamed, "it is open. We are saved . . . saved."

He broke into a shambling run, Constance and the doctor following as best they could, but he rapidly outdistanced them. There was the gate white and tall, shining in the moonlight. It was like the fence, a steel frame covered with a fine wrought mesh.

It was, as Mr. Deeling had shouted, wide open and the white road ran through it down the valley to freedom.

They stumbled on to the road. Constance was by this time half carrying her almost unconscious companion. Mr. Deeling had outstripped them by thirty yards.

"Saved," he shouted again, as he ran towards the gate.

He was within five yards of it when it began to move. Inexorably it swung forward, as they gazed towards it.

There was a click. The gate shut fast, just as Mr. Deeling, running fast, flung himself frantically against it.

Chapter XIV

I

The doctor sank to the ground, while Constance stared over his head at the gate, which only a moment before had opened the way to freedom. She scarcely yet realised what had happened.

Mr. Deeling did not cry out. He was fingering the gate, as a sick man fingers the counterpane, touching it here and there along one of the sides where it fitted closely into the steel post.

"We have made a mistake," he muttered. "It was to open at 5,000, and not to close . . . 4,927, 4,928, 4,929. . . ."

His silk hat stood well on the back of his head, and a large amount of white cuff showed upon his wrists.

"Stop that counting, for God's sake," said Constance.

The sound of the dry husky voice was maddening. He took no notice.

"Help me with Dr. Murchison," she begged.

"4,998, 4,999, 5,000," he concluded with a shout.

He stepped back and threw his arms wide. The gate

was still shut.

"It is jambed," he muttered, and he began to finger it again.

"It's no good, Mr. Deeling," said Constance, who had by this time succeeded in helping the doctor to the side of the road and was propping him against a tussock of rough grass.

"We must have counted wrong," said Mr. Deeling. "We have only to count up to five thousand and the gate will open. We must start again. One—two—three—four—five—six . . . "

"His brain has gone," said Constance to herself.

She said it mechanically, for she was past emotion now. She had made her effort, and she had failed. It was all to do again. She felt suddenly a great weariness, and she hardly noticed at first the shadowy figure which leapt suddenly from a thicket near to the fence, or that other which followed a few paces behind. The first figure, carrying something in its hand, a stick or a club, rushed forward, uttering a bestial cry. It flung up its club, and, as it did so, Constance saw that it was Mr. Curtis. His face was white, the lips drawn back exposing the teeth in a snarl.

He paused a moment, gazing with indecision first at Mr. Deeling, who stood beside the gate still counting monotonously, then at Murchison, who had risen to his knees and was swaying slightly.

The next moment, before Constance could move or realise what was happening, Mr. Curtis was rushing towards her. He pushed her roughly aside, so that she almost fell, and brought his club down on the head of the doctor. Murchison dropped without a sound, and Mr. Curtis raised the club again.

But the second figure by now had drawn level with him. It seized him by the throat.

"You fool," said the voice of the Rev. Mark Hickett, "you triple fool. Have you forgotten what he said to us. There is to be no more killing. You will have to answer for this."

Mr. Curtis lowered his club and gazed bewildered, first at his companion, who had thrown back the dark cloak that covered him and was looking him full in the face, and then at Constance, who was kneeling beside the doctor, trying to stay the flow of blood from his head.

"307, 308, 309," said Mr. Deeling.

"What shall I do?" moaned Mr. Curtis. "He will never forgive me. He will drive me away. I shall be shut out. What shall I do? What shall I do?"

Mr. Hickett gazed at him compassionately.

"I will help you," he said.

"They'll find the body if it lies there," said Mr. Curtis, "and he will want to know who did it."

"Come," said the Rev. Mark Hickett. "Do exactly as I tell you."

Mr. Curtis rose from his knees, and together they approached Constance, who was still bending over the doctor. The Rev. Mark Hickett laid a hand on her shoulder and pulled her back roughly, so that she staggered and fell.

"Take his legs," he said to Mr. Curtis, and, bending down, he seized the doctor by the shoulders. Together they lifted him.

"Into the bushes," said the Rev. Mark Hickett.

They stumbled over the grass for a few yards, and, swinging the helpless form between them, let it go. Turning in the air, it fell head downwards in the rough scrub.

"No one will see him there," said the Rev. Mark Hickett.

"No one will see him there," echoed Mr. Curtis.

They turned and came back to Constance. She had risen and now stood facing them. This was the end of the tether, but she would make one more effort.

"What do you mean by wandering about the grounds at this time of night?" she said sternly. "You know perfectly well you ought to be in your rooms, both of you. Go back to the castle at once."

Mr. Curtis gazed at her sheepishly. The Rev. Mark Hickett, however, taking no notice of her words, produced a dark blue silk handkerchief, which he handed to Mr. Curtis.

"Tie her hands," he said, "and see that she doesn't get away. I will be back in a moment."

Mr. Curtis approached her, seized her wrists with sudden violence, so that she bit her lips to prevent herself from crying out, twisted them behind her back and tied them together with the handkerchief. She fell against him as he completed his task; the world began to spin; she realised that she was on the edge of fainting.

There was a creak of wheels. Was it, by some miracle, a trap or cart coming up to the gate? But the hand of Mr. Curtis was on her shoulder, and there on the road beside her was a light handcart, a mere flat board on two wheels. The Rev. Mark Hickett had taken it from a little shed that stood by the lodge.

"That will do," he said.

She felt herself lifted and laid upon it, flat, so that her bound hands pressed into her back.

"810, 811, 812," said Mr. Deeling, but his voice broke off abruptly.

"You must come too, Mr. Deeling."

It was the voice of the Rev. Mark Hickett.

"And you shall push the cart—," it continued.

Constance turned her head. She could just see the two of them. Mr. Deeling had left the gate and was coming towards the cart. His lips still moved. He adjusted his top hat, and obediently laid hold of the handle and started to push. The Rev. Mark Hickett went in front and Mr. Curtis brought up the rear, and in this order they moved slowly down the road. There was no sound except their feet shuffling in the dust, the creak of the wheels and the voice of Mr. Deeling:

"850, 851, 852."

By the time they arrived at the castle he had reached 3,500.

At the castle they halted. She was taken off the cart, pushed up the steps and taken straight through the main door into the hall.

The door of the library was open, and they forced her to enter.

"He has gone," said Mr. Curtis. "I thought he would still be here."

"I will go and fetch him," said the Rev. Mark Hickett. "Untie her hands. He will not like to see them bound."

Fingers were picking at the handkerchief behind her back, and a moment later she was free.

Then, in the moonlight, she saw a figure bending over the desk. It was clad in a fantastic dressing-gown, gold and green, and it was very still. She approached it, as yet hardly knowing what she expected to find, but drawn to it irresistibly.

She laid a hand on its shoulder, and the head of Mr. Clearwater fell back. The eyes were open and the face was very white. His rigid hand was shut tight upon his chest, where there was a large irregular stain.

"He's dead," she thought. "They've murdered him. He kept his promise."

And suddenly she felt the tears, the first she had shed since she came to Château Landry, raining down her cheeks.

The head rolled heavily in the crook of her arm. Then, as she watched, the eyelids fluttered a moment, the lips moved. She bent down.

". . . cars drawn by rainbow-winged steeds
Which trample the dim winds . . ."

His voice died away, but the lips still moved. Constance bent lower.

"And yet I see no shapes but the keen stars," whispered Mr. Clearwater, and so died.

Someone was counting—1,008, 1009, 1010. Why
were they counting? Couldn't they go away and leave
her in peace. And the wood was thick, too thick . . .
and dark. Impenetrable, that was what it was, impenetrable. But she had to penetrate it. And that man
was dragging on her and holding her down. What a
fool he was. If he wanted her to help him, why did he
hold on to her like that? She tried to tell him to put his
hands on her shoulders, but he would not understand.

"On my shoulders," she kept repeating, "on my
shoulders," but he would not, and still he clung
obstinately round her knees. She could not move a
step. She struggled desperately. She turned round to
tell him to let go. Then she saw that it was not Dr.
Murchison. It was a green thing—all arms, with a
great eye dead like the eye of a fish, that looked at her
unblinkingly. Under the eye was a mouth with foam
round it. She shrieked and found that she was awake.

Her head was throbbing. Where was she? Her lips
were dry and sticky; the back of her neck ached as
though she had been struck. She was lying on the bed
in a nightdress and dressing-gown.

The events of the night began to come back to her,
slowly at first, disjointedly in a series of pictures: the
dark corridor and herself tapping at Mr. Deeling's
door, his grotesque appearance in top hat and frock
coat, Dr. Murchison's collapse in the meadow, the
moonlight on the road, Mr. Deeling's counting, his
black figure against the gate, the bleeding form of the
doctor as Mr. Curtis stood over him, the creaking two-
wheeled cart. But these visions quickly gave way to

one more terrible, more cruel than all the rest—the crumpled form of Mr. Clearwater in his embroidered dressing-gown, dead at the desk where she had placed him. There was the real horror.

In her agony of mind she jumped from her bed and began walking up and down the room. She had killed Mr. Clearwater just as surely as if she had struck him down herself. She had put him there. She had given him his instructions, and had made light of his strange foreboding.

"To the death," he had said, and he had kept his word.

For the first time the full meaning of all that had happened during the last twenty-four hours rose up and confronted her. She was appalled by her responsibility, for everything lay at her door. She had come to that place as a doctor, professing an interest in mental cases, and yet she had been unable to discover that the Château had been in charge of a madman for weeks! She had even rejected the evidence of the real doctor till it was too late. She had allowed herself to be fooled and fascinated like any schoolgirl. And these were the consequences, two patients murdered, one sacrificed to the awful delusion of the lunatic she had failed to detect, the other dying as a direct consequence of her own act. And the real doctor, he was dead too. She felt sure of it, struck down and tossed into the bushes. "They will never see him there"—that was what Mr. Curtis had said. He would be lying there now, a sightless corpse, while the great mountain buzzards swept with beating pinions above him, and swooped and fought and tore.

She shuddered from head to foot, and, pausing in her aimless pacing, looked round her with a start. She had not yet even begun to wonder where she was. But this was not her own room, these grey padded walls, this single window closely barred, the bed clamped to the floor with no sheets on it nor coverings of any kind. That did not matter. She had nothing on but her nightdress and dressing-gown, but it was hot enough. Heavens, how hot it was! And wasn't that thunder she had heard! It came again, that distant rumble. The heat was about to break at last, perhaps!

She realised now where she was. This was the room of Dr. Murchison, the real Dr. Murchison, where he had been confined as Godstone for weeks. She went to the door and turned the handle. As she thought, it was locked. She was alone, utterly alone now. Dr. Murchison was dead, and Mr. Deeling's mind had given way. Perhaps he was dead, too. She was alone, with the knowledge of what was in store for her. "In two days the ceremony will take place," Miss Truelow had said. It was now the evening of the second day.

She glanced at the window. The evening sun was striking a tall pillar of rock, thrust up at the sky, the only thing that she could see, for the window was high.

She leaned back wearily against the door, her hands outspread. This, then, was the end. She was beaten. There was nothing more that she could do. Why had she not shared the fate of Dr. Murchison or Mr. Clearwater? Why was she not already dead? Death at any rate was oblivion, rest, a release from the fantastic horrors in which she lived.

She drew herself up and walked firmly to the chair. She put her hand out, and then paused. There was nothing on the chair, her clothes were not lying there, and with them had gone the little phial which she had taken from the medicine cupboard on the day she had poured away the hyoscin.

Then she realised why she had been put in that particular room, the room reserved for dangerous patients. She was not to be allowed to die. That way out, also, was barred.

She fell on her knees by the bed.

"God," she whispered, "God, can you hear me? You know what is going to happen. You see me where I am. I am alone and without defence. But you will not suffer this thing to come to pass."

She stopped abruptly on the last phrase. Why did one always address God in archaic language as though he could not understand modern speech? She was praying from the heart, and yet it sounded unreal. It was simply that she could not, after the first few words, pray anyhow else.

But she had prayed, as blindly and as sincerely as any soul had ever prayed to God. Would she be answered, or was it true that the Devil was master and that he would that night enjoy his victory?

She rose from her knees, and, as she did so, she heard thunder again, nearer this time, and a moment later came the sharp swish of rain. The weather had broken then, and the parched earth would drink in the flood and soak it up and become green again.

She was thirsty, too. Heavens, how thirsty she was. Her mouth was dry. She looked round the room.

There was something standing in the corner that she had not noticed before. She walked across to it. It was an enamel mug full of water. She seized it and drank it off without taking it from her lips. That was better, much better. She pulled her dressing-gown round her, and sat on the edge of the bed.

The rain was pouring down, but already it was less, and soon it dwindled to a light pattering, and then ceased altogether.

It was only a sharp shower, not nearly enough. Something much heavier than that was needed.

Why had the cup held so little? She was still thirsty—thirsty and sleepy, very sleepy. And still it was so hot.

She slipped sideways and lay, half on the bed, half on the floor, breathing heavily.

III

It was dark when she awoke. The night was very still outside. There was a patch of moonlight on the floor, and through the bars she could see three stars, immeasurably remote.

She got to her feet, very stiff, and almost helpless with cramp. A distant drumming beat on her ears, monotonous, rythmical. When had she heard it before?

She turned towards the window. As she did so, there came a knock on the door, and the sound of a key turning in the lock.

Miss Truelow was waiting at the foot of the steps leading down to the meadow. It lacked three-quarters of an hour to midnight. The full moon, which had risen early, was riding high, and the raindrops on the grass sparkled in its light. The sky was still not quite clear. Heavy patches of cloud were drifting slowly across it, caught every now and then upon the peaks of the mountains. The air was hot and steamy, almost tropical, and far away the thunder sulked and rumbled. The evening storm had brought no relief.

Miss Truelow was dressed in a robe of green and yellow velvet. Her thin arms were bare and loaded with jewels, bracelets of paste, torques of imitation gold. On her head was a paste tiara, perched on her greying hair.

She was tired, but in her excitement she was hardly aware of it.

For the last two days she had been constantly busy under the direction of the Master. She had swept and cleaned the white stone and bound about it a garland of vervain, and there had been other things—the making of candles from fat, set in two candlesticks of black wood shaped like crescents.

The Rev. Mark Hickett had been most active in all these preparations. He had helped her with the candles, and with the mingling of various spices which the Master had prescribed—incense and camphor and aloes. These she had placed in a copper bowl, and Mr. Curtis, taking the bowl, had returned presently and handed it back to her full of other things, which he had mixed with the spices. She did not know what they were, but the mixture was dark and sticky and pungent. The bowl was beside her now, on the steps, and she was to take it with her to the ceremony. She did not know its purpose, but that was no matter, for everything would be explained. The Master had told her that she had merely to be patient, to watch and on no account to cry out.

There would not be many at the ceremony, for some had proved unworthy. That poor silly Mr. Clearwater, for instance, had been killed—killed for disobedience. Miss Truelow shuddered. She might herself have disobeyed, for she did not like being ordered about by the Rev. Mark Hickett. But she, thank goodness, had been wise enough to realise that the orders of the Master must be carried out to the letter. They were all part of the great plan.

The Colonel, too, was in disgrace. He had been ordered to keep watch over the door of the bride, and he had deserted his post. The Master had been very angry with him, and had forbidden him to be present that night. Well, it would serve him right. She wished him no harm, but men were so careless. It did them good to be taught a lesson sometimes.

There was a sound of footsteps. She raised her head. At last they were coming. She moved a few steps to the left, rustling in her flamboyant dress, while the moonbeams gleamed upon her jewellery. She picked up the copper bowl and held it to her breast as they came down the steps towards her.

First walked the Master, very noble in his black

sleeveless robe, with the leaden cap on his head emblazoned with strange signs. In his right hand he carried a sword, bright and sharp and gleaming in the moonlight. In his left hand was a forked stick of hazelwood. He reached the meadow and moved steadily on towards the belt of firs. Behind him was Mr. Curtis and the Rev. Mark Hickett, bearing the bride on a litter between them. They, too, were in black, with dark cloaks of the form and pattern prescribed, which she and Miss Collett had cut out and made for them.

The girl was in white as a bride should be. There was a wreath on her head, which Miss Collett had been asked to make. It was unfair to ask Miss Collett. As bridesmaid she herself should have been allowed to make the bridal wreath. The wreath was not of orange blossom but of vervain, for so the Master had decided.

Miss Collett herself followed. She, too, carried a bowl, and a branch of birch tree, together with four iron nails.

Miss Truelow fell in beside her. The bride was very still, lying inanimate on the litter, her head hanging over the back of it. Her face was white, and her mouth moved now and again when she uttered a kind of moan.

Constance did not come to herself till they were entering the wood. Up to that moment she had lived in a mist, incapable of movement, but seeing in a blur everything that went on around her, like a man sitting at a window who looks out into the cold world from a warm room.

First her door had been opened. Mr. Curtis and the Rev. Mark Hickett had come straight inside and seized her by the arms. Then Godstone had arrived, and she had felt a prick in her arm. After that she had been lifted and carried out. And now here she was, numb in every limb, though she was not insensible, merely impotent.

Her mind would not work properly. Everything was remote and nothing seemed to matter. She remembered vaguely what was going to happen, but it seemed now of little consequence.

That was the moon up there, sailing high above the valley. How queer were the shadows of the fir trees on the grass. They were in the wood now. It was very dark in there, and impenetrable as it had been in her dream. How much further would they carry her? The path was long, and she would never be able to find her way back to the castle. She would have to tell Dr. Murchison about this in the morning. For it was all most unusual, and she ought to make an effort, she supposed, to stop it. But that was impossible, for she had no power to move or even to think. That idea of telling Dr. Murchison, for example. It was merely silly, for Dr. Murchison was Godstone, and Godstone was the lunatic.

They had reached the clearing now. Yes, there it was, bright in the moonlight. And the stone, the queer stone that she had seen on her walks, in the brightest spot of all. The stone was garlanded like her own head. How had her own head come to be like that?

What had happened?

She felt herself lowered to the ground, and she was propped against a tree, half sitting, half lying.

What were they doing? What curious clothes Miss Truelow wore. They were getting to their places now. Godstone was tracing a circle about the stone with a sword in his hand and a forked stick. The others were helping. They all had bare feet, and the clearing itself was bare.

Miss Collett and Miss Truelow were kneeling together in a little circle within the large one, and the two men were helping Godstone. It was all very childish. Faust and Mephistopheles, Paracelsus and all that quaint mediæval nonsense which no sane person believed in now. But these people were not sane. They really expected the devil to appear. How disappointed they would be when nothing happened.

Godstone was drawing a triangle, a great triangle within the circle. In the centre of the triangle was the white stone, and at the apex Mr. Curtis placed a brazier which the Rev. Mark Hickett kindled with flint and steel. A thick bluish white smoke rose, and an acrid smell of spices filled the air.

Her mind was growing clearer and her limbs were beginning to feel warm. She could smell the smoke quite strongly, but she did not yet feel that she could move.

What was Godstone doing now? He was laying strips within the circle, strips of what looked like parchment, and now and then he hammered something into the ground to keep the parchment down. Mr. Curtis was setting things in place outside the circle opposite the points where Godstone had nailed the parchment. She could not see what they were—four dark objects. One looked like the horns of a goat.

Godstone had signed to his two assistants. One of them was tendering him a bowl. He had taken a little branch of wood from Miss Collett and was sprinkling the ground all about them. The drops fell dark in the moonlight. Again there came the sound of flint on steel, followed by the crackling of wood. The Rev. Mark Hickett had kindled another fire on the bare ground, in another angle of the triangle. Then he and Mr. Curtis moved to one side, and, drawing a circle about themselves, knelt down.

Meanwhile, Godstone was tracing strange signs on the ground. But presently he stopped, and, turning, faced the stone a little distance off, so that his back was now towards her. For the third time she heard the rasp of flint on steel, and she saw him bend to left and right and light two candles standing on the ground beside him in queer crescent-shaped holders. Their thin spear-points of flame pointed straight upwards, for it was deathly still, and there was no wind. The smoke from the brazier and from the fire bellied upwards in thick coils. There was dead silence. No one moved. What curious clothes Miss Truelow was wearing.

Godstone was standing with bowed head, like a great black bird drooping on a perch. Suddenly he raised his arms and called out with a loud voice. The others in the circle shivered, the two women drew closer together. Again he cried out something that Constance could not understand, and then a third time. What was that he was shouting?

"Ai saraye! ai saraye!"

But she knew those words. She had known them somewhere before? Yes, they were written in that dreadful book which she had read in the library that night when he had found her there alone. They were the cries of the sorcerers at the Sabbath. She shuddered violently and looked round bewildered.

She remembered everything now, remembered, not in the distant fashion of a moment before, but in a way that made everything imminent and real. This was the ceremony from which she had somehow to escape, which she had prayed to God might never come to pass. And God must have heard that prayer. He could not allow this thing to happen. For now she was able to move. In a few moments she would be strong enough to run away, to fly anywhere, anywhere from the horror that was closing in upon her.

Again the madman shouted. He was speaking now an unknown tongue. What was it, Greek, Hebrew, Latin? Words poured from his lips. Some she could understand.

The demons of the heaven of Gad. . . . By Gibor. . . . Come, come, come."

There was a moment of silence. The figure by the stone had dropped its hands, the smoke bellied up more thickly, the air was pungent with the scent of spices. Then it raised its arms once more.

"Come," it shouted again, and the voice rang through the forest. *"I command thee by the key of Solomon and the Great Name."*

She was leaning now against the rough trunk of the

316

fir tree. Still she could not fly. She was not yet strong enough to rise, and at his shout there had come a change. The moonlight was vanishing. It was growing darker. No longer could she see the tops of the fir trees against the sky. The stars were going out one by one. The face of the sky was withdrawn. It was too dark now to discern even the column of smoke. All that she could see was the crackling fire, and the dim form crouching beside it.

The darkness was coming down. But that was only a coincidence. . . . Or was it something more?

The madman made a slight gesture, and two dark shadows leapt to their feet and came towards her. She felt a hand on either arm, hot breath upon her cheek.

"*He is here*," said a voice, exultant and ringing proudly.

She knew now that her hour had come, and she awoke at last to action. She wrenched her arms and fought madly, but she was helpless in the grip of these creatures. They seized her, lifted her aloft to the full stretch of their arms, as though she had been a child, and moved with her towards the circle and the white stone. Godstone stood there, his hands outstretched, his eyes gleaming in the light of the brazier.

"He has come," he shouted. "He has entered me. Your Lord, your Master, the Prince of Evil is here. I am filled with the life of hell. I am lord of the depths of the sea. I am the mighty and the strong."

He flung wide his arms again.

"The moon is covered," he said. "Her light is put out."

A strangled cry burst from her lips. She was carried

317

nearer to the stone, jerked to and fro.

"God, God," she said, "kill me now. Do not let me live."

She was already close, and moving ever closer, to the stone. A skull daubed with blood grinned at her from near the brazier. And there was the head of a black cat, the lips twisted back from the white pointed teeth. She touched something hard. That was the stone, the stone of sacrifice. He was waiting beside it, and had turned towards her. His hands were outstretched. His body gleamed white between the folds of his dark robe. His face was working, and blasphemies poured from his lips. He reached towards her, and a hand gripped the top of her gown and tore it. The face was nearer now, bending over her, working. There was foam on the lips.

No, not foam. It was a still quiet face, a face full of pity and concern, the face of an elderly man with a short grey moustache and spectacles. What was this?

They had stopped holding her. She was free. She moved an arm. What was all that noise, those footsteps and the cries?

Over the shoulder of the unknown man bending over her she saw dark figures running. They were dressed in some kind of uniform. The tops of the fir trees were visible again, and the moon was sailing serene in a star-sown sky. That darkness from which she had just broken clear had been only a cloud. That was all, a cloud which had blown for a moment across the moon. All was clear again.

But no, the cloud was again creeping up the sky. It must be stopped, it must not move like that, or there would be darkness a second time. . . .

"She has fainted," said Dr. Edwardes. "Carry her at once to the castle. I will come to you as soon as I can."

V

He was running desperately, flying rather, borne up on the sable wings which streamed from his shoulders. And behind him were men in pursuit. Fools, to think he could be caught like any common fugitive. The Master would help him, the Master who had answered his call and who had for one glorious moment possessed himself of his body.

Godstone paused on the edge of the belt of firs. Above him clear in the moonlight towered the rocks. Noises below him in the wood showed where his pursuers were at hand. He listened for a moment, then turned his face to the mountain and began to climb, sometimes on hands and knees, with catlike agility.

"*Mon dieu*, there he goes, Etienne," said a voice from the edge of the wood.

Two men in dark uniforms paused and gazed upwards. They shouted, but Godstone did not even turn to look at them.

It was not much further now, only another hundred feet or so. There at last was the summit, clean and bare. There he would stand and the Master would come to him again. They would fly together over the world, borne on black pinions.

His breath came in gasps, his hands were torn and bleeding. Twice he stumbled, but yard by yard he fought his way upwards. Now at last he was on the top. He stood on a ledge of rock just below the highest pinnacle. Underneath him was the forest, and at his feet a precipice that dropped sheer towards the valley.

The watchers stopped in their scrambling pursuit and gazed. They saw a figure with arms flung wide in a sable cloak. A voice came down to them, faintly through the clear mountain air:

"Into your arms, Master. You shall bear me up."

He leaped forward into the empty air, and fell like a stone, his great cloak streaming behind him.

Chapter XV

I

"Yes, Sir," Warder Jones was saying, "jumped clean off the rock 'e did. Just like as if 'e was some big bird that was going to fly. I've sent the men we brought along from Annecy to recover the body. But it'll take 'em some time to find it."

Dr. Edwardes was sitting at his desk—the desk from which he had ruled Château Landry for the better part of a lifetime. Warder Jones was standing at his elbow.

"Very good, Jones," said Dr. Edwardes wearily. "Tell them to let me know as soon as they have found it."

"Yes, sir," said the Warder, turning on his heel.

He paused a moment.

"Begging your pardon, sir," he said. "About the doctor."

"The doctor?"

"Dr. Murchison, sir."

321

"He will recover, Jones."

"Lucky we found 'im, sir."

"Lucky indeed."

"If I 'adn't noticed that them bushes were a bit disordered."

"Yes, Jones."

But still the Warder lingered.

"Well, Jones, what is it?"

The Warder seemed to be swallowing something hard. Then suddenly he moved clumsily towards the doctor in his chair.

"Excuse me, Doctor, but I should like to say as 'ow I . . . as 'ow . . . well, it's a matter o' fifteen years as I've been 'ere, and I know as 'ow you're feeling it, Doctor . . . and . . . well, that's what I wanted to say."

The old man at the table put his hand on the Warder's arm.

"Thank you, Jones," he said.

"Are the patients all quiet?" he added after a pause.

"Yes, sir. All except Curtis, who 'ad another fit when we took the jacket off 'im. 'E's running round now trying to murder Stimson, saying as 'ow it's all Stimson's fault that we broke up that party in the clearing. Miss Truelow is back again in her black, and behavin' like a perfect lady, and Miss Collett is inquiring after a rubber ball what she lost previous to what 'appened. The Colonel is quite 'is old self—polishing 'is braces as he allus does on the thirteenth of the month and the Rev. 'Ickett is saying 'is prayers most of the time. 'E did want to tell me of a bad dream as 'e had 'ad, but I 'adn't time, and 'e was asking me whether I'd seen a cross what used to 'ang in 'is room and telling me as 'ow 'e'd lost 'is bible. He seemed terribly upset about it, so I got him a bible out of the chapel, and 'e was pacified."

Warder Jones now stood stolidly at attention beside the doctor's chair.

"Anything else, doctor?" he added.

"Nothing to-night, Jones."

"Thank you, sir. Good-night, sir."

"Good-night."

Dr. Edwardes was alone. He looked at his watch. Two o'clock in the morning. This, he knew, was the end. To-morrow the patients would be removed to the asylum at Annecy. There would be official inquiries, a sensation in the press. Thank God, he had arrived in time—only just in time. But Château Landry was finished. Perhaps that was just as well. He was getting old. And there were all those files to study and put in order—the big book to be completed, the results of a lifetime.

His work at Château Landry was closing in failure, but he would pass on the fruits of his experience to the new men. There was that young Murchison, for example, of whom Freud himself had spoken so highly. The work would go on. He must edit his notes and diaries, publish them for the benefit of those who would follow him in the task.

There was a rustle beside him and he looked up. Constance was standing in front of him.

"My dear young lady," said Dr. Edwardes, springing to his feet. "What on earth are you doing here?

You must go back to bed at once."

She put her hand out with a gesture of refusal. She was, he noted, fully dressed.

"For pity's sake, Doctor," she said, "tell me what happened."

"Another time," he said, "another time."

"Can't you understand," she burst out, "I must know at once. I shall go mad if I don't know what happened after . . . after I fainted."

Dr. Edwardes moved towards her and laid a hand on her shoulder.

"Nothing happened," he said. "Go back and try to get some rest. You have had a terrible experience, but it's all over now, and you will be none the worse for it in a week from now. I will give you a sleeping draught."

She shook her head. "No more drugs, Doctor," she said. "Godstone has drugged me once already to-night. Please tell me everything."

"Very well," he said, "but you must be quiet."

Mechanically the doctor tore off the back leaves from the big calendar on his desk.

He pointed to a chair. She sat down obediently.

"My arrival is easily explained," he said. "Warder Jones came straight to me when he was sent away. I was not very far off, you know, only at Aix-les-Bains. He told me the circumstances of his dismissal. He also told me how the man confined as Godstone had claimed to be Murchison, and of the crosses that had appeared on his feet since his arrival. As soon as I had heard his story I came straight back, and I arranged with the head of the asylum at Annecy to lend me some of his men. We came here in a car, and we scaled the fence with ladders brought from the village.

"We were only just in time."

"And . . . and where are they all now?" said Constance.

"The patients are in their rooms," replied Dr. Edwardes. "Now that Godstone's influence is removed they will soon be normal again, even Curtis, though at present he is having a bad attack."

"And Godstone?"

"He escaped towards the mountains behind the clearing and flung himself from a high rock. They are looking for the body."

Constance listened. Her head ached abominably, and there had been something urgent she had wanted to say. It came back to her suddenly.

"Doctor," she said, "there's something I meant to tell you. You must send at once to the gate and search the bushes on the side of the road. Dr. Murchison. . . ."

Dr. Edwardes interrupted her.

"Dr. Murchison has been found. He was unconscious, but he will recover. It was a heavy blow, but he was only stunned."

It was the first good news she had heard, and she felt suddenly very weak, almost to tears.

At that moment there came a tap at the door.

"Come in," said Dr. Edwardes.

It was Mr. Deeling.

He was wearing the clothes in which Constance had seen him first, the black suit with the striped trousers carefully creased. His hair was neat again, his manner precise and formal. He stood at the door for a moment in surprise.

"Excuse me, Doctor," he said. "But I saw a light in this room, and in view of the fact that it is past two a.m. I thought it well to ascertain. . . ."

He broke off suddenly. He was staring at the big calendar on the desk.

"August 11th," he said. "There must be some mistake."

"No, Mr. Deeling. Yesterday was the 10th."

Mr. Deeling passed a hand over his forehead.

"Loss of memory," said the doctor aside to Constance. "The days since your arrival here are a complete blank."

But Mr. Deeling was still staring at the calendar.

"Dear me," he said. "I must have forgotten how to count."

"Thank God," said Constance under her breath, and fell to laughing weakly in her chair.

II

Pierre and Germaine were walking slowly up the road leading from the village. It was an autumn afternoon in late October. Soon the snow would fall on the mountains, but meanwhile it was warm and mild.

They walked in silent content. Below them, as they slowly mounted the narrow road, already showing signs of neglect, stretched the green valley and the rooftops of the little village. A thin haze of smoke was hanging blue in the quiet air.

They paused at the last bend of the road. Before them stretched a steel fence broken by a gate of the same material, propped open by a stone. Just beyond stood a little lodge, its white paint dilapidated, its door discoloured.

The road wound on through the fence, across the green upland meadow to where the castle stood half a mile away on its mound. For a moment in the rays of the setting sun the grey walls were tinted with rose and the windows were touched with fire. Then the sun sank for another day behind the barrier of rock beyond, the windows of the castle became blank, and it lay heavy upon the ground, like a great head with sightless eyes.

The two at the gate stood silent in the fading light, looking up the road, already covered here and there with growing weeds; and, then, moved by a common impulse, they turned towards each other, and Pierre took Germaine in his arms and kissed her.

"We shall be in the great Paris in two months from now," he said. "There will be no more of this," and he made a vague gesture.

The girl looked doubtfully towards the castle.

"Would it not still be better to take service with the rich American who is coming to live at the Château?"

Pierre shook his head violently.

"No," he replied, "you will never see me there."

"But consider the wages."

"No," he repeated. "We must leave all this. For you and me, it is the new life we shall begin. We will go to the great town where there is laughter and happiness and people in the streets."

Germaine drew a little apart from him. She rubbed one of the steel gateposts with her finger.

"Look," she said. "Already it begins to be rusty."

"Let it rust," he said. "Come, sweetheart."

He drew her again into his arms.

When, a little later, they turned to go down the hill, the castle behind them was a shadow among the gathering shadows of the night.

Epilogue

Grand Hotel des Libellules,
Monte Carlo,
December, 1926.

Dearest Helen,

Monte is a perfect dream. I never saw such flowers. You know they actually uproot any dead or dying plants in the public gardens over night and put fresh ones in. John says that they comb the grass and dust the leaves every morning with a feather broom.

John has had three goes at the tables, and has so far been lucky. I have had three new frocks, the evening one a perfect duck (a page of details is here omitted), and two hats (two irrelevant paragraphs are again omitted), and John has still got a thousand francs over. So you see what a lovely place it is.

A funny thing happened yesterday. We were walking on the terrace, and John was using strong language about the pigeon shooting, which is really rather horrible, my dear, when I happened to notice a man and a girl sitting on a seat. I would not have given them a second glance, though the girl was quite pretty, and had on the darlingest frock, if I had not thought I had seen the man before. And then I had quite a shock, for I realised who it was. You remember that adventure we had this summer on our honeymoon. Well, this was the very man I had seen lying on the road unconscious—the lunatic who had been knocked on the head with a spanner.

Well, there was this same lunatic, talking quite happily to the pretty girl. John recognised him too, and we wondered whether we ought to do anything about it. In fact, it worried John quite a lot, and we mentioned it at lunch that day to the Baxters, and old Tommy Baxter told us the story. There's simply nothing that man doesn't know, and it is the most incredible tale.

It seems that the man we saw lying by the motor car was not the lunatic at all, but the real doctor, and that the lunatic had knocked him out and pretended to be the doctor himself. What's more, he actually took charge of the asylum. And the best of it is that John, who prides himself on his medical knowledge, was himself taken in and, as you remember, actually helped the lunatic to take his doctor to the madhouse. Of course, I laughed like anything, but old Tommy Baxter was quite grave. It was no laughing matter, he said. For the most awful things had happened. It appeared that the lunatic, who was quite sane except on one subject, was also a doctor, and that he kept the real doctor shut up for weeks, and ran the place by himself with the assistance of the pretty girl who was new to her job.

All went well for some weeks till he had one of his fits and tried to raise the devil. For it seems he was a diabolist. I don't quite know what that means. I always thought it was a game that you played with a cone and a piece of string and two sticks, but John says I am mixing it up with diabolo.

Of course, it wouldn't have mattered very much, only unfortunately, he murdered two of the patients and nearly killed Dr. Murchison himself (that was the real doctor's name). And then, in the nick of time, the old doctor to whom the establishment really belonged (I can't remember his name) turned up. Otherwise I gather no one would have been left alive, though John says something worse would have happened, but he won't tell me what it was.

Well, the real doctor, who had been shut up by the lunatic, was, of course, released, and he and the pretty girl (a Miss Sedgwick, and a cousin of the Yorkshire Sedgwicks, I believe) fell in love with one another. They have only just been married, and are now on their honeymoon.

It is extraordinary how you keep meeting people you have seen before, isn't it?

I must stop now or I shall be losing the post. We are moving on next week to Bordighera and Alassio.

My best love to you all,
Always your affectionate
Susan

**Mysteries from the
Masters of Suspense**

By Sax Rohmer

DAUGHTER OF FU MANCHU (1818, $3.50)

THE DRUMS OF FU MANCHU (1617, $3.50)

THE INSIDIOUS DR. FU MANCHU (1668, $3.50)

THE TRAIL OF FU MANCHU (1619, $3.50)

SHADOW OF FU MANCHU (1870, $3.50)

By John Dickson Carr

THE MAN WHO COULD NOT SHUDDER (1703, $3.50)

THE PROBLEM OF THE WIRE CAGE (1702, $3.50)

THE EIGHT OF SWORDS (1881, $3.50)

Available wherever paperbacks are sold, or order direct from the Publisher. Send cover price plus 50¢ per copy for mailing and handling to Zebra Books, Dept. 2002, 475 Park Avenue South, New York, N.Y. 10016. Residents of New York, New Jersey and Pennsylvania must include sales tax. DO NOT SEND CASH.

THE BEST IN GOTHICS FROM ZEBRA

THE BLOODSTONE INHERITANCE   (1560, $2.95)
by Serita Deborah Stevens

The exquisite Parkland pendant, the sole treasure remaining to lovely Elizabeth from her mother's fortune, was missing a matching jewel. Finding it in a ring worn by the handsome, brooding Peter Parkisham, Elizabeth couldn't deny the blaze of emotions he ignited in her. But how could she love the man who had stolen THE BLOODSTONE INHERITANCE!

THE SHRIEKING SHADOWS OF
PENPORTH ISLAND   (1344, $2.95)
by Serita Deborah Stevens

Seeking her missing sister, Victoria had come to Lord Hawley's manor on Penporth Island, but now the screeching gulls seemed to be warning her to flee. Seeing Julian's dark, brooding eyes watching her every move, and seeing his ghost-like silhouette on her bedroom wall, Victoria knew she would share her sister's fate—knew she would never escape!

THE HOUSE OF SHADOWED ROSES   (1447, $2.95)
by Carol Warburton

Penniless and alone, Heather was thrilled when the Ashleys hired her as a companion and brought her to their magnificent Cornwall estate, Rosemerryn. But soon Heather learned that danger lurked amid the beauty there—in ghosts long dead and mysteries unsolved, and even in the arms of Geoffrey Ashley, the enigmatic master of Rosemerryn.

CRYSTAL DESTINY   (1394, $2.95)
by Christina Blair

Lydia knew she belonged to the high, hidden valley in the Rockies that her father had claimed, but the infamous Aaron Stone lived there now in the forbidding Stonehurst mansion. Vowing to get what was hers, Lydia would confront the satanic master of Stonehurst—and find herself trapped in a battle for her very life!

Available wherever paperbacks are sold, or order direct from the Publisher. Send cover price plus 50¢ per copy for mailing and handling to Zebra Books, Dept. 2002, 475 Park Avenue South, New York, N.Y. 10016. Residents of New York, New Jersey and Pennsylvania must include sales tax. DO NOT SEND CASH.